D1519909

MUTED

ERIK CARTER

ISBN: 9798861904988

CHAPTER ONE

Death Valley National Park, California
The 1990s

THE PLACE WAS CALLED Death Valley.

How fitting.

Adrian Hirsch hadn't chosen this U.S. national park because of its name. In fact, he hadn't chosen it at all; he'd delegated that decision to his contact. Hirsch wouldn't have done something as whimsical as staging the intensive operation based on clever wordplay. His international reputation was one of practicality and efficiency. A man like Hirsch had no inclination or even tolerance for silly indulgences.

Still, he couldn't deny there was a certain poetry to the notion that his murders were to take place in a land named Death.

The view through the windshield before him was a raw, awe-inspiring expanse, overwhelming isolation, a level of nothingness so vast it approached sublimity. His eyes traversed a rugged desert stretching unbroken in all directions. Towering rocks sprouted from the earth in the distance, casting shadows under the relentless sun, while a bombastically blue sky contrasted with the brown-and-red palette below. A smattering of twisted, hardy plants dotted the endless landscape—brittle monuments of survival.

The interior of the geriatric pickup truck vibrated with the unsteady rhythm of the engine, a grating dissonance. The vinyl upholstery was torn, and its once cheerful reds and yellows were now faded to murky pinks and browns. Seated on the passenger side of the dry-rotted bench seat, Hirsch found the rustic simplicity of his surroundings both jarring and mildly amusing. His world was one of crisp suits, polished manners, and calculated brutality. In the desolation of Nature, in the middle of America, seated in a rattling American vehicle, many incongruities were announcing themselves. Yet, he felt a sense of anticipation that made the blood thrum in his veins. Today was a day of work.

Dark work.

He glanced beside him at the driver, Luca Westlin, who looked slightly more at home amidst their surroundings. Westlin's profile was hardened, his eyes focused on the road ahead, the corners of his mouth twitching in a semblance of a smirk atop his square jaw. He wore a gray T-shirt, appropriately American blue jeans, and scuffed hiking boots. The sunlight pouring through the windshield glinted off his ever-present leather wristband, highlighting its engraved symbols.

The windows were shut, and the sprawl of desert surrounding Hirsch was an empty void, yet the cabin roared from the noise of the motorcycles outside. There were eight Harley-Davidsons in total—four ahead of the pickup, one on either side, and two taking up the rear. Oversized men sat on each bike. Loping arms dangling on the handlebars. Equally loping legs in black leather and black denim. Sunglasses. Faded tattoos. Hair flapping in the wind along with the light blue bandanas on their foreheads and tied to their biceps.

The bikes and the truck formed a motley crew of a caravan barreling down a highway in an appropriately end-of-the-world environment. Everywhere, chrome glinted brightly against the rocky backdrop, making Hirsch squint.

Though Hirsch typically orchestrated his activities from a distance, he sometimes went into the field for important operations like this. But the previous experiences hadn't been this rough, this crude, this uncouth. All the same, the image of the motorcycles tearing through the desert landscape of the American West—untamed and unapologetic—echoed Hirsch's ruthless drive.

He reached forward and turned the air-conditioning dial to its highest setting. Even cranked to its limit, the old truck's system struggled to spit out anything better than lukewarm air. Hirsch adjusted his sleeves, rolling them up another rotation's worth past his elbows. As the hot sunlight melded with the belching semi-cool putters from the vents, Hirsch eased back into the seat as his eyes grew heavy behind his mirrored Persols, an involuntary moment of serenity, a calm before the storm.

Then he shot forward, straightening in his seat, alert.

He'd caught sight of their mark.

A growing speck on the distant horizon.

The tour bus materialized over a rise in the barren vista, right in the middle of the glimmering heat mirage, at the far end of the highway stretching before Hirsch. The bus lumbered forward, oblivious to the impending danger. With the reveal of the massive vehicle, Hirsch's pulse quickened, and he glanced at Westlin, whose professional facade had not altered, though his hands tightened on the steering wheel.

This was it. It was time.

The roar coming from the desert outside intensified as the motorcycles bolted ahead. Two of the four in front took off faster than the others, lunging for the distant target. The pickup, too, growled with renewed vigor as Westlin stomped the gas pedal, jolting Hirsch in his seat. The caravan rocketed off.

Hirsch's heart pounded, mirroring the rhythm of the motorcycle engines. His hands clenched into fists as the motorcycles fanned out into an even wider formation, encompassing the entire width of the highway—an attack pattern.

As the caravan closed the gap, the tour bus grew clearer in Hirsch's view—a blue stripe encircling its girth, sun shining off the polished steel panels. It was metallic prey, unaware of the hunters closing in.

The growl of the motorcycle engines echoed in the barren landscape. Rising, falling.

Hirsch's gaze never wavered from the bus.

Nearer.

Nearer.

He could read the writing on the bus's backside now: *LEGACY ROUTE TOURS*. He tapped his fingers on the window frame beside him, like a beat, a countdown.

Westlin smashed the accelerator again. The truck lunged ahead.

More motorcycles zipped past the pickup on either side and joined the others in an orchestrated maneuver circling the bus. The trap was setting. The Harleys moved into position—one to the bus's left, one directly in front of it, and another several yards behind the bus's rear bumper.

Finally, the bus driver sensed danger and gunned the engine, desperately trying to squeeze the hefty vehicle between the Harleys. But he was too late. The bikers had closed the gap.

Hirsch smirked.

He tracked their progress until all the bikes were in perfect formation, then he gave a signal to Westlin—a subtle dip of his head—and Westlin jammed a fist into the steering wheel, blaring the horn.

The bikers understood. They tightened around the bus as they simultaneously slowed and pulled to the right.

Yard by yard.

Foot by foot.

Slowing, slowing...

...until the bus's tires left the highway and hit rock. A plume of dust rose, obscuring the bus from view. Brakes squealed.

With a jolt, the pickup truck left the smooth surface of the highway, falling into line behind the other slowing vehicles. Hirsch whacked into the passenger door, the window crank striking his knee. He grabbed hold of the bench seat. With a final shake, the truck came to a stop.

All the vehicles were now still—the bus and the bikes and the truck.

Westlin put the gear selector into park, reached under the seat for his firearm, and stepped outside. The weapon was a Heckler & Koch MP5. Specifically, among the many MP5 variants, this was an MP5A3, a solid weapon. Hirsch hadn't taken long choosing the weaponry to be used by Westlin and the others for this operation. The MP5 was one of the most popular submachine guns in the world, utilized by governments, military forces, law enforcement, intelligence groups, and security agencies. Its ubiquity and reliability made it the perfect, obvious choice.

Hirsch threw open his door and stepped outside as well. He coughed. Dust everywhere, obscuring his view. The desert was hotter even than it had been that morning when Hirsch left his hotel. In the aftermath of the chaotic chase, the landscape returned to quietude as, one by one, the motorcycles clicked off. The dust slowly settled back to the ground. The bus sat motionless as it reappeared out of the swirling tan haze, a metallic monolith against the grandeur of the desert.

Hirsch now found himself surrounded by the bikers as they dismounted their rides. All of that black leather. All of those beards and tattoos. Each man held an MP5A3 like Westlin's, which, to Hirsch, created an almost amusing visual. He imagined men like this carrying different types of weapons: sawed-off shotguns, revolvers, battered 1911s with filed-off serial numbers.

One of these bikers was Hirsch's contact, and a subconscious portion of Hirsch tried to draw his attention toward the man, but he suppressed the urge. The other bikers didn't know who the contact was. Not even Westlin knew who the contact was.

Even among the swarm of testosterone-fueled American toughs, Westlin stood out, a formidable figure who commanded attention without leather clothing or metal-studded gear. He was Hirsch's only confidant for this operation, the only individual he had even informed, the only person who'd hopped across the ocean with him. Secrecy was vital, and Hirsch's decision to trust Westlin was just as natural as his choice of H&K MP5s for the mission weapon.

Stepping toward the bus but angling himself outside the ring of bikers, Hirsch watched as Westlin crunched across the rock, leading the other men.

"Get out!" Westlin bellowed at the bus's main door on the passenger side.

The bus remained silent.

"Get out, or we'll come in!" Westlin yelled, his patience wearing thin.

No movement from the bus, only a stifled whimpering of multiple voices.

A smirk touched Hirsch's lips as he watched Westlin control the situation. The standoff lasted mere seconds longer before Westlin fired a round into the air, the deafening blast of the gunshot echoing around the landscape.

Screams erupted from inside the bus, high-pitched and panicked. Then a shuffling sound. Then the hiss of the bus's pneumatic doors opening.

A man in an all-navy-blue uniform, presumably the driver, stepped out. His hands were raised, face pale, eyes wide with terror.

"Get them out!" Westlin said.

But the driver just stood there, paralyzed by fear.

Westlin leveled his gun at the man with a swift, irritated-yet-controlled motion. "Now."

The driver jolted into action and hurried back inside. Moments later, he reappeared, herding the passengers out. They stumbled off the bus—sightseers whose vacation had suddenly turned into a nightmare. Quivering, crying, whispering.

It was an old group. The youngest was the driver, and even he had gray streaks through his hair and wrinkles around his eyes and mouth. Among the passengers, no one was under the age of sixty-five. Legacy Route offered several tours exclusively for senior citizens. This was one of them.

Fear radiated off the group as they descended the steps out of the bus and met the armed bikers, who took them a few yards into the desert and positioned them into a long column. Elderly women were rudely shoved forward, frail bodies stumbling, as the bikers roared with laughter. Men, protective instincts flaring, tried to intervene but were met with slaps and backhands. Every plea, every brave word, only added to the bikers' sadistic enjoyment.

Hirsch remained on the sidelines, the picture of composed observance. His eyes scanned the line of terrified tourists as they were forced out into the unforgiving brightness of the sun, their cries and pleas for mercy providing a discordant soundtrack to Nature's silence.

Westlin stalked up and down the line, asserting his dominance, his H&K jabbing sharply into trembling bodies, invoking fresh bouts of tears. A white-haired woman cried out as he grabbed her arm, squeezing until she crumpled in pain. A bespectacled man with a bushy mustache swung at Westlin, only to be knocked back with a vicious blow.

Hirsch watched the pageant impassively. In fact, he hardly noticed any of it. His attention was locked on two figures among the line of captives, just a seemingly ordinary pair of old men among the fourteen tourists.

Scott MacLeod and Milton Shapiro.

Hirsch had never seen them in the flesh, but they'd impacted his life immensely. He'd read their stories and heard their voices through recordings and interviews over the years, which afforded Hirsch's mind only a fraction of the men's sentience, the hazy half-reality of mass media.

Yet here they were, standing in front of him in the desert, far from their homes and far from safety. The men had found anonymity among this tour bus crowd, just as they'd found anonymity in the rest of the world over the last dozen years. But within their element and within the annals of history, MacLeod and Shapiro were legends of a sort.

They didn't look so legendary now in this desert called Death.

Both of their faces were drawn with dread.

He studied them in turn, starting with MacLeod.

The man was about six feet tall with thick white hair that tossed in the hot desert breeze. Wrinkles creased his face, and his eyes were wide and wet. He wore a Hawaiian shirt, cargo shorts, and sandals.

Hirsch's gaze then shifted to Shapiro, who stood beside MacLeod. Shapiro was a bit shorter, a bit slighter. He wore a fedora, a plaid shirt, and khaki pants. He was every bit as frightened as the other man. His hands shook. His silver mustache twitched.

Both men were prominent figures on the other side of the continent, but now, they looked like lost old men far away from the comfort of home and family, about to die in the middle of nowhere, surrounded by rock and shrub plants and Harley-Davidsons.

The bikers finally retreated from the tourists, having marshaled the old people into a line, barking orders and threats all the while. Raucous laughter merged with the broken cries of the captives. The scene was set, the actors ready.

All that remained was Hirsch's deadly command.

But Hirsch was in no state to offer the order.

Rather, his state was trancelike.

Oblivious to the panic around him, his focus remained pinned on MacLeod and Shapiro. Their fear, their confusion, thrilled him. Everything was happening so quickly, so simply. A concept that had always entranced Hirsch was that of life frequently offering a drawn-out build-up to an event, only for the moment in question to occur abruptly and suddenly, in mere seconds.

This was about to be one of those moments.

Hirsch's rumination was shattered by Westlin's deep voice addressing him.

"Sir?"

Hirsch jumped, pulled his attention from MacLeod and Shapiro, and turned, locking eyes with his lackey. A silent conversation passed between them. Hirsch inclined his head —a subtle nod like he'd offered in the truck, this time bearing much more gravitas.

Then it began.

The valley exploded in a cacophony of gunfire, a hailstorm

tearing through the terrified captives. Bodies dropped, crumpling to the ground. Gut-wrenching cries were abruptly silenced, replaced by the relentless roar of the submachine guns. Westlin and the bikers advanced, their faces masked in a brutal, detached satisfaction as they continued to fire at the fallen bodies.

Hirsch watched, his eyes never leaving.

The air grew thick with acrid smoke and the coppery smell of blood. When the gunshots finally died, a deafening silence swallowed the surroundings. Hirsch's ears rang with the guns' echoes while death, shit, and gunpowder filled his nostrils.

And though his eyes remained locked on his two targets, his peripheral vision couldn't deny the other thirteen corpses surrounding MacLeod and Shapiro.

It wasn't supposed to happen this way.

They weren't *all* supposed to die.

Something in Hirsch tried to pull his attention toward his contact again—realizing now that the man's identity must not be a mystery to the other bikers after all—but it was only a tiny fraction of his consciousness, quickly overruled. His eyes remained locked where they had been: on MacLeod's and Shapiro's mangled corpses, inconspicuously mounded near the center of the line of bloody flesh.

They'd been torn to shreds.

Faces shot to mush.

Hirsch would have stared at them for an hour.

But he couldn't.

The rational, latent portion of him fighting against his surging emotions, against the onslaught of relief and hedonistic joy, demanded that he address his contact, to find out what the hell had gone wrong here, why they'd all been slaughtered.

But not now. Not here.

He would address his contact soon enough.

Wordlessly, he turned, his shoes crunching on the earth as he walked back to the idling truck. Westlin followed, his expression unreadable as he cast one last glance over the gruesome scene behind them and climbed into the driver's seat.

The roar of engines filled the desert again as Hirsch, Westlin, and the bikers took off, continuing down the highway.

Hirsch pivoted to look out the rear window. The bodies were a berm of limbs and blood, a splash of bold crimson against the streaks of paler red in the surrounding desert.

He turned around, rested the back of his head against the glass, and closed his eyes, waiting for the hot sunlight to lull him into a well-deserved nap.

CHAPTER TWO

Pensacola, Florida

SOMETIMES EVEN WORLD-CLASS assassins need a little help.

Sometimes they need to hire a private detective.

Silence Jones sat alone at a small outdoor table of a dock-side restaurant, tucked away in the Sanders Beach neighborhood, a slightly-less-trodden corner of Pensacola, Florida, his city of residence. The Moonlight Shore Bar & Grille was neither a dive bar nor a family restaurant but something in between—a cozy bayside pub with a hint of brackish water in the air. A place where you can either lurk around the bar or grab an outdoor table, pound a few beers and taste the freshest of seafood. An ideal spot for summer nights of all types, from wild to subdued.

Neon lights from the restaurant danced off the dark surface of the water, the playful ripples in contrast to the gravity of Silence's thoughts. An occasional breeze rustled the palm tree fronds to Silence's right, just past the rope railing. The din of nighttime city traffic was but a distant, muted hum here in this tucked-away spot where Bayou Chico merged with the expanse of Pensacola Bay.

While Silence waited, his gaze fixated on the gravel parking lot. He watched as a nondescript Ford pulled in, settling into the pebbles with a squeal from the brakes. The man who emerged from the sedan was barely out of his early twenties, yet he carried himself with an air of seasoned experience. To this point, Silence had not seen the man—neither in person nor via photos —but from the hint of a Scottish accent Silence had heard on the phone earlier, he knew this individual with close-cropped red hair and a freckle-spattered face must be Andy Elsher.

As the younger man approached the patio area, he found Silence's gaze, grinned, waved, and changed trajectory. Silence waved back and studied Elsher carefully.

The guy had a relaxed but not too relaxed appearance— linen shirt, chinos, leather flip-flops—as though aiming to strike a balance between professionalism and comfort for an after-hours meeting at a bar and grille. His blue eyes were sharp and inquisitive, and despite the time of day and an hour-long drive from Mobile, Alabama, Elsher showed no signs of fatigue. Instead, he seemed energized, the prospect of an exciting case visibly spurring him on.

"You must be the man I'm looking for," Elsher said, his voice seasoned favorably with that hint of a Scottish accent.

Silence stood, nodded, and they shook hands.

"Pleasure to meet you," Elsher said.

"Pleasure's mutual," Silence said, nodding at Elsher to take the stool across from him on the opposite side of the whiskey barrel table.

As Elsher sat, he narrowed his eyes in slight bemusement. Even though Elsher had heard Silence's voice once already— an hour and a half earlier when Silence first called him—there was still palpable confusion in the man's eyes.

Years ago, an event nearly took Silence's life, leaving him with a permanently injured voice box. His voice now rumbled and crackled like a dissonant storm, terrifyingly unusual. First-time listeners inevitably reacted when they heard his voice; their eyes would grow wide, their faces would contort, or they'd instinctively step back. They couldn't help but respond in shock.

Speaking caused intense pain to the glut of scar tissue in Silence's neck. The more syllables he attempted, the worse the suffering, leading him to swallow frequently to soothe his throat.

"Sorry for the..." Silence said and swallowed. "Late notice."

Elsher's lips quirked in a half-smile. "The hundred bucks you promised made it more than tolerable."

He looked at Silence, waited.

Silence retrieved his wallet, slid a hundred across the smooth yet slightly grimy wooden topper. Elsher's grin widened as he took the bill, studied it momentarily, and transferred it to his own wallet.

The waitress, Mollie, approached. Bright yellow tank top, denim shorts that were frayed at the edges. Her curly dark hair was pulled back into a high bun, and she flashed a bright smile as she glanced at Elsher.

"What can I get ya, hon?"

Mollie's slight Southern accent was a pleasant compliment to Elsher's slight Scottish accent as the latter looked from Mollie and back to the table—seeing Silence's condensation-dappled bottle of Heineken resting on a warped paper coaster with Dos Equis branding—and said, "I'll have what he's having."

"You got it," Mollie said and left.

Elsher watched her leave—intrigued, perhaps—then he

blinked clarity back into his light blue eyes and faced Silence, leaning closer, crossing his forearms on the table.

"What kind of situation requires a private investigator to be contacted in the middle of the night and asked to drive an hour across state lines?"

"Leaving town tomorrow..." Silence said, swallowed. "But can't risk hiring..." Another swallow. "Someone in Pensacola."

"Sounds naughty," Elsher said and raised an eyebrow before immediately negating it with a shrug. "I don't judge. Obviously. It's not in my interests to judge. So you want an out-of-towner—an out-of-stater, actually—to watch something for you while you yourself are out of town. You don't want to hire someone in your own town. So you grab the phone book for Mobile, Alabama, the nearest city of size, only an hour away, flip to the private detective listings, start making calls, and I was the first one to answer the phone at eight o'clock at night. Do I have that about right?"

"You were the second..." Silence said and swallowed. "To answer. Didn't like..." Another swallow. "First guy."

Silence had purposefully omitted a couple of words. Along with his frequent swallowing, the use of broken, shortened English was another technique to help with his throat condition.

But the shortened explanation he'd offered Elsher for why he'd eschewed the first private detective he'd called—*Didn't like ... first guy*—was complete in its brevity. Silence had always been good at reading people, and something had rubbed him the wrong way about the first nocturnal Mobile private detective he'd managed to reach via telephone. The guy had had a devious, almost deceptive quality to his voice. Silence hadn't liked it. So he'd moved on.

Elsher smirked. "Well, I'm honored."

Mollie arrived with Elsher's beer, placing it in front of the detective on another used, moisture-warped Dos Equis coaster that she pulled from the pocket of her waist apron.

"Thanks," Elsher said.

He watched her leave again, his eyes lingering a beat as they had moments earlier, before looking back at Silence.

"So, is this a business or personal matter?"

"Personal."

Elsher took a long swig from his Heineken, watching Silence, waiting for more.

Silence pulled his NedNotes brand PenPal notebook from his pocket. Though small, PenPals held a substantial number of pages. Their plastic covers came in various bright colors, often with bold patterns; this one bore blue-and-gray zebra stripes.

He flipped the notebook open to the first page of his prepared notes and handed it across the table. As Elsher took it, Silence tapped his throat, then pointed at the PenPal.

Elsher nodded his understanding.

"I get it," Elsher said and squared up the notebook on the tabletop in front of him.

Silence watched as Elsher began reading the several-page handwritten account of what had happened a few hours earlier.

———

It had been dusk.

Silence had been at Pensacola Beach, a few-minute drive away from Pensacola proper. But he hadn't been seaside, enjoying the purple-pink magnificence along the famous "Whitest Beaches in the World." Rather, he was at a tucked-away joint, not so very different from the Moonlight Shore Bar & Grille.

He was parked inconspicuously on the opposite side of

the parking lot from where a warm, golden glow spilled out from the windows of The Sand Dollar, a quaint eatery nestled around the corner from a strip of bars and beach shops, a place known for its shrimp and grits. The scent of frying seafood permeated the air, the salt-and-grease tang making Silence's stomach rumble.

But Silence wasn't there for food.

He was there for a glimpse of Marvin Tanner.

C.C.'s voice came to him in his mind.

Love, she said. *This is creepy. Super creepy.*

I do this all the time, Silence replied internally.

C.C. wasn't convinced. *That makes it* more *creepy, not less.*

C.C. was his fiancée, and she'd been dead for years. Murdered. Since then, Silence convened with her in his mind. In life, she'd been wise well beyond her years, and Silence relied on that wisdom even after her death. His mind's version of C.C. often appeared at times of high stress —which were frequent in Silence's line of work as a vigilante assassin—but sometimes she materialized simply to scold him.

She particularly disliked when he did this—when he followed his old friend and mentor, Marvin Tanner.

And Silence didn't like being judged.

I know what I'm doing, he told C.C.

Silence took a deep breath, held it for a moment, and released it, exhaling his frustration at the phantom version of his dead fiancée. Ironically, C.C. had taught him this deep-breathing technique.

He refocused.

And yawned. He hadn't slept much the past week—only a few fitful hours each night.

From his position in the parking lot, Silence could see the familiar figure several yards away, hunched over a table, plowing through a plate of fried shrimp. It was a quiet evening, and the restaurant was half-empty, making Tanner stand out even more.

In another life, years earlier, Tanner had been something much more significant than a mere silhouette behind glass. Back when Silence had been known as Jake Rowe—before the series of events that stole his former identity, ruined his throat, and left C.C. lifeless in a puddle of blood—Tanner had been Jake Rowe's lieutenant, his mentor, and to some extent, a father figure.

Tanner was a seasoned officer with the Pensacola Police Department, a man who'd dedicated his life to upholding the law. African American. Salt-and-pepper hair. Mustache. Dark eyes that held a weary sort of wisdom. His frame bore the evidence of a lifetime of tough police work, muscular but softened by age.

Since the incident and Silence's conscription into the Watchers, Silence was forbidden to have contact with Tanner. But Silence yearned for the past—his frequent brainscape conversations with C.C. evidencing this more than anything else—and so he sometimes followed Tanner, watching the man from a distance.

He'd done this often enough that he knew the man's patterns.

On most Thursday nights, Tanner trekked out to the beach to take advantage of The Sand Dollar's shrimp and grits deal. The bargain offered a mere dollar off the standard price, but that was enough to draw Tanner out for an extra thirty-minute round trip on his way home. Tanner was a creature of habit. This was helpful in Silence's trailing of the man.

This is stalking, C.C.'s voice said. *You're stalking someone you care about.*

So? Silence replied.

You just followed him last week.

So?

You get like this sometimes, love, C.C. said, *when your thirst for the past intensifies.*

Silence repressed more frustration. *You know there's a very specific reason I'm following Tanner again this week.*

If you say so, C.C. said. *Or maybe you're just looking for an excuse to cling to the memories. What do I always tell you?*

Silence didn't reply.

I tell you to let go, C.C. said. *You need to let go of the past.*

Silence ignored her.

Yes, his mind's version of C.C. frequently told him to let go. She was correct about that. Years earlier, the real-life woman had also insisted he learn to let go, but her post-mortem rendition was even more bullheaded about the idea.

A non-corporeal version of a dead person in Silence's head, instructing him to let go—there was something ironic about that.

Or maddening.

He pushed the notion aside.

In the restaurant, Tanner's face broke into a smile as he said something to the waitress. Watching the man now, Silence felt a sharp, bittersweet tug. In the former life, Jake would have sat across from Tanner, swapping stories over plates of dollar-off shrimp. They would have talked about the job, their shared passion for serving their community.

But that was before.

Before Silence had been nearly killed. Before C.C. *had* been killed. Before the wretched voice. Before the reconstructed face. Before Silence became an Asset for the Watchers, a group of individuals embedded within U.S. government who illegally corrected errors in procedural justice. Now that he was no longer Jake Rowe, Silence Jones, the Watchers assassin, wasn't afforded any familiarity with his former mentor.

So he cheated like this.

It helped.

Tanner stood, went to the counter, paid his bill, gave a final wave to the staff, and exited The Sand Dollar, the door jingling merrily behind him.

Silence eased back into the shadows of his BMW's cabin, but this was an unnecessary precaution. After the incident, a Watchers plastic surgeon had completely remade Silence's face. The visage that Tanner had known as Jake Rowe had been erased from existence.

Silence keyed the ignition while, across the parking lot, Tanner climbed into his Lincoln. It was the same vehicle Tanner had driven years ago when Silence had been his underling and mentee. Regular oil changes. Dutiful mainte-nance. Always with a fresh set of Dunlops.

As the Lincoln rolled out of the diner's parking lot, Silence eased his vehicle onto the road, maintaining a comfortable distance between them, tracing through Pensacola Beach's lights and condo towers, across the bridge into Gulf Breeze, and across another bridge—Three Mile Bridge—back into Pensacola proper.

After years of following his routine-driven friend, Silence knew Tanner typically returned home after getting his discount shrimp and grits at the beach. Last week, however, Tanner *hadn't* gone straight home. He'd gone somewhere very out of character, so much so that it was alarming.

That's why Silence, to C.C.'s chagrin, was following the man again, only one week after his latest indulgence.

Just like the previous week, Tanner didn't go east toward his home upon exiting Three Mile Bridge. He instead went west.

Silence's heart sank.

Going west didn't necessarily mean that Tanner was headed to where he had visited the previous week. But it sure felt like it.

Silence's grip tightened on the steering wheel as Tanner's car moved westward on Gregory, then Garden. They crossed through downtown. Continued several more blocks.

And turned.

On *that* street.

The same one as last week.

Shit.

The soft glow of street lamps illuminated the aging, graffitied bricks of the buildings they passed. The streets were narrow and littered, the smells sharp with the stench of rotting trash and stale alcohol.

The Lincoln pulled up in front of a grimy, nondescript establishment—a rough, *rough* bar called Black Jack's. The single-story, windowless building was squeezed in between a shuttered pawn shop and a row of shabby apartments. Its walls were a drab grey, covered with layers of soot and neglect. The flickering neon sign was missing a few letters, accentuating the threatening aura.

A hulk of a man stood guard at the door, his massive frame blocking the entrance like a wall of human flesh in a black leather jacket. Tanner exited his Lincoln and approached the man, their exchange hidden in the gloom. After a moment, Tanner was let inside. A flash of light strobed in the night, revealing tables and beers and a line of liquor and slovenly, laughing faces before the door snapped shut again.

Tanner was gone.

...vanished into Black Jack's for the second time in two weeks.

Parked a block back, Silence observed from the shadows, his heart pounding. He'd been tailing Tanner for years, studying his patterns. The man was predictable. His regular visits to The Sand Dollar, a plate of shrimp and grits, friendly banter with the staff—that was all familiar.

But Black Jack's?

This was a new development.

Via his long-time residency in Pensacola and his brief tenure on the Pensacola Police Department and his resource-wizard connections at the Watchers, Silence knew that nothing good went on inside Black Jack's.

But he didn't need insider knowledge for that.

Anyone could glance at a place like Black Jack's and know that it was a dark pit, a spiritual vortex.

As a Watcher, though, Silence had to work on absolutes, not gut feelings. Regarding Black Jack's, there was one thing he knew for sure, one absolute: unsanctioned gambling took place in that shithole.

With the headlights extinguished, Silence edged the BMW forward, nosing close to the dank alley adjacent to the building. A group huddled there, their faces lit by the faint glow of a flashlight upended by their feet. Dice clattered onto the concrete, followed by groans and curses. They glanced up as Silence's car moved near, hostility flashing over their eyes. Immediately, they scattered deeper into the shadows, their illegal game vanishing with them.

One of the characters lingered a beat longer than the others, staring in Silence's direction. A moment earlier, this man had stood to the side of the group, watching the gambling but not taking part. He was cleaner than the other men, too, and neater, so much so that, in another less deprived setting, the man could be mistaken for a young military officer, a sharp-suited businessman, or a fresh-faced computer software pioneer.

He was in his early to mid-twenties. Caucasian. Dark hair and piercing blue eyes. While his clean-shaven face, gym physique, and fresh attire painted a picture of refinement—relative to the surroundings, at least—those intense eyes spoke of malevolence.

In the few scant moments Silence observed, it was clear the man had a tic, a tell: he kept clenching and unclenching his jaw, the masseter muscles at the corners of his face bulging and then relaxing repeatedly.

Silence was well concealed within the shadows—training and years of experience in the field left him acutely aware of such details—but still, those blue eyes on that muscular, twitching face felt like they were locked right in on Silence's own eyes.

The long moment passed.

And the man disappeared into the darkness where the others had.

Another sinking shot of dread settled in Silence's stomach. For a week now, he'd entertained the idea that Tanner was working undercover, infiltrating the gambling den to gather information. But it felt like a flimsy hope. As a high-ranking cop who'd been in the city for decades, Tanner was well-known, his face familiar to those in the criminal underworld.

It made no sense for Tanner to be undercover.

It made no sense for a lieutenant like him, perennially on the cusp of retirement, to be in the field at all.

Silence's cellular phone chimed, startling him out of his grim musings. The caller ID revealed a very familiar number. It was Falcon, a Watchers Prefect, Silence's boss.

A moment of hesitation as Silence glanced again at Black Jack's shrouded entrance and the alley where he'd seen the men disappear. His instinct told him he was on the brink of a distressing truth about Tanner. But duty called, and he was a man who answered.

One more lingering look.

Then he put the car in gear, took off, and flipped open the phone.

"Sir?" he said.

———

"So what's the job?" Elsher said as he snapped the PenPal shut and reached it across the table. Silence took it. Elsher stowed away the microcassette recorder he'd used to verbally jot down a few of his own notes as he read through Silence's.

A waitress in denim shorts even shorter than Mollie's scurried past them, balancing a tray laden with plates of steaming grilled fish. Laughter and pleasant conversations emanated from the surrounding tables while a classic rock tune carried over the inky water that lapped against the wooden patio.

"I'll be out of town," Silence said and swallowed. "Track Tanner for me."

Elsher's eyebrow arched upward. "That's it? Just keep tabs on someone for you?"

"I need to know if..." Silence said, swallowed. "He's gambling illegally."

A shadow of confusion crossed Elsher's face. "And if he is?"

"If he is..." Silence said and swallowed. "I'll handle it..." Another swallow. "When I get back."

Elsher's eyebrow ascended even higher.

"What does that even—" He stopped abruptly, cutting himself off with a shake of his hand and a shake of the head, looking away from Silence's gaze. "Never mind. I'm breaking my own rule. No questions. It's not my business."

"Good man," Silence said.

"So ... this guy's a cop?"

Silence nodded. "A lieutenant."

Elsher sighed as he leaned back in his chair, looking at the water. His fingers drummed against the table in an absent rhythm, his gaze unfocused. A small huff of laughter escaped his lips.

"If I'm found out..." Elsher trailed off. A moment passed. "This is hot work, man. Really hot."

The tone of his Scottish accent had wandered into the muddled depths of ambivalence, losing its way.

To right him, Silence said, "Not an issue for..." He swallowed. "A pro like you."

Elsher smirked, one corner of his lips lifting in a smile that said he recognized both the sincerity of Silence's praise and also its true purpose of subtle manipulation. The guy really was a pro.

After a moment, Elsher sighed and nodded, "All right, I'm in. I'll find out what your cop is up to."

Silence drained the rest of his beer, climbed off the chair.

"I want frequent reports," he said and swallowed. "Call me."

He flicked a fingernail against Elsher's Heineken—*clink*—pulled a ten from his wallet, and dropped it on the table.

"Beer's on me."

He left.

CHAPTER THREE

Death Valley National Park, California

WEIRD SHIT HAPPENED within the U.S. national parks.

Often enough, people died.

And, perhaps worse, many simply vanished.

Mitch Lockwood had never wished suffering upon anyone, but he'd always loved the allure of the parks' macabre mysteries.

The National Park System boasted broad expanses with millions of acres, often featuring wild and undeveloped landscapes. Over the years, riddles had shrouded these parks—unexplained phenomena and various tales that captured the imaginations of perceptive individuals.

One prominent element: the accounts of people who had mysteriously disappeared. The vastness and rugged terrain contributed to some of these cases, but the peculiar nature of a few disappearances led to much speculation. Some believed these events could be attributed to natural causes or accidents, while others suggested more bewildering reasons.

Mythical creatures—notably the famous Bigfoot, aka

Sasquatch—were synonymous with national parks. They'd been part of local legends for centuries, with indigenous communities also sharing tales of such beings. Beyond Bigfoot, other cryptids were associated with the NPS, such as the Snallygaster in Shenandoah, the Wendigo in Voyageurs, and the Slide Rock Bolter in Rocky Mountain.

Given the remote nature of many of the parks, individuals had surmised that the areas served as grounds for covert government experiments or even hidden bases. These claims ranged from testing cutting-edge aircraft to mysterious clandestine operations. There were reports of UFO sightings and alleged alien encounters, with some asserting the existence of undisclosed government-alien collaborations.

Natural phenomena, too, often got swept up into the realm of the supernatural within these parks. Similarly, the rich tapestry of cultural and historical narratives associated with national parks added another layer, while legends, ghost stories, and other tales contributed to the allure and mystique.

For years, Mitch had delightfully devoured all of this intrigue.

He loved it so much he made a career out of it.

The RV's moonlit interior was soothing but offered scant comfort to Mitch as he paced in a loop, wincing at each soft squeak of the floor, trying not to wake his wife. Despite his attempts to remain quiet, he couldn't resist the urge to move. When his thoughts raced, so did his feet.

Carmen lay in bed at the back of the RV, motionless, curled in a ball beneath the comforter. As he watched her sleep, he felt another wave of the warm-fuzzies they'd shared before turning the lights out. Just before bed, her enthusiasm for this upcoming tour had noticeably improved, as if a renewed spark had lit up inside her.

Dim moonlight streamed through the blinds, casting a

dance of shadows and lights across the walls, playing off the items tacked haphazardly to form a sort of chaotic wallpaper —newspaper clippings, scribbled notes, photographs, and a map or two. Much of it was related to previous tours, with names like Grand Teton, Crater Lake, and Glacier Bay looking back at him. An average person would have taken the items down, but Mitch left them where they remained— remnants of adventures past. Plus, you never know when they might come in handy.

Instead of tossing the materials out, he tacked new materials right on top of the old. Two words tied to the latest tour stared back at him from all directions.

Death Valley.

He stepped closer to one article that stood out to him. A bold headline read, *DEATH VALLEY BUS SLAUGHTER*. Mitch's finger traced the clipping, his mind swirling with thoughts.

The incident had been the talk of the nation. A bus of tourists heading to a Death Valley landmark had been ambushed. No survivors. No viable leads. A complete mystery.

Mitch had his theories, of course, and those theories had set the direction for Unseen Path's latest tour. The bus tragedy drew the attention of idealogues and truth-seekers from all over the country. To many, it was a morbid curiosity. But for Mitch, it was a lucrative opportunity.

The tickets for this upcoming tour were snatched up quicker than any before, despite being available for only a few days. People from all backgrounds had joined Mitch, each eager to know what the authorities weren't telling them. Though Mitch hadn't had much time, he'd been meticulous in his planning process, knowing this would be his most significant and possibly most dangerous tour yet.

Even with his thorough preparation behind him, doubt

festered inside Mitch. Was he genuinely seeking the truth, or was he exploiting an atrocity? The line had blurred, and the weight of that realization bore down on him.

His gaze returned to Carmen, sleeping so peacefully. She had been with him every step of the way, long before Unseen Path's nascent days, before it was even a whisper in Mitch's mind. He remembered the late-night discussions, the way her brow would furrow as she expressed her concerns about Unseen Path's direction. While she believed in his cause, she often questioned his methods. Their debates would heat up, but by the night's end, they'd always find a middle ground.

But this tour, this exploitation of the Death Valley incident, had strained their bond. They hadn't argued, not explicitly, but he could sense the distance growing between them. Until hours earlier. She'd finally acquiesced, telling Mitch that she felt the sincerity in her husband's demeanor. She'd climbed into bed with a look of relief and peace.

Now that Mitch had his wife on his side, his damn conscience had taken her place, nagging him, questioning him.

Suddenly, the RV felt claustrophobic, the walls lined with his obsession pressing in on him. He needed air. He needed clarity.

With a final lingering look at Carmen, Mitch quietly made his way to the RV's door and stepped out into the dry nighttime desert air.

He exhaled.

The vast expanse of Death Valley consumed Mitch's view. A carpet of moonlight-blued rock stretched infinitely, merging with a star-studded sky at the horizon. Those celestial bodies shimmered more vividly in places like this—with clear, natural, wild skies—than anywhere else.

In the rustic parking area surrounding his RV was a handful of vehicles, each one a member of his group. Unseen

Path had Mesquite Spring campground all to themselves.
Mitch's motley crew of hobbyists and truth-seekers had come
not just to seek out clues of some decades-old conundrum
like usual, but to be a part of history, to step out into the
immediate wake of the latest national park mystery.

Some of the vehicles were RVs like Mitch's, some were
rugged 4x4s, and others looked barely roadworthy. All the
windows were dark save those of a camper shell on the back
of a Toyota pickup, where a soft glow hinted at late-night
reading or a hushed conversation.

The desert had a distinctive smell at night—a mix of
warm rock, scraggly plant life, and the ancientness of the
earth. This moment of serenity was precious, especially
considering what loomed on the horizon, and it was then that
Mitch pinpointed his apprehension.

It was guilt.

Guilt not for the upcoming tour—which some might label
as "exploitative"—but for what he had planned, shortly after
the tour began.

Carmen had given her full support for the tour only hours
before she went to sleep.

But Mitch hadn't even *mentioned* to her the other plan of
his, the one that would take place the morning after next, in
about—he checked his watch—twenty-nine hours.

Somehow he'd rationalized it to himself, deluded himself.
But now, the reality of it had come upon him in full force.

He looked out into the desert.

Clicked his teeth absentmindedly.

Well, as long as Carmen didn't find out about it—if he
didn't have a slip of the tongue in the next twenty-nine hours,
if she didn't catch him in the act the morning after next—
then he'd come clean and tell her what he'd done when this
was all over, when they were miles away from Death Valley.

Yes, that would work.

That should sate his conscience. That should keep his honor intact.

Yes.

He sighed. And smiled, his guilt dissipating. He had a full day and a few hours remaining; in that time, the guilt would fully subside, he was certain.

Contented, he turned and went back into his RV, heading for the bed.

CHAPTER FOUR

Pensacola, Florida

SILENCE EXITED the BMW and took the path to his mid-century, shotgun-style house nestled within Pensacola's eclectic East Hill community. Years earlier, the Watchers had given him the place as a starter home when he first joined the organization. There was a good reason Silence hadn't since moved.

The house's exterior was unremarkable in the soft glow of the streetlights. Inside, though, it was a carefully crafted zone of respite, somewhere Silence could unwind from his business of killing people for a living.

Or, at least, *usually*, it was Silence's sanctuary.

But not for the last week.

Ever since he'd returned from Ohio after completing his latest mission, his tranquil sphere of solace was in disarray. A situation had been thrust upon him.

It was past ten o'clock now, so East Hill was even quieter than its standard gentle vibe. The neighborhood was a sprawling affair where stately oaks contrasted with slender, swaying palms, weaving a tapestry of the aged and the tropical that mirrored the eclectic mix of architectural styles. With many homes already darkened for the daily trip to dreamland, only the gentle cadence of nocturnal insects and distant laughter from a lingering conversation graced the air.

As Silence stepped onto the deep, concrete porch, an unwanted thought flashed through his mind. Tanner. His trusted father figure. Two weeks in a row at Black Jack's. It was a mental paper cut, agitating Silence's always-chaotic mind space. The weight of despondence tugged at Silence, but he pressed it down.

He yawned again. Tanner was one of three reasons he'd had sleepless nights all week. The sight of Tanner heading into Black Jack's on Silence's initial night back in Pensacola, immediately upon returning from Ohio seven days ago, meant he hadn't had even a single night of solid sleep.

This was made all the worse by the fact that the Ohio mission had been so impacting.

Literally impacting.

Silence had been lost in a muddy cornfield outside Caledonia, Ohio, in the middle of the night when a fist had shot out from the darkened stalks. He was infinitely more trained than the Whitman cousins...

...but they knew the cornfields.

And Silence had only one shoe. The other had gotten sucked off his foot, the thick mud he'd stomped into suctioning it with an unbelievable grip.

The fists and boots had kept coming out of the darkness, into the cold evening air, still thick and damp after the earlier rain shower.

A fist, out of the corn. Gone again. Impact. Pain. Fist. Boot. Punch. Pain. Boot.

Silence had killed both Whitmans—double taps to each

of their heads, courtesy of his Beretta 92FS—but they'd put him through the Whac-A-Mole from Hell first.

Stepping inside his house, Silence got a glimpse of the crisp aesthetic that made the house his place of recovery— grays, blacks, and whites punctuated by gleaming chrome, stainless steel, and brushed nickel. The smattering of lush green tropical plants provided just the right amount of color contrast. Every square foot resonated with Silence's sense of order and cleanliness.

However, for a week now, the grayscale sanctity of his home had been utterly violated.

His gaze swept across the open floor plan and took in an accumulation of garish blankets, their patterns faded with age, sprawled across his pristine gray sectional sofa. Frayed towels adorned his kitchen chairs and other surfaces. At the center of it all was a vintage quilt with a bright pattern of reds, blues, and greens draped across his armchair.

A few of the dark towels belonged to Silence. Everything else—all of those gaudy, clashing colors, the hideous patterns, the wayward strings and the tattered edges—belonged to Rita Enfield, Silence's next-door neighbor. Mrs. Enfield was blind. And ancient. Neither style nor colors nor wear-and-tear bothered her much.

Mrs. Enfield was why Silence had never moved out of the small house in East Hill. He watched over her. And, in her own, blind way, she watched over him. Their friendship provided them both with a sense of comfort and security.

But even the best of friendships can be trying at times.

Or invasive...

Silence narrowed his eyes as he studied his assaulted space. The eyesores spread over every square inch of his furniture made for a jarring, blasphemous sight. A slap in the face.

At the epicenter of this disarray was the culprit—Baxter.

Mrs. Enfield's thickset orange tabby lay stretched out in carefree bliss on the sectional. The standard cat-smile was there on Baxter's face, accentuated by a line of drool trailing out of the corner of his mouth. Silence was taking care of Baxter for a week while Mrs. Enfield was out of town. He'd deployed the towels and blankets as the primary line of defense in his dayslong battle against fur and drool.

Drool.

Baxter was a drooler. A constant drooler. A line of saliva forever dangled out of the cat's cheerful face.

Silence's eyes trained on the current iteration of Baxter's ever-present string of saliva. As if aimed by a laser-guided system, the drool had somehow found the half-inch gap between the yellow-and-brown afghan Baxter was curled up on and the dark gray towel beside it.

There was a small puddle of cat spit...

...right there on the sectional's exquisite gray upholstery.

Silence's face tightened.

Twice. *Twice, now.* This was the second incident in a week, despite Silence's covering every square inch of his furniture.

Ugh.

He made his way to the linen closet on the opposite side of the living area and retrieved one of the few remaining hand towels that hadn't been conscripted into furniture-protection detail. A moment later, he was at the sofa, on his hands and knees with Baxter a foot and a half away, watching him, purring. Smiling. Possibly laughing.

As Silence methodically blotted the slobber—dabbing at it, not rubbing—he tempered his vexation with the knowledge that the drooling monarch's temporary reign in his household had nearly reached its end. Mrs. Enfield was to return that night.

The old woman's former caretaker and dear friend, Lola, visited several times a year from out of state. Though Lola typically spent the entirety of her visits within the Pensacola area—overnighting in Mrs. Enfield's house—this time, Silence's neighbor had succumbed to the travel itch, which manifested itself as a hankering for a road trip around the Southeast region beyond Panhandle Florida—a few days touring Alabama, Mississippi, and Louisiana, with a three-day finale in New Orleans.

Naturally, Lola had been happy to be Mrs. Enfield's chauffeur. If their itinerary had held true, the two women would be on the Interstate highway at that very moment, heading home, knocking out the final leg of their tour—the three-hour drive between the Big Easy and Pensacola.

Silence had been counting the hours until the moment he could hand the tabby back to Mrs. Enfield, strip away the blankets and towels, and get his home back to normal. The mission in Caledonia, Ohio, had been rough and left him in need of recuperation, decompression, a few moments of rest. But life hadn't obliged him. On the very first night of his return, he'd both received Baxter and trailed Tanner to Black Jack's, which led to the week-long nagging anxiety in his gut.

Yes, mental recovery had been scant the last seven days.

And then tonight, Silence had both trailed Tanner to Black Jack's for a second time and gotten the call from Falcon, telling him his next mission was to commence tomorrow.

...on the other side of the country.

R&R would have to wait a while longer.

A giant wet mark now graced Silence's beloved sectional—which, in its typical, non-blanket-and-towel-covered state, was a long, gray, squarish stretch of non-tufted fabric with firm but comfortable cushions—but Silence was satisfied that the remaining blemish was purely water-based with no remnants of Baxter's saliva. He pulled the afghan and the towel into tighter alignment, overlapping them, closing the gap.

He looked at Baxter.

Their eyes met. A man and a cat in silent communication. Baxter's immutable cat-smile seemed even more pronounced.

With the drool addressed and his house back in some semblance of order, Silence stepped away from the sofa to his table off the kitchen—glossy with stainless steel chairs. Spread across the surface were the case materials Falcon had sent to the fax machine in Silence's bedroom after their phone call earlier in the night. Maps, lists, photographs, charts.

On the left-hand side of the table was his PenPal. Silence picked it up, flipped past the Marvin Tanner-related notes he'd made for Elsher, and readied the more recent notes he'd taken during his phone call with Falcon. On the last page of the fresh content, he'd written a simple bulleted list: the primary components of his upcoming assignment.

Often, Silence created mind map diagrams of a mission's facts. It was one of the techniques C.C. had taught him to help organize the chaos of his mind. With the upcoming Death Valley affair, however, the concepts were so disparate that he needed to make a broader examination before he could consider crafting a mind map.

Hence, the bulleted list.

- *Death Valley NP bus tragedy, three days ago*
- *multiple unauthorized searches in FBI databases*
- *woman seen asking questions in region*
- *Raven's Ride*
- *Adrian Hirsch???*
- *Boston Legacy Center canopy collapse tragedy???*

At the mission's core was the Death Valley National Park

tour bus incident the previous week. As expected, national and international media had clambered to the story of fourteen elderly tourists and their bus driver being forced off the road and slaughtered with automatic weapons.

It occurred shortly after the start of this year's Raven's Ride motorcycle rally, an event that brought thousands of bikers and dozens of outlaw motorcycle clubs into the Southwest United States, localized near the convergence of California, Nevada, and Arizona, with the unofficial boundaries encompassing such locations and landmarks as Las Vegas, the Mojave Desert, and long stretches of Route 66, I-15, and I-40.

And, of course, Death Valley National Park.

For the last several years, Raven's Ride culminated in a final celebration at Ridgecrest, California, a city that no biker gangs called home, making it a neutral location, a Switzerland of the desert, negating much of the potential violence. Much, but not all. Not nearly all.

But the Watchers hadn't initially considered the Death Valley attack worthy of their covert efforts. Typically, Silence's organization allowed standard law-enforcement and judicial systems to run their course. It was only when people or entities escaped true justice that the Watchers stepped in and administered their brand of righteousness, sending out assassins like Silence to put things in proper order.

However, during the last few days, the Watchers—through their intricate web of technological and personnel wizardry embedded illegally within all levels of U.S. government—had gotten word of multiple unsanctioned FBI database queries regarding Death Valley. Naturally, the Bureau had been conducting its own research in conjunction with the National Park Service; this was not what had caught the Watchers' attention. Rather, for several days, FBI personnel had exchanged a flurry of panicked phone calls and emails regarding several unauthorized and unattributed computer searches in seemingly random offices throughout the United States: field offices in Memphis and Phoenix and a satellite office in Peoria, Illinois.

At the same time, a mystery woman had been spotted throughout the Raven's Ride area, asking enough questions to draw attention, to create a pattern. The right questions. Or maybe the *wrong* ones. The questions related directly to intel linked to the bizarre and unsanctioned FBI database queries.

This alone was enough to pique the Watchers' interest, but what warranted *immediate* action—in the form of mobilizing Silence—was the fact the woman was also asking people about two topics seemingly unrelated to the tour bus incident: Adrian Hirsch and the 1983 Boston Legacy Center architectural tragedy.

Both topics were glaringly incongruous with anything the Watchers—or the FBI or the NPS or the media—had yet discovered about the slaughter of the elderly tourists. Adrian Hirsch was an international criminal, one with a penchant for forged documents and brutal torture methods, and while his list of attributed crimes was prodigious, spanning decades, he was more the mass-smuggling and corporate espionage type, not anarchy and outright killing. In fact, Hirsch was known, perhaps infamously, to have never committed nor sanctioned a murder, despite moving in the same circles as the most murderous people in the world.

Even more confounding was the other topic the woman's investigation had disentombed: the Boston Legacy Center event, an architectural disaster from the previous decade. The only connection between the Boston tragedy and the recent tragedy in Death Valley seemed to be a loss of life. No one in the Watchers' massive, surreptitious think tank had decoded a connection between the two.

But for the last couple of hours, since getting the call

from Falcon, Silence had been trying to do just that. Reaching his hands to opposite sides of the table, he pulled the photocopied newspaper article alongside the photocopied encyclopedia article, aligning them neatly. He narrowed his eyes.

The newspaper article began with:

Tour Bus Attacked in Death Valley During Raven's Ride Rally: 15 Dead, Investigation Underway

DEATH VALLEY NATIONAL PARK — A tour bus carrying fourteen elderly tourists and its driver was found attacked in Death Valley National Park yesterday, with all on board confirmed dead. As the incident occurred during the Raven's Ride motorcycle rally, authorities are considering the possibility of motorcycle club involvement. As investigations are underway, no group has been officially named, but authorities are urging anyone with information to come forward.

And the encyclopedia article began with:

Among Boston's notable developments in the late 1970s was the Boston Legacy Center, a pinnacle of cultural and social endeavors. However, on November 7, 1983, this icon became the site of a catastrophic event, known thereafter as the Boston Legacy Center Canopy Collapse. Mirroring the devastation of Kansas City's Hyatt Regency walkway collapse in 1981, this incident at the Legacy Center resulted in the loss of 46 lives and injuries to over 90 individuals. The tragedy cast a shadow on the image of urban revitalization efforts of the late 1970s. It became a somber reminder of the implications of overlooking rigorous safety measures in architectural designs.

Silence closed his eyes. Visualization was another of the techniques C.C. had taught him, and it was instrumental in the beginning stages of a mission, particularly when the parameters were unclear, hazy. He envisioned the grandeur of Boston's cultural hub, the glittering attendees in evening gowns and tuxedos, rich scents of high-end catering, the horrifying noise of twisting metal, the tinkling of glass shards raining down from above. He then juxtaposed that with the barren Death Valley landscape, the unsuspecting tourists, the merciless gunfire cracking over the barren landscape.

While both events carried the gravity of unexpected catastrophe, the contexts felt worlds apart. The architectural negligence in Boston was disgusting, but it was an accident all the same; it stood in stark contrast to the outright murders in Death Valley.

As if things weren't confusing enough, there was also Hirsch.

Adrian Hirsch, with his East German roots and a track record of calculated, often geopolitically driven crimes, seemed worlds apart from the brutality of the recent massacre in the desert. From arms smuggling in Hungary to the ruthless extortion of a Spanish judge, his operations carried a signature of cold, methodical precision. The Watchers had been watching Hirsch for decades. So had the FBI, NSA, and other alphabet agencies. So had INTERPOL. The randomness of the bus slaughter was so uncharacteristic of Adrian Hirsch as to be confounding, even laughable, were it not so gut-wrenching.

Silence's hand drifted away from the articles to a photograph at the top of the table amid the other scattered mission materials. It was Hirsch, seated at a cozy outdoor bistro amid picturesque Europe. There was an ageless quality to the man, youthful but mature, as if time had no effect on him. His salt-and-pepper hair, immaculately styled and with a fine beard to match, bore the hallmark of an expensive salon. His tailored suit, too, suggested a designer's touch. Yet, the way he wore it —with the shirt casually unbuttoned at the top in the absence of a tie—added an air of relaxed confidence. Hirsch was lean, his physique telling a story of discipline and control. Every aspect of him was exact, down to his clear, unblemished skin.

From the pile, Silence's fingers next latched onto another pair of faxed photographs, these depicting a tall blonde woman. The grainy images were purloined from security cameras—one from an I-15 truck stop and another from a motel's dimly lit parking lot. Watchers data Specialists had massaged the clues, crunched the data, milked the details until they were confident this woman was the individual who'd been asking all the bizarre questions. The individual who seemed to be tied to unsanctioned FBI computer searches. The individual who'd brought the confoundingly out-of-place concepts of Adrian Hirsch and the Boston Legacy Center Canopy Collapse into an already opaque mass murder investigation.

No name.

No age.

No background.

Just two blurry images.

Silence squinted and leaned in closer. The details were difficult to discern, the shadows of the low-res pictures obfuscating the woman's features. She was Caucasian; that much was clear. Her height was undeniable, too, as was her robust yet unmistakably feminine build. Long, muscular legs carried her confidently in both shots. Dark blonde hair. But beyond these broad strokes, Silence struggled to extract any specifics.

He took a step backward from the table.

Sighed.

His thoughts whirled—*Death Valley, fifteen people slaughtered, FBI, mystery woman, Adrian Hirsch, Boston tragedy, 1983*—and he reached instinctively for more of C.C.'s mind methods. But he knew that while those techniques were invaluable, they wouldn't help when his thoughts were this torrential.

There was another method Silence had developed on his own, without C.C.'s help, *after* C.C.'s death, that could very well help. He kept this method stored away in his spare bedroom.

It was his floating pod, otherwise known as a sensory deprivation chamber.

Inside the pod, with the world's distractions muted, Silence found the clarity and focus that often eluded him elsewhere. It was more than just a place of calm; it was where his mind could untangle the most intricate of webs, providing insights into missions and problems that had previously seemed insurmountable.

Turning from the table, he walked past Baxter—who cat-smiled at him, drooling, purring—and made his way to the rear of the house. The first door off the hall was open six inches, blue light pouring out of the room beyond.

He entered.

CHAPTER FIVE

THE FLOATING pod dominated the confines of the small bedroom, nearly reaching the walls. Its surface was smooth and polished, oval in shape—a confluence of organic curves and state-of-the-art precision. Blue luminescence from the six-inch gap in the pod's lid transformed the bedroom into something otherworldly, like a decontamination chamber in a sci-fi spaceship.

Silence stripped naked, then stuck his hand in the bright glow emitting from the gap and pulled open the lid. A small shelf inside held the necessary supplies. He inserted the flanged silicone earplugs, then smeared petroleum jelly on the nicks and scrapes on his hands and face. This kept the salt water from stinging his wounds. He never skipped this step; Silence was always scratched up from his line of work.

The surface of the ten-inch pool of water before him was perfectly still, glowing a brilliant, artificial azure. Its temperature was skin-receptor-neutral 93.5 degrees, and it was loaded with eight hundred pounds of Epsom salt.

Silence stepped in, reclined, and immediately bobbed.

With that much salt in the water, anyone floated, even people with low buoyancy like Silence.

He grabbed the lid's inner handle and pulled down, sealing himself inside the blue glow. After a moment of this transitional stage, he reached for the buttons on the wall to his right, pressed the center button, and the blue light vanished.

All was dark. Entirely black.

Silence stretched out, his muscles relaxing as his body lolled with the subsiding undulations. The waterline fell at his chest, around his neck, halfway up his head, covering his ears. The flanged design of the earplugs, coupled with the coverage from the water, siphoned all sound from his perception.

After a few moments, the bobbing lessened, and, as per usual, as per the pod's purpose, Silence began to drift off. With the perfectly controlled water temperature, the pitch-black surroundings, the lack of sound, the lack of a sense of gravity, Silence simply melted away, losing track of where his flesh ended and the water began. He'd been absorbed into it. Or it had been absorbed into him.

This was one of his favorite parts of the experience—losing track of his physical form.

He blinked once, twice, three times. And grinned. This was another of his favorite aspects—registering no difference between having his eyes open or closed. His vision was an empty black void either way. The positioning of his eyelids no longer mattered.

Nothing mattered.

All the same, he closed his eyes.

C.C. had always said he was too uptight, and he hadn't disagreed. Even now, with C.C. long gone, he knew he still carried that rigidity within him. C.C. had always told him to let go. The pod helped him let go.

He used the pod not just to help with his uptightness but also as a bridge to the memories of C.C. This went against

C.C.'s notion of letting go, and his mind's version of her often
scolded him for doing it. But he continued nonetheless.
Immersed in the depths of the pod, C.C.'s presence became
tangible, even if just for a moment. It was worth the repri-
manding.

Beyond its uses of philosophical detachment and senti-
mental tethering, the pod also served a more practical, career-
minded purpose for Silence: as a sanctuary for his thoughts, a
place to clear the chaos. Right now, he needed it more than
ever—to help sort out the Death Valley situation before
embarking on the mission.

Visuals danced before his eyes, coming out of the darkness. A barren desert, mountains in the distance. Corpses, the
bloody mound of bodies he'd seen in the crime scene photo
that was among his mission materials. The mystery woman in
the surveillance images. Tall. Blonde. Obscured. People in
1980s-style eveningwear screaming as metal and glass rained
down on them.

The tour bus murders, those fifteen slaughtered souls.
Adrian Hirsch, not seen in the United States for years. The
Boston Legacy Canopy Collapse. 1983. The links were frag-
mental, puzzle pieces that wouldn't fit together, *couldn't* fit
together. Just as the tangled web of clues started to over-
whelm Silence, a sharper, more immediate thought pierced
through the confusion.

Tanner.

The idea that his old mentor, the man who'd shown him
the ropes, could be involved in illegal gambling somehow
overpowered everything happening on the other side of the
country. It was a shard of doubt wedged into the foundation
of trust Jake Rowe had built with Tanner years earlier.

New imagery appeared, starting with a week-old memory.
Tanner, walking into Black Jack's. Not exiting for an hour. A

week later, only hours ago, back at Black Jack's. Vanished once more. The men in the alley. The dice. The guy with the strong, twitching jaw and the piercing blue eyes staring at Silence out of the darkness for a long moment before retreating, disappearing.

A cogent part of Silence's mind asserted itself, recognizing the need to refocus, to pull his thoughts back to the matter at hand: Death Valley. But overall clarity could ultimately help him with his upcoming mission as well, he conceded. If he could temper his nagging suspicions about Tanner, it would help him with Death Valley.

So he let go.

The pod didn't lend him any clarity to the immediate mysteries.

Instead, it took him into yet another memory, this one even further back in time.

————

Years earlier. When Silence was Jake Rowe.

Across a battered desk, Jake faced Tanner. The lieutenant's office was just a box with a single window. Frames covered the side walls—certificates, a college diploma, faded photos of cops. Some framed family pictures sat on a shelf. A corkboard littered with papers and mugshots was in the back.

Jake was agitated. Leg bouncing. Fingers squeezed into fists, fighting off the shake. The folder was open on the desktop in front of him, one of many such folders brimming with materials related to Martinelli.

Jake had been in the office for nearly ten minutes, and Tanner continued to stare back at him, a stoic facade that occasionally broke out into a slight smile, which only confused Jake and amplified his frustration.

He jabbed a finger and, nearly shouting, told Tanner that the numbers didn't lie, that Martinelli was undoubtedly crooked. Fraud. Embezzlement.

Tanner's hands had been resting under his chin, fingers interlaced, while Jake pontificated. He removed them now, placed them on his desk.

"Jake," he began, voice firm yet not devoid of empathy, "sometimes, the most unexpected people keep the boldest secrets. But secrets aren't always insidious."

Jake threw his hands up. Stared at Tanner for a moment. Then tore into the contents of the folder before him, almost violently. Shouting now, he listed off the filth in the paperwork: financial discrepancies in Martinelli's accounts, high-end goods beyond his known income, and anonymous tips about his alleged illegal dealings.

Another one of those slight grins came to Tanner's face. "If it was as bad as you think," Tanner said, "we'd have gotten the warrant already."

Jake exhaled, nostrils flaring. Tanner's guidance sometimes bordered on condescension.

Still shouting, Jake contended that formalities weren't paramount —the truth was. His eyes flicked to the folder and back to Tanner before he continued in a quieter, almost defeated tone, rattling off the good Martinelli had done in the city, years' worth, a lengthy resume of charitable work with children.

All of it was a farce.

Tanner's nod was one of understanding. "Part of the job, Jake. It's never easy when you flip a guy end over end and find a dark side of him you never knew existed." He stabbed one of his beefy fingers at the documents. "But are you sure you're right about Martinelli? Or is your anger clouding your judgement?"

———

BUZZ! BUZZ! BUZZ!

Silence jolted, sending waves sloshing against the pod's

curved inner walls. He reached out, pressed a button, and the buzzing stopped.

He took a deep breath to calm his rapid breathing and rapid heartbeat after the sudden shock from one reality to another.

With one hand, he palmed the wall and steadied himself against the sloshing water, and with the other, he reached up and opened the lid. Blue light flooded over him.

Though floating pods were soundproof, Silence had made a crucial modification to his: a blaring chime. It was linked to a series of nearly invisible motion sensors on his house's exterior, which ensured he was never entirely cut off from the outside world. One sensor kept tabs on the gravel drive between his home and Mrs. Enfield's. Often, he disabled the system, but this time, since he was anxiously awaiting Mrs. Enfield's return—as it meant he could hand Baxter back to her—he'd left it on.

Emerging from the pod, water streamed down his six-foot-three frame, cascading in rivulets onto the teak flooring and gurgling in the drains beneath. Though the pod took up a significant portion of the room, there was just enough space for a lavish rain shower head installed in one corner, complete with its own drain. Silence hurried to it and took a thirty-second rinse, ridding himself of the salt water. He then grabbed his robe from the adjacent hook and exited.

As he crossed to the front of the house, Baxter watched him from the same spot on the sectional. Smiling. Purring. Drooling.

Silence smiled back at him. A slightly dark smile. The cat's time in his house was almost over.

At the side window, Silence peeked through the blinds. Outside, in the soft glow of the evening, Lola was stepping out the front door of Mrs. Enfield's Victorian home onto the porch. Her Taurus was in the drive. Her face turned in Silence's direction.

Silence yanked his finger out of the blinds.

Lola's voice—muffled through the glass but still piercingly clear—cried out.

"I saw you, jackass!"

Silence groaned.

He looked at Baxter, who seemed to be laughing at him again. A moment of frozen paralysis at the window. Then Silence went to his door, opened it, and thrust his head out into the night.

Lola was now standing by the Taurus, arms crossed, leg kicked out, eyes narrowed. She was mixed-race Asian, thirty-something, and a natural beauty. She wore shorts, a T-shirt, and a bangle bracelet.

"You weren't gonna say hi?" Lola uttered.

No, Silence hadn't at all planned on saying hello.

Lola had moved out of Florida years ago and now lived in Knoxville, Tennessee, five hundred miles away. When she'd still been in Pensacola, her relationship with Mrs. Enfield had become more than just that of a caretaker—they'd become dear friends—so now Lola visited at least once a year.

When she did, she always pushed the limits with Silence. She spoke a little too sweetly. She stood a little too closely. Even though she knew Silence was engaged, Lola seemed to have somehow deciphered the fact that Silence's fiancée was no longer among the living, despite neither Silence nor Mrs. Enfield having told her.

Case in point: right now. She'd just demanded to know why he hadn't said hi. They were friends of a sort, yes, but nothing said Silence had to say hello to his elderly neighbor's former caretaker when she visited from out of state.

Silence leaned a bit farther out the door, revealing more of himself.

"I'm in a robe," he stated simply, as if that explained everything.

Lola rolled her eyes. "Really? That's your best excuse, Si? A robe?"

Silence didn't respond.

Lola uncrossed and recrossed her arms. "Why didn't you say hi when I first got here a week ago, huh? Wearin' a robe then, too?"

No, Silence had been even more cowardly that time, shutting off all the lights, acting like he wasn't home, and telling Mrs. Enfield that he'd have to pick up Baxter shortly after the two women commenced their road trip.

Silence didn't respond.

Lola shook her head. "Whatever. Well, lucky for you, I got work tomorrow, so I'm taking off now, driving halfway home."

She opened her driver's-side door.

"Safe travels," Silence said.

Lola shut the door behind her, looked at him through the passenger window, and rolled her eyes again. The Taurus backed out.

Closing the door behind him, Silence immediately brought his gaze to Baxter.

"Time to leave," Silence said, a hint of mirth in his ruined voice.

———

As soon as Silence entered the house, Baxter squirmed, eager to be back in familiar arms. Without hesitation, Silence transferred the bulky orange tabby into Mrs. Enfield's waiting embrace. Purring filled the room.

"Oh, my precious boy!" Mrs. Enfield exclaimed, her withered old voice wavering with emotion. She cuddled the cat close, fingers running through his fur. "Baxter, baby, look at you! Were you good for Si? Oh, how I missed you!"

She nuzzled her face into his neck, whispering endearments that only the two of them would understand.

Silence watched. The simplicity of their bond, the depth of their connection, made the complexities of his own world seem distant, if only for a fleeting moment.

Mrs. Enfield was tiny, shriveled, black, and blind, with eyes as blazing white as her hair. They were in her living room. Despite its beauty, the old house's antique atmosphere and outdated furniture, combined with the blind woman's perpetually dim lighting, always made it feel eerie.

When she finally pulled her attention away from the cat, Mrs. Enfield's smile dipped slightly as her lifeless, milky eyes "looked" at Silence.

"You have a cloud over you," she said. "I noticed it the moment you stepped through the door. You seem ... burdened. And I doubt it's just Lola's doing."

No matter how often she did this, Silence was still caught off guard. She could read him almost as well as C.C. had. Maybe even better. Silence was good at reading people too, which made him appreciate her ability all the more.

The confusion of the upcoming mission was heavy on Silence's mind.

But he knew it wasn't Death Valley that Mrs. Enfield was perceiving.

With a heavy sigh, he confessed, "An old friend ... Someone I trusted." He swallowed. "Beginning to wonder if..." Another swallow. "I ever truly knew him."

It was all the detail he could offer. Not only did Silence's ruined voice discourage long explanations, but he couldn't inform her of his work or his past. Mrs. Enfield, in her intuitive way, had long ago discerned that Silence belonged to some sort of violent, secretive profession; she'd never pressed him on the specifics of his job nor the life that came before it.

But she still perceived the truth of things.

The room grew quiet as Mrs. Enfield absorbed his words. Sensing the change in mood, Baxter curled up tighter in the old woman's arms, his purring a comforting background to the heavy stillness.

After a few moments, Mrs. Enfield spoke.

"Oh Si," she said, "Sometimes, we see the version of a person they want us to see, or maybe the version we choose to see. But there are multiple sides to each and every one of us."

Silence turned away, looked at the hardwood floor.

Mrs. Enfield was wise.

Like C.C.

But also unlike her.

"Thank you," he said.

He gave one more glance at Baxter, a parting shot, a look of triumph. Baxter was unaffected. He smiled. A line of drool dangled from his mouth.

"Have to go," Silence said to Mrs. Enfield. He swallowed. "Business trip tomorrow."

He placed his hand on her shoulder, squeezed, then turned.

"Si?" Mrs. Enfield said.

Silence stopped at the door, faced her again.

"Be safe."

Silence nodded. "Yes, ma'am."

He left.

CHAPTER SIX

Las Vegas, Nevada

THE NEXT DAY.

The pawnshop was an outcast, banished to the periphery of Las Vegas, miles away from the world-famous casinos and attractions, among a collection of other such structural refuse. In faded letters, the sign proclaimed *FREDDY'S FORTUNES PAWN & JEWELRY*. The windows were an all but meaningless affair, their visibility obscured by a one-two punch of iron bars and a spattering of announcements like *WE BUY GOLD* and *12-WEEK LAYAWAY* and *CASH LOANS*. The river rock veneer must have been chic back in the '60s or '70s before the place was reduced to its current state.

Leah Bloom emerged from the Chevy Nova. Not even noon yet, and the temperature was already blistering, though the air was so dry it was bearable. The blazing sun gave her an excuse to lower her ball cap further, while the true reason was the pair of security cameras she'd spotted perched in the corners of Freddy's awning—sleek, modern, jarringly high-tech.

A bell on a mangled strip of metal offered a sad rendition of a clang as she entered. The place smelled of decay, body odor, and desperation. A tower of electronics rose from a corner. Handbags and VHS tapes were locked in an eternal struggle for dusty shelf space.

Twitchy eyes surreptitiously assessed Bloom as she entered. There were murmured exchanges, the kind only initiated by unexpected shifts in a room's dynamics. The three patrons—all men—glanced at each other, nodding slightly in Bloom's direction. Their not-so-covert exchanges wouldn't have worried her a couple of days ago, but by this point, she'd become increasingly concerned about the reputation she knew she was fostering.

Was she merely a stranger to these men, a rare outsider in Freddy's Fortunes?

Or were their minds hard at work linking the tall woman before them to the rumors floating around the Raven's Ride region?

Though trepidation tugged at her, a more important notion—her reason for this visit to the pawnshop—overpowered it.

The trail had gone cold.

She couldn't make out the men's low, rumbling voices, but the paranoid part of her filled in the blanks, offering dialogue, an exchange of rumors about the individual with a distinctive height and build who'd been roaming the desert, asking questions.

That's her, ain't it? one of them might be saying. *I heard she's real tall, kinda muscley.*

That's what they say, the other could reply. *Over in Enterprise, I heard she's five-foot-eleven.*

Subtly angling away from the men, Bloom did a quick

scan of the ceiling, the corners of the space. More security cameras. They matched the ones she'd seen outside—small and matte black with flashing red lights, clearly expensive. Instinctually, her face lowered just a fraction more to obscure her features beneath the brim of her hat. She hadn't removed her sunglasses upon entering. And she wouldn't.

Funny how destitute places like this never skimped on security. Throughout this self-imposed mission, Bloom had become accustomed to dodging the probing eyes of surveillance, acutely aware of how formidable her organization was at sifting through visual data.

Including visual data that didn't belong to them.

Behind a clear acrylic counter housing rows of jewelry and watches labeled with circular paper tags on strings, a round man with a red-and-gray beard in a cutoff T-shirt watched her approach. His bearing said he owned the place. Freddy.

Freddy's squinting eyes settled on her, and she could tell he was evaluating her height if not her build as well. The staring wasn't overt, but Bloom felt the vacuum of the room's attention, amplified now with Freddy's curiosity, as though the proprietor's dubiousness had been a stamp of approval for the others. Again, paranoia whispered to her that it was folly for someone with a distinctive appearance to conduct an illegal covert op.

Bloom ignored the men's murmurs, her focus narrowing on Freddy. Despite his lassitude, there was a spark in him, clearly evident in the eyes. Not a man to be taken lightly.

Bloom stopped at the counter, and Freddy smiled.

"What can I do for you, pretty lady?" He jabbed a beefy fingertip onto the scuffed-up acrylic, indicating the wares below. "Got some real nice necklaces. Sterling silver. Got some Black Hills gold in yesterday."

"No jewelry," Bloom said. "Information."

One of Freddy's bushy eyebrows lifted. "Information?"

"I need to find a biker gang."

Freddy snorted. "There are plenty of those around the area. We got Raven's Ride goin' on right now. It's a big motorcycle rally. Huge. Wraps up in Ridgecrest tomorrow night, a big 'ol party."

"I know. I'm looking for a specific gang. The Lost Jackals. Where can I find them?"

The man's laughter surprised her—a barking sound, full of irony and disbelief, ricocheting off the walls of his establishment.

"Lady, this is a pawnshop. I buy and sell shit. Stereos. Tear-stained promise rings. Get it?"

"Yeah? Well, you bought *that*," Bloom said, pointing across the room.

Freddy looked.

Bloom was pointing at a Craftsman radial arm saw wedged between a pair of 1980s arcade stations—*Pac-Man* and *Space Invaders*.

Freddy returned his attention to her. "And?"

"The Lost Jackals knocked over a truckload of Sears merchandise a month ago."

"And?"

She pointed at the saw again. "*And* that saw was on the truck. *And* a Jackal sold it to you two days ago."

Freddy's response threaded a fine line between patience and menace. "I believe I was clear."

He then glanced at a man in the back, and when Bloom looked, she noticed a striking resemblance between Freddy and the younger guy. The set of the jaw, the slope of the nose. Like a beefed-up, clearer-eyed, less Jabba the Hutt version of the man behind the counter.

Family.

Li'l Freddy Jr., no doubt.

Junior shifted his weight, reacting to Freddy's subtle nod.

As Bloom watched him draw nearer, her fingers drummed on her thigh. She'd been at this for a couple of days, but there was still much work to do. Any altercation with Junior would risk further cementing the unwanted reputation she was inadvertently crafting in the shadows of the region. This was a concern.

The shop grew quiet. Bloom took a measured breath, eased her right foot back into position, and settled her weight, while her mind assessed options, calculating angles and trajectories.

Junior's smile was both irked and amused, revealing yellow teeth with nicotine stains. She saw physical intent in his eyes, but not violence. He probably expected Bloom to back down, to be cowed by his sheer size. A yard away, Junior reached out, a bear paw going for Bloom's shoulder.

"All right, lady, it's time—"

Bloom sidestepped, avoided his grab, shifted her weight into the foot she'd planted behind her. Momentum betrayed Junior. So did mass. A practical lesson in physics.

Or a practical joke, perhaps.

Unable to arrest his forward motion, Junior's arms went flying in circles. His footsteps *thump-thump-thumped* forward two yards until he crashed face-first into a stack of cheap Japanese miniature TVs. A cacophony of creaking plastic and shattered glass echoed through the space.

The other two men in the back gasped. Freddy pulled his girth off his stool, leaning over the counter, looking across the space with wide eyes.

"You broke my inventory, bitch!" Freddy spat.

Then Bloom noticed the angle of his sightline—aimed not at his presumed son but a fraction of a degree past Junior at the pile of mostly broken six- to eighteen-inch televisions.

"You're paying for those. You—"

"No, I'm not."

"You instigated a fight in my shop, and—"

"I didn't touch him. You want to blame someone, blame gravity. Or his fat ass."

On the floor, Junior was groaning among the consumer culture rubble. His "fat ass" was on full display, half hanging out of his now bunched-up jeans—sweaty, pink, jiggling as he tried to right himself.

Freddy's eyes studied Bloom. His expression changed. "How did you do that? You ... moved so quick-like."

She stepped back to the counter. Now that Freddy had gotten himself off his stool, their faces were only inches apart.

"I didn't touch him," Bloom repeated. "Think that through."

She paused, letting Freddy's mind do the work for her as he looked back into the darkness of her sunglasses, allowing the implication to germinate.

Then she continued. "Now, where can I find the Lost Jackals?"

The shop was silent, save for Junior's grunts as he attempted to extricate himself from the televisions.

Freddy swallowed. He glanced again at Junior, then back to Bloom.

"Pahrump," he whispered, the name escaping his lips like a plea. He pointed at the radial arm saw. "The ones who brought that were going to Pahrump."

"How many of them?"

"Two."

"What'd they look like?"

"One of them was a Mexican-lookin' guy. The other was white, tall, skinny as hell, buzz-cut hair."

Damn. Neither of the descriptions came close to the man Bloom wanted. But the intel was enough to get her closer to the Jackals, to keep her on the trail.

Bloom nodded, acknowledging Freddy's cooperation, then turned away from the counter.

Junior had managed to flip himself right-side up. He watched her—arms crossed on his knees, sitting among the tiny TVs—as she passed.

The bell clattered again. Sunlight. Heat. Pausing in the doorway, Bloom cast a glance back inside, looking over the men one by one—Customer 1, Customer 2, Junior, Freddy. She conveyed menace, a warning, something to ward off potential gossip.

It was an attempt, but it was also largely pointless. The men would surely talk, and the rumors of the woman roaming the Raven's Ride region asking suspicious questions would surely grow.

But it was worth it. She'd gotten a lead. She knew where to find the Lost Jackals.

Anyway, if she was going to see this thing through, she wouldn't be able to hide in the shadows forever.

She went to her car.

CHAPTER SEVEN

"YEAH, I SEEN HER."

The old gas station attendant had barely looked up from his dog-eared book of crossword puzzles as he replied. His face was a map of wrinkles. Early seventies. Native American ancestry. Red flannel shirt, open halfway down, exposing white chest hair. Don't-give-a-shit white stubble beard.

Sunlight poured through the windows, casting a long shadow of Silence's figure across the dingy linoleum. It was one of those stretched-out shadows that Silence had long ago come to identify with the American West, like the ominous silhouette of a gunfighter on the brink of a shootout—only flash-forwarded to the late twentieth century in a grimy convenience store stuffed to the gills with beer and Little Debbie's snack cakes and a dozen or so varieties of chewing gum. The scent of stale coffee and two-day-old corn dogs wafted over from the stainless steel counter in the back.

Silence used a finger to retrieve the printout, dragging it back across the scratched glass surface between him and the other man. It was one of the security images of the mystery woman, the one from the motel parking lot, the one in which she was not wearing a ball cap, her blond hair on full display. Silence doubled, then quartered the paper along the folds he'd established and returned it to the back pocket of his chinos.

He looked back at the old-timer and blinked, inviting the man to continue.

"She pulled up in a beat-to-hell Chevy," the man rasped, scratching his stubbled chin. "Wanted to know where she could find ...which one was it? ... QuickPawn. No. Not Quick-Pawn. Freddy's, it was. Freddy's Fortunes."

A pet parrot, vivid emerald in color, ruffled its feathers from its perch a few feet behind the counter, interrupting the conversation with a sudden squawk of, "Bingo!"

The attendant shot the bird a sidelong glance.

"Damn bird," he muttered, following it up with a chuckle.

There was an odd camaraderie between the two. When Silence entered, the old man had been talking to the bird. The latter had replied almost like it understood. Their casual banter was more akin to two old pals than man and beast.

"What kind of Chevy?" Silence said.

"A banged-up Nova. Fifth gen. Or was it the fourth?" He waved it off with a knobby hand. "Doesn't matter. The last generation. Not one of the cool ol' muscle car types. Hideous thing."

Silence couldn't talk cars with the guy, but he was inclined to agree. The final Novas didn't hold a candle to the old ones.

"Color?" Silence said.

"Blue. But plenty of orange rust, too."

The man emitted a dry laugh at that.

The bird said, "Bingo!"

The attendant responded by leaning back and giving the bird an indulgent pat, grinning a piano key pattern of teeth.

"Thanks," Silence said. He pulled a crisp twenty from his

wallet—the promised remuneration—and slid it across the glass.

As Silence pushed through the door, he heard the parrot one more time.

"Bingo!"

———

Silence approached the entrance of Freddy's Fortunes Pawn & Jewelry, immediately noting the eerie absence of activity. The place didn't just seem deserted; it had the marks of recent turmoil. Debris—broken glass, cracked television casings.

There was a sensation of earlier-that-day chaos still crackling through the air, like pulses of static electricity, the echoes of violence. C.C. had always said that events leave spiritual reverberations. Although Silence honed his natural empathic abilities in a much less hippie-ish way than his deceased fiancée had, he still listened to his intuition when it had something important to say.

And it was speaking to him now.

Something had happened in this pawnshop.

Silence was shrinking the gap. The woman was close now. He could sense her, smell her.

Endorphins flushed through him, emboldening his stride, straightening his spine. The thrill of the chase.

The moment he stepped through the threshold, a broomstick swung in his direction, going for his head.

Silence put out a hand—*thwack!*—and absorbed the impact with his palm, bringing the rod to a dead stop. A grizzled-looking man released the broomstick and lunged at Silence. Just a few steps behind was a younger man with a large bruise on his face who looked like the grizzly fellow's son. He lunged, too.

But Silence deftly sidestepped the attack, swinging the broomstick in a broad stroke that scraped across both of their shins. It wasn't a devastating move—Silence had sensed immediately these men were frightened, not dangerous—but it certainly hurt like hell, evidenced by the fact that both men dropped to their knees, howling.

In this now-free moment, Silence assessed the pawn shop's interior. The air carried a distinct aroma of dust, aged metal, and over-taxed motors. A shit-ton of second-hand novelties surrounded the groaning men, and among the not-so-gently used items was a pile of broken TVs—the sort of miniature televisions kept on a desk or in a child's bedroom. Glass and cracked black plastic littered the floor beneath the mound. A second broom was propped against the wall, and the mess had been contained to a tight circle but not yet discarded. Recent destruction, but not too recent.

Silence reached a hand out to the older man—a rotund individual who wore a tank top and sported a fading red beard. He was in his sixties. Or possibly a hard-livin' fifties. Silence guessed the latter.

The man hesitated, not out of pride but bewilderment. A moment passed. Then the man took Silence's hand. Silence helped him up, then the younger one as well.

Panting, the older man leaned against the display case. The acrylic creaked. There was a strange sort of unease smeared all over the man, not just due to the moments-earlier scuffle, but as though he'd swallowed another heaping helping of humble pie earlier in the day during the event that had been the cause of the shop's disquietude, a tough guy who'd been caught in two mortifying moments of vulnerability.

The younger man retreated to a rickety stool in a poorly lit corner where an ice pack was already waiting. He put it to his bruised forehead.

"You're with her, aren't you? The lady who was in here

earlier?" the older man—Freddy, no doubt—said as Silence stopped in front of him. "You gotta be, 'cause you fight like her. Are you, like, a fed or something? I figure you are, dressed like that."

Freddy's eyes looked Silence up and down.

Silence glanced at his outfit as well. He had chosen a pale gray linen shirt, short-sleeved, an appropriate choice for this stage of his investigation in the desert when he'd be spending a considerable amount of time outdoors. On his lower half, he wore tailored Ted Baker chinos in a muted navy hue, selected for their lightweight fabric—breathable yet sophisticated, ideal for the biting heat. The brogues on his feet were from Cole Haan, and the model bore a particularly thick sole, better to fend off the scorching pavement.

The bead bracelet? Well, that was just pure indulgence. Slightly counterproductive, actually. Tiny spots of perspiration had surfaced beneath the beads.

Freddy must have believed Silence was some sort of investigator. Which, of course, he was, but not in the way Freddy or others often assumed during Silence's work. People thought he was a police officer or a federal agent or a private eye or hired muscle working for some criminal outfit. Often, it was in Silence's best interests to let the assumption ride.

So he looked back up at Freddy and said, "Talk."

At the sound of Silence's voice, Freddy's eyes went wide, apprehension amplified.

"I ... I already told her all I know, brother. Okay? Just ask her."

Silence didn't respond.

"I got nothing else. I swear! Look what she did to my boy!" Freddy said and pointed.

In the back, the younger man stirred but didn't look up, only adjusted his ice pack.

Freddy's expression slackened by a fraction, and a sparkle

of realization flashed across his eyes. "Wait. Wait, you're not *with* her, are you? You're *following* her."

Silence didn't respond.

"Okay, man. Okay! She asked about the Lost Jackals," Freddy said. "You know, the motorcycle gang? I told her she'd have a hard time tracking them down, what with Raven's Ride goin' on."

Freddy gestured toward a handmade sign hanging by the cash register. The cardboard was discolored from time, scrawled with: *BIKERS WELCOME*. The subtler text beneath—with a less-than-subtle misspelling—said: *We Love Ravin's Ride*.

The mystery woman had narrowed down the specific motorcycle gang associated with the tour bus slaughter: the Lost Jackals. This was no small feat, given the preponderance of gangs in orbit around the region for days on end during Raven's Ride.

A pulse of intrigue throbbed in Silence's mind. The Lost Jackals were an outlaw motorcycle club based in Bakersfield, California, one of the notorious one-percenter gangs. Their gang color—displayed on bandanas and patches—was a light blue. They were infamous for their brutality.

But the senseless murder of tourists? It wasn't their style.

Silence didn't respond.

"I told her to go to Pahrump," Freddy said. "That's it! That's all I know. A pair of the Jackals came in here two days ago. They said they was on their way to Pahrump."

Silence didn't respond.

He waited.

After a moment, he looked at the injured young man in the back, then returned his attention to the beleaguered Freddy.

There was nothing else to be had here.

He nodded.

And left.

He threw on his shades as he stepped back into the desert sun. There was a feeling of abandonment in the air, as if time hadn't stopped for this part of town but skipped over it entirely. Nondescript cars lined the roadside with no accompanying signs of life. Beyond was a ramshackle neighborhood with peeling paint, boarded windows, and dilapidated porches.

But past the rooftops, in the distance, Silence could just discern the bookshelf outline of the Las Vegas Strip. As fortune dictated, his years of missions had taken Silence to the Strip multiple times. He had a lot of memories out there in the glitzy distance. Most of them brutal. But a few of them pleasant, too.

Walking away from Freddy's Fortunes Pawn & Jewelry, he segued his thoughts from the past to the present. He'd hunted down many individuals, but this mystery woman was proving to be an enigma. He'd known that she must be connected in the right places—having somehow gotten the information from the illegal FBI database searches—but now, after meeting the men in the shop behind him, he knew something else about her.

She was also dangerous.

Violent, even.

Silence would need to recalibrate.

CHAPTER EIGHT

Death Valley National Park, California

IT HAD BEEN hours since the sun edged over the distant mountain range, and it now blasted across the vast expanse of Death Valley and the collection of vehicles at the Mesquite Spring campground.

The day's tasks swirled in Mitch's mind. His hair ruffled gently in the dry breeze as he leaned over the extra-wide steel carrier rack at the back of his RV that held a matching pair of dirt bikes facing in opposite directions. One was his; one was Carmen's. His and hers.

A battered toolbox, a bucket filled with towels and fluids, and a five-gallon red plastic gasoline can stood at his feet. He'd been servicing the bikes for the last several minutes. For what he had in mind—not that day's Unseen Path tour, but his solo work the following morning—his bike needed to be in tip-top condition. He couldn't risk waking Carmen tomorrow morning, on the day of the task, so he was getting everything ready ahead of time.

He checked his watch.

Less than eighteen hours.

The Unseen Path tour was scheduled for early afternoon, and many of the vehicles surrounding Mitch were stirring with life—trailer doors opening, sun shades retracting and collapsing out of windshields, people milling about outside.

Mitch cursed himself.

He should have started this process earlier to draw less attention before the sun peeked over the mountains. But he'd been *damn* tired when his alarm had woken him up. Last night, guilt hadn't subsided as much as he'd optimistically believed, so after he'd climbed back into bed with Carmen, he'd remained awake for some time.

He'd need to remedy that tonight. Sleep was necessary for his upcoming work. He had to remain sharp.

He pressed the dipstick back into the 200cc engine, grimacing as he saw movement in his peripheral. Though he'd tried to be inconspicuous, his actions were a beacon attracting the attention of the ever-curious Unseen Path members. Of course, that's why Mitch loved these folks— their skepticism, their well-intended distrust, their constant vigilance. But right now, the benign paranoia of his hangers-on was problematic for Mitch.

"Mitch!" a voice echoed across the campground. It was George, one of the more enthusiastic tour members.

Mitch's heart sank a little as he watched the burly man in a cutoff T, gym shorts, and splayed-open galoshes stomping toward him, his broad smile almost reaching his twinkling eyes.

"Morning, George," Mitch called out, striving to keep his voice casual. He watched as George's gaze fell onto the dirt bikes, a question forming on the man's lips.

"Planning a bit of off-roading later, Mitch?" George said.

Mitch shrugged. "Just keeping up on things. You know how these bikes can be. Need a lot of love."

George's laugh filled the morning air. A smoker's laugh. By the cigarette odor, it was clear George had already enjoyed his morning treat.

"Can't wait for the tour," George said. "This one's gonna be wild."

He stomped off.

George was a veteran of four previous Unseen Path tours. He was hyper-paranoid but also one of the friendliest people Mitch had ever met.

There was the creak of a door from the other side of the RV. Footsteps crunching on rock. Then Carmen appeared. She was still wearing the T-shirt and shorts she'd slept in, though she'd put on a bra before stepping out into the public space of the campground. Her dark hair was piled in a loose, just-got-up bun atop her head, its glossiness shining in the bright morning sun. Unlike Mitch, however, the light wasn't making her squint; her dark eyes were practically impervious to brightness, though she loved wearing sunglasses.

Those dark eyes registered a sort of skepticism as she looked right at him. Before meeting his wife, Mitch had never dated a Latina, but a buddy of his, Sammy, had had relationships with more than one, and he'd advised Mitch, *Don't try to pull any shit on Carmen, man. You won't get away with it. Never get sneaky with a Latina.*

Carmen raised an eyebrow in an all-too-familiar expression. She took in the fuel cans, the bucket of additives, Mitch's hands on the bikes, and sighed softly.

"Only a few hours until start time," she said. Her English was flawless, but her Mexican accent was prominent, holding on strong for all these years, a permanent fixture. "Surely you weren't planning on going for a ride. Not without telling me." A pause. "So what are you up to?"

"Just maintenance, babe," Mitch said, injecting as much assurance into his voice as possible. "Just maintenance."

"What are you up to, Mitch?" Carmen repeated.

Sammy's words sounded in Mitch's mind once more. *Never get sneaky with a Latina.*

Mitch smiled, stepped away from the bikes—as though distancing himself from the machines might quell the situation, a foolish idea—and approached her.

"Maintenance," he said and dropped his hands on her shoulders. "I want us to take some rides after the tour."

Carmen looked up at him from way down there at her five-foot-two apex. She lowered the eyebrow, but she didn't smile back at him. She frowned. And left.

Mitch leaned around the corner and watched as she disappeared back into the RV. After a moment of looking at the closed door, his gaze settled back on the dirt bikes, their presence whispering of tomorrow morning's secretive work.

He stepped back toward the bikes, where he reached down and plucked out the folder he'd wedged under the bucket. Inside was the single-sheet printout he'd distributed last night to every vehicle in the campground—the day's itinerary. He flipped past that sheet to tomorrow's itinerary, the final and most important day of the tour, the real reason everyone had forked out the not inconsiderable price Mitch had charged.

Mitch and Carmen, in their RV, would lead the Unseen Path caravan, retracing the route taken by the ill-fated tour bus less than a week prior. The journey would begin with them rolling eastward, eventually exiting both Death Valley and the state of California. Once they crossed into the tiny town of Beatty, Nevada, the group would halt at a greasy spoon called Dusty Vittles. It was more than just a spot to scarf on locally renowned breakfast; it was where the doomed bus's passengers had their final meal. Mitch and the others would dine on the same eggs, bacon, and buckwheat pancakes.

After Beatty, the journey would pivot, returning to California and Death Valley National Park. The Legacy Route bus's destination had been Ubehebe Crater, so Mitch would take Unseen Path westward on 190 before taking a right turn onto North Highway.

Along the way to the NPS highway barricade, Mitch planned several sightseeing detours. While the stops would be scenic—the perfect opportunities for photographs, stretching, hydrating, and snacking—Mitch would spice them up with eerie stories from the annals of national park mysteries.

These tales would have nothing to do with the grim shadow of the previous week; it was a tactical way to stretch the tour out a bit. If he was being honest with himself, there was really only so much he could provide on a tour like this. By day's end, they would settle in at Mesquite Spring Campground, and hopefully they would have the place to themselves again.

All of this would be accomplished *after* Mitch's secretive solo work.

He glanced across the campground now. Isolated. Rustic. It was the perfect staging location for what he had planned the following day.

That is, if he could slip away unnoticed.

Carmen's suspicions had already been piqued, and Mitch had learned long ago that it was in his best interests to not piss her off.

I know, Sammy, Mitch thought. *You're right. But I can make this work.*

CHAPTER NINE

Pahrump, Nevada

SILENCE SHIFTED INTO SECOND, the tactile response providing a satisfaction he rarely savored: driving a manual transmission. The *thunk* as the stick dropped into place was enough to make him grin. There was something instinctive and natural about driving a stick shift, feeling the vibration as the vehicle responded directly to one's command.

He was in a Jeep Wrangler, something quite different from the posh interiors and smooth rides of the luxury machines to which he was accustomed. The Watchers had arranged for the Jeep to be waiting for him when his flight touched down at the Las Vegas airport, accommodating Silence's request for a 4x4. His mission centered on the desert of Death Valley National Park, and he might need to leave the comfort of paved roads.

Silence glanced down momentarily, catching sight of his Cole Haan brogues working the trio of pedals. A stark juxtaposition struck him: the pristine leather shoes against the utilitarian rubber pads. This mirrored the contrast between the rugged Jeep and the sophisticated sleekness of his BMW back in Pensacola. Each had its purpose, its own language, but one spoke of city streets and high-speed chases; the other whispered tales of desert tracks and rocky pathways.

The BMW at home was a fantastic ride, but it hadn't been with him long. And it wouldn't be for much longer, either. Every six months, without fail, the Watchers provided Silence a new set of wheels. The reasoning was layered—sometimes it was about upgrades, other times for anonymity's sake. Silence had learned early on not to become overly attached to his vehicles.

His preference was for luxury machines, with BMWs high on his list, their blend of performance and sophistication aligning with his tastes. On occasion, for the hell of it, he would opt for a sports car. Now, as the Jeep thumped over a particularly rough patch of cracked street, its suspension absorbing the bumps with ease, he pondered a future with a similar vehicle. This Jeep—silver in color and fortified with a hardtop—had grown on him in the scant hours they'd been acquainted.

Maybe his next six-month vehicle would be neither a luxury machine nor a sports car.

Maybe it would be a Wrangler...

Hmm.

Dusk had settled in, and the dim outlines of the Pahrump, Nevada, cityscape started to blend into the violet canvas of twilight. Silence kept a measured distance from the faded blue Chevy Nova ahead of him. In practice, the drive between Vegas and Pahrump was less than two hours, but it had taken the Nova and the Wrangler several additional hours.

First, the mystery woman had stopped at McDonald's. Then she'd taken a three-hour nap in a discount store parking lot. Silence didn't need to guess at her reason for such a lengthy midday sleep; he'd conducted enough investigations to know that you gotta get shut-eye when you can get it. Upon waking, the woman had gone into the store, emerging a few minutes later with plastic sacks of what looked to be snack foods or supplies. She wore different clothing now, too, undoubtedly having changed in the restroom—a tight white tank top and even tighter jeans. Finally, they'd left the Las Vegas metro area and taken Nevada State Route 160 through Pahrump Valley to the smaller city.

As the waning light of dusk shone dimly through his windshield, Silence observed the red glow of the Chevy's taillights. The passenger-side light was dimmer than the other. It even flickered out entirely occasionally. This made the Nova convenient to follow—a flashing beacon that guided him through the streets of an unfamiliar city.

But before the woman had turned on the Nova's lights, it had been increasingly difficult to track her. It seemed she'd detected the tailing vehicle in her rearview mirror because while her driving hadn't been *overtly* evasive, her sudden rights and lefts and her late turn signals hinted that she was aware.

Silence filed this notion away in his mind, right next to the image of the skittish pawnshop owner in Vegas, his injured son, the pile of broken televisions. More and more, the mystery woman was looking like a pro.

They'd been in Pahrump for a couple of hours now. Though Silence hadn't gotten out of the Wrangler for the entire second half of the day, he wasn't growing weary. Quite the contrary. He was enjoying this. Usually it was *him* climbing in and out of a vehicle, asking questions, roughing up scumbags. This time, he was letting the mystery woman do the dirty work. Under such conditions, the Wrangler's rugged interior felt luxurious, like someone should be massaging his feet while he sipped a glass of champagne with a moist terrycloth towel draped over his eyes.

The first stop in Pahrump had been a dilapidated dive bar nestled between abandoned warehouses. Its brick exterior bore painted-over windows, and dim lights barely illuminated the faded lettering on the sign above the entrance. The parking lot was dotted with pickup trucks in varying states of disrepair. Even from a distance, Silence could hear the discordant hum of a jukebox mingling with raucous laughter.

The woman had breezed through the swinging doors, her pace confident yet unassuming, almost as if she was a regular patron of such joints. She'd emerged fifteen minutes later, having changed her demeanor. Her stride was hurried and tense then. Whatever intel she'd gathered had raised either the stakes or the danger or both.

The second location was seedier: a worn-out bowling alley in a forgotten corner of town. The cracked parking lot boasted defiant weeds, and the building's peeling blue paint was scarred by faded graffiti. Above, a neon sign once spelled *BOWLING*, but now only a flickering *B* and *L* remained. Here, the woman spent even less time. She entered, only to reappear within eight minutes, a small slip of paper clutched tightly in her hand.

But the third stop was what piqued Silence's curiosity the most. He'd expected another shoddy establishment. Instead, the woman led him to the Pahrump Public Library, a modern two-story structure with large glass windows. Silence pulled the Wrangler into the trailer park across the street, allowing him a concealed but unobstructed view of the library's entrance.

He watched as the woman paused at the doors, glancing at her wristwatch. In contrast to their other stops, she seemed to be in a rush. It was 6:47. The library must have been closing soon. She entered.

And Silence settled in for the wait, feeling like a cop on a stakeout.

His chaotic mind went to work, wondering if the woman was in there scouring local data of some sort or if she had gone in to use an Internet terminal, in which case she could be researching materials related to any conceivable topic from resource banks worldwide—historical records, news articles, group forums.

Or...

Maybe she was doing something more tech-savvy. More clandestine.

Perhaps she was authoring another illegal FBI database search.

As the minutes dragged on, Silence consulted his notes—both the written ones in his PenPal and the ones stowed away in his mind—and his theory of the woman's status as a well-trained professional further solidified. His mission materials compiled by Watchers Specialists had offered the idea that she could be a rogue FBI agent; after several hours of surveillance, this is precisely what Silence thought she was. Bars and seedy bowling alleys and even public libraries were predictable stops for someone chasing clues, a person who seemed to be some sort of experienced investigator. For just a moment, Silence's thought process was neat and organized—a well-structured mental spreadsheet.

But a few terms came whooshing back at him out of the darkness of intellectual ether—*Boston Legacy Collapse; 1983; Adrian Hirsch*—tearing through the columns of his spreadsheet, collapsing his momentary clarity.

He was just about to close his eyes for a five-second meditation—to restore order, to temper the torrent—when a sharp ringing noise jolted him out of his mental haze.

His cellular phone.

The number bore a Mobile, Alabama, area code.

Silence flipped the phone open. "Elsher?"

The detective's Scottish-tinged accent replied with a bit of coy sparkle. "The one and only. I have an update on your friend Tanner. The old-timer doesn't go to Black Jack's only on Thursdays after he gets his shrimp and grits on the beach. He went again tonight."

A knot tightened in Silence's stomach.

Outside at the library, the mystery woman emerged. She had nothing in her hands—no borrowed books, no printouts. Silence thought again about the unwarranted FBI searches.

The woman went to her Nova, climbed inside. Silence disengaged the Wrangler's parking brake and readied the stick.

Elsher said, "So that's *at least* two nights in a row Tanner has gone to this bar-slash-gambling den."

Back east, in Pensacola, it was two hours later than Nevada's Pacific Time Zone—night, as Elsher had said, instead of dusk.

"I did some digging on Black Jack's," Elsher continued. "Lately, the place has advanced beyond mere unsanctioned gambling. They're movin' on up, you might say. Labyrinth is establishing a cell in Pensacola, and Black Jack's is the base of operations."

By the slight emphasis on the word *Labyrinth*, it was clear that Elsher was subtly asking if Silence was familiar with the term. Of course, Silence couldn't reveal his line of work to Elsher.

So he played stupid by not responding.

But he knew Labyrinth's background, already aware of every detail that Elsher rattled off.

"Labyrinth is an organized crime syndicate," Elsher said, "known primarily for their involvement in illegal gambling rings. They're named for the confusing trail they leave behind —like a maze, a labyrinth. Makes it almost impossible for the police to pin them down. They're based out of New Orleans, but they have no fixed headquarters. They're nomads, setting up operations in a set of constantly shifting locations so their trail goes cold before the law can catch up. Now they've made their way to Pensacola."

Yes, Silence knew all about Labyrinth, already familiar with all the details Elsher offered.

...except for the fact Labyrinth was making moves in *his* city.

Labyrinth's influence extended far beyond New Orleans, with satellite branches strategically situated in Beaumont, Texas; Biloxi, Mississippi; and, at the easternmost point, in Elsher's own Mobile, Alabama.

And now, evidently, they'd crept even farther east to Pensacola, Florida.

Across the street, the Nova took off. Silence gave it a moment, then he put the stick into first. The Wrangler crunched out of the trailer park's gravel. Turning left, he kept the flickering taillight in sight, a half mile in the distance.

Maintaining his quasi-ignorant facade, Silence said, "That's... interesting."

"You could say that," Elsher said. "Especially since Tanner left Black Jack's out a different door than he entered."

"What do you..." Silence said and swallowed. "Mean?"

"He went in the front door, the *legitimate* entrance," Elsher said. "But he exited from a door in the back that led to an alley."

Silence's mind flashed on the illegal gambling he'd seen in Black Jack's back alley the night before. Rattling dice. An upturned flashlight. Cash changing hands.

And the man who'd stared toward Silence's vehicle for several long moments after the others had scattered like startled rats.

The man's bright blue eyes, his twitching jaw muscles.

Labyrinth...

Tanner...

Silence swallowed, as much from apprehension as to soothe his throat, and said, "Was Tanner gambling?"

"Not sure," Elsher said. "But ... he's gone there at least three times that we know of, two of those nights sequential, so the pattern's too significant to ignore."

Silence nodded to himself. Elsher was right.

"And before Tanner even went to Black Jack's tonight..." Elsher continued before trailing off with a tone of voice that said he'd had second thoughts about what he was about to say.

"Go on," Silence said.

Elsher sighed. "I'm sorry, man. You said this guy was a mentor, so I hate telling you this." A long pause. "Before he went to Black Jack's, Tanner stopped at an ATM, took out a small stack of cash."

"Shit..." Silence groaned.

"I'll keep you posted."

"Thanks."

Beep.

Elsher was gone.

Silence hadn't noticed during the call, but as he collapsed the phone and dropped it onto the passenger seat, he found that his hand was shaking.

Tanner...

Ahead, the flickering of the Nova's tail light morphed into a purposeful blink as it took a turn. Using one of C.C.'s techniques—compartmentalization—Silence pushed the notion of his mentor's dark side from his mind and focused on the task that was literally right before him.

The dimming embrace of twilight had deepened, and now the Nevada sky was cloaked in an indigo blanket, pierced by glimmers of starlight. The Nova pulled into another establishment, this one resting at the classier end of the dive bar spectrum. It was a low-and-wide, sprawling place with a parking lot to match, loaded to near capacity with dozens of vehicles and a row of motorcycles. The neon sign overhead buzzed with electricity, the words *BLUE BARREL LOUNGE* cutting through the growing darkness.

As Silence watched the Nova roll to a stop, he pulled his Wrangler over on the side of the adjacent street, just past the sprawling lot. He squinted at the Blue Barrel's entrance, the dim light from the neon sign barely illuminating the figure standing guard.

The bouncer was massive, with shoulders that spanned the doorway's width. But it wasn't his size that caught Silence's attention; it was the tattoo. A rattlesnake coiled its way up and around the man's tree trunk neck.

The mystery woman approached, now wearing a kicky jean jacket over her tank top—not just fashionable, but also practical given that, outside, the desert was cooling rapidly. The bouncer allowed her entrance to the bar, and as he closed the door behind her, his gaze snapped in Silence's direction, finding the Wrangler beyond the Blue Barrel's parking lot.

This visual lock occurred so quickly, so intently, that Silence knew what had happened a moment earlier: while the bouncer was checking the mystery woman's ID, she must have played scared, put on the face of a frightened lady in danger.

You see that Wrangler over there? she would have said. *No, don't look now! I think that guy's, um ... been following me through town. Can you, like, watch him for me?*

Not only would that get a pair of eyes on Silence—of whose presence this woman was clearly aware now and whom she'd undoubtedly assessed as an enemy—but it would almost certainly ensure that the bouncer permitted her entrance to the Blue Barrel, where she could continue with the next step of her investigation.

Smart.

As SnakeNeck continued staring in Silence's direction, it felt like they were locking eyes. But Silence knew—from the positions of the nearby streetlights and the angle at which the Wrangler was parked—that from the man's perspective, Silence was nothing more than a silhouette.

It had been like this the previous evening. In Pensacola. Outside Black Jack's.

The man with bright blue eyes and bulging, twitching jaw muscles. He'd been staring in Silence's direction as Silence sat parked a few yards away in his BMW. Silence had known the man couldn't see him in the shadows.

But still, somehow, their eyes had locked.

It felt like they had, anyway.

Those bright blue eyes.

On that cold face.

The face of the man who'd stayed behind when the others fled. The man who *hadn't* been gambling with the others. The man who seemed to be in some position of authority.

He must've been with Labyrinth. That would explain why he'd had the bearing of a young professional. He was someone the organization had sent out to the upstart market, someone to ensnare the initial round of Pensacolans into the grip of illegal high-stakes gambling.

...including Tanner.

Silence sighed.

In his previous life, he'd been inspired by Tanner's determination and ambition, but now the older man had gotten himself involved in something illegal, something wickedly dark and dangerous. Perhaps Tanner had been living a double life for years, not just recently. Perhaps Silence—or Jake Rowe, rather—had been too damn naïve to notice.

Marvin Tanner—taking routine trips to Black Jack's, of all places, withdrawing cash money from an ATM...

...at the very time Labyrinth was moving into town.

Silence's Jake Rowe memories had been assaulted. This was a betrayal! This was—

C.C.'s voice came to him, *Focus, love.*

Silence's mental spiral came to an abrupt halt. He closed his eyes. Breathed. Felt the air move through him. Exhaled.

It was the five-second meditation he hadn't been able to complete earlier. And it cleared his mind entirely, brought him back to the present.

Thank you, his internal voice said.

C.C. left.

He brought his attention back to the Blue Barrel. Snake-Neck nodded at a pair of women—both in miniskirts and high heels—opened the door for them, then brought his attention back to Silence, a malevolent gaze.

If Silence's earlier assumption was correct, then Snake-Neck was operating on the idea that Silence—the "man in the silver Jeep across the street"—was some sort of creep who'd been following the mystery woman. As such, SnakeNeck was only doing what he was supposed to do, both as a bouncer and a man of chivalrous honor.

Nonetheless, Silence couldn't deny the naturalistic bristling of antagonism.

He stared back in SnakeNeck's direction.

Yeah, I see you, too, shithead, he thought.

SnakeNeck's dark, almost taunting gaze—as warranted as it might be—would help Silence stay rooted in the present...

...and out of Pensacola, away from notions of betrayal.

CHAPTER TEN

Bakersfield, California

Luca Westlin leaned against the wall, his gaze settling on his employer, Adrian Hirsch, who was at the floor-to-ceiling window, framed against a cityscape. The sun was dipping below the horizon, casting an array of oranges and purples over Bakersfield, a city that looked smaller than it truly was.

Westlin had done his research; he was that kind of man. The most recent American census in 1990 revealed a count of 175,000 Bakersfield inhabitants, a substantial growth from the 105,000 recorded in the 1980 census. A mere two decades earlier, in 1960, the population had stood at only 55,000. Going in the opposite direction, looking forward in time, experts predicted a doubling to 400,000 people in the upcoming thirty years.

Through the window before Westlin, Bakersfield seemed almost quaint despite its climbing population. The buildings were low-profile, and the energy was subdued, peaceful, more typical of a small town than an up-and-coming city center. This effect was further heightened by the city's surroundings

—the rugged nature that enveloped it. The unassuming charm of Bakersfield brought Westlin back to the European cities and towns he'd known his whole life, an abstract but striking resemblance.

He was in the suite's kitchenette on the tenth and top floor of downtown Bakersfield's Blue Enclave Hotel. It was Hirsch's suite. Westlin's, a smaller unit, was down the hall. Hirsch had summoned Westlin for the imminent phone call.

Westlin glanced at the clock ticking over the oven/range. 7:13. Two more minutes. The caller was always punctual if nothing else.

The suite bore the trademark luxury that Adrian Hirsch was fond of—a spacious expanse adorned with opulent décor and art, reflecting the man's tastes. Rich velvets, dark woods, and gold accents whispered of wealth and power. And while Westlin had grown accustomed to such luxury in his employer's presence, he never took it for granted. Thanks to Hirsch's tutelage, it was a world Westlin had come to know and understand, a stark contrast to his more modest beginnings.

Hirsch finally turned around from his lengthy assessment of Bakersfield.

"Well, it's better than Las Vegas, *ja*?" Hirsch shook his head and wiped at his arms as if trying to rid himself of something unpleasant. "I thought I'd catch chlamydia just strolling through that city."

Westlin snickered. "Yes, sir."

Now that Hirsch and Westlin were unexpectedly stuck in the American Southwest, conventional logic would dictate that they stay in Vegas, not Bakersfield, as the prior was only two hours from Death Valley National Park, while the latter was a three-hour drive. But not only did Hirsch have a distaste for Sin City, but, more importantly, Bakersfield was the Lost Jackals' home. The Jackals were providing Hirsch and Westlin a sphere of protection. At that very moment, three motorcycles were rumbling through the surrounding streets, patrolling a five-block region around the Blue Enclave.

Westlin was amazed by Hirsch's ability to remain unperturbed despite the intense pressure. But then again, that was what had brought his boss so far in the criminal underworld. Calculated. Professional. Refined. Ice-cold.

With these thoughts, Westlin's hand came to rest on the wear-slicked leather of his wristband. His fingers traced the engraved symbols. He was reminded of another man near Hirsch's age, whose presence lingered.

Westlin's father.

The wristband was the only remnant of the man who'd vanished from Westlin's life in his teenage years, replaced by Adrian Hirsch. A simple strip of leather had become a link between father and father figure, between coarse and refined. The contrasts were stark. Adrian Hirsch was a titan, commanding respect in circles that mattered; Westlin's father was not even a footnote in the annals of European crime.

But without his father, Westlin would never have met Hirsch. So while he owed Hirsch everything he had, he also owed his father for indirectly bringing him to Hirsch.

The trill of a cellular phone's ringtone pulled Westlin back to the present. Without hesitation, Hirsch took the phone from his jacket pocket and activated the speakerphone function as he breezed over to Westlin in the kitchenette. He laid the phone flat on the granite countertop between them.

"Draper, where the hell have you been?" Hirsch said. "It's been five days."

Even knowing Hirsch's renowned steadiness, Westlin was astounded by how well the man kept himself together after being left in the dark for nearly a week.

"My apologies," Draper's voice crackled through cellular

distortion. "The reception out here is piss-poor, as you saw last week."

Hirsch looked up at Westlin, and they communicated non-verbally, both saying the same thing: *It took him five days to arrange a phone call? Bullshit.*

Hirsch straightened as he brought his attention back to the phone lying on the granite, and his eyes narrowed with a bit of sculpted power. It was as though he was staring at Draper himself, not the phone, asserting dominance in a situation that left him in an extremely rare position of strategic vulnerability.

"You've been off organizing your own affairs, haven't you, Draper?" Hirsch said. "You've not been at Death Valley at all."

A long pause. Then Draper's voice came through the static again. "Sorry, what? I'm having a hard time hearing. Tellin' you, the reception here is awful."

Westlin detected a hint of snark in Draper's tone, like a mischievous child taking irresistible pleasure in his own antics.

"You told me this would be a clean operation," Hirsch said.

"I told you they'd be taken care of, and they were."

Hirsch's nostrils flared. "It was only supposed to be MacLeod and Shapiro. You were going to rough up the others so they wouldn't talk."

Draper laughed, a sudden sharp bark. "We *did* rough 'em up, man. Roughed 'em up bad. And they sure as hell aren't gonna talk."

A vein pulsed in Hirsch's temple, his trademark restraint slipping. "Listen to me, cocksucker. You double-crossed me. Manipulated the situation. Do you really want to cross a man like me?"

There was a pause on the line, and Westlin could almost imagine Draper weighing his next words carefully.

"Relax, okay? We're on the same side here. I know you're probably getting restless in that hotel, but just, I don't know, try to enjoy the pool, the city. It's a nice area. The plan was always for you to stay in the States for a few weeks until the heat subsided, anyway. The only difference is more people died than you'd planned, so now you need the Jackals' protection. You gotta be specific when you place an order, Adrian. Details matter. Now you're gonna have to deal with the consequences."

Westlin winced. Draper's language had been more than cavalier; it had been insulting. Brazenly so. He'd even used Hirsch's first name.

Hirsch flared, but before he could reply, Draper continued. "Speaking of consequences, we have a situation in Death Valley."

Hirsch's eyebrows furrowed. "And what might that be?"

"We've detected someone scouting the bus tragedy site from a distance."

"So what? There have been plenty of people trying to get a glimpse of the crime scene. Why should one more matter?"

"Well," Draper said, pausing for effect. "This one's different."

"In what way?"

Through the audio distortion, Draper's voice was almost a whisper, filled with gravity. "Ever heard of Unseen Path?"

CHAPTER ELEVEN

Pahrump, Nevada

THE DEEPENING TWILIGHT draped Pahrump in indigo and obsidian, washing away the last traces of the simmering Nevada day. As the stars began to prick the vast desert sky, Silence sat motionless in the driver's seat of his Wrangler, still positioned across the street from the Blue Barrel Lounge's sprawling gravel lot. He'd cracked the window to taste a bit of the dry air as it mixed with the Jeep's pumping A/C. Through the window's gap, he heard the familiar beats of a Michael Jackson song merged with distant chatter, the hum of nightlife contrasting with the emptiness of the quiet city.

Silence yawned. All day long, the thrill of the chase had made him forget how damn tired he was after his week of awful sleep in Pensacola—after returning from the beating from the Whitman cousins in Ohio, then being met with the shocking news that his former mentor was a corrupt officer, then, to top it off, being the unhappy recipient of a drooling cat who tarnished his home for days on end.

He rubbed some life back into his cheeks.

As he watched the Blue Barrel, the bar watched him back in the form of the hawkish stare of the bouncer with the tattooed rattlesnake coiling up his neck. SnakeNeck's gaze—broken only by his duties to the coming and going Blue Barrel patrons—was like a red-hot brand, igniting an irritation deep within Silence. He could taste the man's animosity even from a distance.

Though he knew SnakeNeck was likely operating off false intel given by the mystery woman, Silence's fingers still curled, wanting to form fists, instinctively preparing for a clash. He glanced at the tautened forearms, willing them to relax, a mental control technique, another of C.C.'s offerings.

As his muscles slackened, he saw the small scar on the inside of his right forearm. Embedded beneath the scar was a surgically installed GPS dot that allowed the Watchers to track him at all times. Someone somewhere was staring at a computer screen, watching as a motionless dot representing Silence slowly blinked on a map of Pahrump, Nevada.

This made Silence think of the item in his lefthand pocket. He patted it—a small, hard lump against his thigh. It might just come in handy.

He brought his attention back to the moment, to his objective, and studied the Blue Barrel. The place bore only two windows—picture windows on either side of the entrance, littered with neon beer logos. Hightop tables sat right on the other side of each fixture, and both windows were frames for a mass of swimming arms and legs and bottles and glasses. The silhouette of the mystery woman appeared occasionally, momentarily, before disappearing again into the undulating swarm of humanity.

These glimpses elicited an unwanted reaction in Silence—a sense of chivalry, protective and potent. From a logistical standpoint, remaining outside the bar was in his best interests. This woman was a federal agent—yes, that much was clear—but through the Blue Barrel's pair of windows, Silence had spotted many burly customers, several of whom had been watching the mystery woman with less than pure expressions on their faces.

Silence's instincts kept trying to propel him to action.

And the recognition of this innate chivalry made Snake-Neck's aggressive staring in Silence's direction suddenly seem even more benign.

Just as suddenly, a memory assailed Silence. The hard floor of a dimly lit room, the salty tang of sweat, and Nakiri, a Watchers Asset, his trainer. Silence could almost hear Nakiri's stern voice chastising him for a lapse into indulgent humanity. Nakiri had warned him repeatedly to eradicate many of his former codes of conduct, chivalry among them.

C.C.'s voice came to him, joining the fray.

Love? she said.

Yes?

You already suspect this woman is an FBI agent. Your employers do, too.

That's right, Silence said.

Then let it go. Stick to your mission protocols. Don't underestimate this woman.

You're right.

In an airy yet slightly smug tone, C.C. said, *I know I am.*

She was gone.

The Blue Barrel's doors swung open, casting a brief splash of beer-gold light onto the pavement. The mystery woman emerged, striding past SnakeNeck and into the gravel lot. Her movements were fluid, each step taken with an air of showy nonchalance, a persona to aid this stage of her investigation. A streetlamp illuminated her face for a fleeting second, revealing nothing of her inner thoughts—a blank facade. She made her way toward the Nova.

The car fired up. The taillights illuminated in their mismatched discordance. And she took off.

Once more, the game was afoot.

Silence shifted the Wrangler's gear into first, pausing with the clutch fully depressed for a few moments to allow the mystery woman a chance to pull away. As the Nova's taillights cut through the thickening darkness, he took off and settled into pursuit.

As he went by the Blue Barrel, he turned his attention to the right, looking through the passenger window. SnakeNeck watched, scowling, as Silence passed.

Silence navigated Pahrump's streets with a predator's patience, keeping the Nova in sight but always at a non-threatening distance. The vibrant lights of Pahrump's bars, motels, and diners began to thin out, gradually replaced by the cold expanse of rocky landscape. The darkness of the Mojave Desert seemed to swallow everything, the world outside narrowing to just the two vehicles and the road beneath them.

The Nova's brake lights flared, and the car abruptly slowed. This wasn't the behavior of an oblivious driver but of someone aware they were being tailed—perhaps even trying to control the narrative. The deliberate nature of the move, the overt invitation to approach, only deepened Silence's suspicion of the woman's FBI ties. The Nova gradually pulled onto the rough earth at the side of the road and halted.

Silence stopped the Wrangler several yards back. Ahead, the Nova's driver-side door popped open, and the woman climbed out, her long figure stretching to its five-foot-eleven height. She stood next to her car, bathed in the faint moon-light. She looked in his direction.

Finally. This fully confirmed Silence's theory that the woman had known she was being followed for some time now.

His mind flashed on his assumption—the one the

Watchers had been operating on from the beginning of the mission—that this woman was a rogue FBI agent. But C.C.'s words ripped through his consciousness as well. *Don't underestimate this woman.* Accordingly, Silence felt the weight of his Beretta in his shoulder holster, mentally readying himself to draw it if needs be.

For a moment, Silence's trained eyes absorbed the details. The woman's towering height. Her athletic build, evident even beneath her out-on-the-town clothing. Blonde strands of hair dancing in the desert breeze, glinting in the moonlight.

Silence opened the door. Stepped outside. His brogues crunched on the rock as he approached, never letting his mind lose sight of that gentle weight against his ribs—the Beretta—just in case.

"Why ... why are you following me?" the woman said, her voice wavering with an unexpected vulnerability.

The raw desperation underlying her words gave Silence pause. This wasn't the confident federal agent he had envisioned; it was a woman on the edge, grappling with uncertainties.

Immediately, another wave of that repressed chivalry washed over him, some remote component of a past version of him—Jake Rowe—wanting to reach out, to offer comfort.

Just as quickly, C.C. chided him, her voice repeating what she'd told him earlier. *Don't underestimate this woman, love.*

Silence stopped when they were an arm's length apart. He showed his hands.

"I'm a friend," Silence said.

The woman jumped at the sound of his voice. But she didn't yelp. Her eyes didn't widen. It was a more subdued response than most first-timers.

Slowly, in a way that showed his intentions were peaceful, Silence lowered one of his raised hands to his back pocket, where he retrieved his wallet. He removed the plastic card and reached it toward the woman.

A moment of pause. The woman's eyes locked onto his. Then she took the card.

The card's size, thickness, and shape—including the round corners—were the same as a swipe card, but no magnetic strip was on the back. Aside from a design flourish on the lefthand side—two angled, blue stripes—the plastic was clear with an opaque, matte finish. A message covered the front of the card in dark blue letters, thick and raised off the surface:

MY ORGANIZATION IS AWARE OF YOUR SITUATION.

WE UNDERSTAND NORMAL CHANNELS HAVE FAILED YOU.

WE HAVE THE MEANS TO ASSIST.

PLEASE EXCUSE THIS FORM OF INTRODUCTION.

I AM NOT MUTE, BUT SPEAKING IS PAINFUL.

I AM HERE TO HELP.

The woman looked up. "What's your name?"

"Kai," Silence said.

Silence adopted a new identity for each mission, always one-syllable names. This helped to lower the number of syllables he ran through his painful throat. Not a significant benefit, but it added up. Every little bit helped.

"You're an agent," the woman said, voice cracking. "Aren't you?"

Once already during this nascent investigation, Silence had let an assumption fly when someone had presumed his type of employment. Usually, this was to his advantage. But this time, since the woman was likely an FBI agent herself, denial was more prudent.

"No," he said.

The woman studied him for a long moment. Then she studied the card again. Another moment passed. Then she looked back up and returned the card.

"I ... I don't understand how—" she began as Silence put the card away.

But in the next moment, her demeanor shifted, and Silence sensed the danger even before she moved. The woman's posture shifted into an aggressive stance as the befuddled, frightened expression dropped from her face.

She lunged forward.

Her attack was swift, a combination of sharp punches and fluid kicks that caught Silence momentarily off guard as he returned his wallet to his back pocket, hand behind his ass. He deflected a strike aimed at his throat, recognizing the precision and power behind it as Krav Maga.

Silence jumped back, one step, two, three, creating space just before the woman struck again. He parried, but even his blinding speed wasn't quick enough to fully deflect the blow, as her fist went scraping up his forearm, blossoming spots of pain.

They circled each other, both looking for an opening. The woman then surprised him again with a low sweep combined with an upward palm strike—a move straight out of Pencak silat. As Silence dodged and countered, grappling with her, he felt the fluidity and leverage techniques that were hallmarks of Systema.

Krav Maga. Pencak silat. Systema.

These combat styles weren't part of the coursework at the FBI Academy in Quantico.

This was a professional on an entirely different level.

A level akin to Silence's.

This was an operator.

And if he didn't get his shit together quickly, he was headed for serious trouble.

Survival and training flooded over Silence, and he mentally bolstered his technique, fortifying his stance into one of Iwama-style Aikido, something to counter the Krav Maga, Pencak silat, and Systema.

The woman lunged at him. Each move she made, each technique she employed, expanded his understanding of her.

Block.

Deflect.

Block.

Damn! She caught him on the ribs, sending a flare of white-hot pain shooting up through him.

CIA? SPECOPS? Silence's mind raced even as his body reacted, countering and deflecting her strikes.

Nakiri's training flashed through his mind again, the harsh insistence on banishing chivalry, and he laid a heavy uppercut into the woman's stomach right as he dodged another Pencak silat strike.

The woman folded and shrieked as Silence felt his fist sink into the depths of her abdomen, practically to her spine. Guilt swept over him. But, as Nakiri would have commanded, he immediately banished it.

Just in time, too.

Because the woman's howl had been only partly genuine, evidenced by the quick return of icy fire in her eyes. She'd been faking it, setting an emotionally predatory trap. She lunged at him again as she tried to catch him off-guard.

You underestimated this woman, C.C. said. *I tried to warn you.*

Oh yeah? Silence said. *Just wait and see what happens next.*

Amid the flurry of movements, Silence found an opportunity. The woman had left herself exposed, one of her missed strikes flying errantly to the side, leaving a wall of open target right in front of Silence.

But he didn't capitalize on the opportunity.

Or, at least, not in the way the woman would expect.

He deftly sidestepped the punch, slid his hand into his left pants pocket, retrieved the loose GPS dot—similar to the one embedded in his arm—and planted it in a pocket in the woman's jean jacket without her noticing.

It was a risk, but one that needed to be taken. Silence could have brought the woman down, sure—subdued her, transported her, and begun a line of interrogation—but at the moment, with this new revelation that she was something much more than a rogue FBI agent, it was better for Silence to continue following her, this time with the aid of a positioning system, letting the woman think he'd been bested.

He allowed the woman's next punch to land. She hit him in the stomach with enough strength that, unprepared, Silence would have been knocked windless. He let out a feigned growl of pain and staggered back from the punch, making it look more impactful than it was. Momentary triumph flashed over the woman's eyes.

Without wasting another second, she darted back to her Nova, the engine roaring almost immediately. The tires kicked up stones and dust, and she sped away, leaving Silence momentarily alone under the vast expanse of the starry sky.

Silence remained still, his hands on his knees, his chest heaving slightly from the encounter. The adrenaline still pumped through his veins, but his mind was already plotting his next moves.

Climbing back into the Wrangler, Silence reached for the duffel bag on the passenger-side floorboard. He plopped it on the seat, opened it, and took out an electronic device—a glass screen with a black plastic bezel.

The Watchers were privy to many ahead-of-the-curve,

twenty-first-century devices, and so-called "tablets" like this
would be a common device in the not-so-distant future. He
switched it on, and pixelation filled the screen, soon clearing
into a crude map. He tapped the touchscreen a few times,
and the map centered on the Pahrump area. The blinking dot
representing the Chevy Nova was heading west, away from
Pahrump and into the wild desert, toward Death Valley
National Park.

Silence grinned.

He wouldn't tail the woman directly; that would be too
obvious, especially after she'd caught onto him once before,
especially after their confrontation, especially now that he
knew she was some sort of elite operator. Now he could
linger back a bit, relying on the GPS dot's signal, letting the
woman lead him to whatever she was involved in.

Putting the tablet on his lap, he reclined the Wrangler's
seat a few inches, savoring this rare moment of pause and
allowing the pain of the fight to throb its way out of his body.

CHAPTER TWELVE

Death Valley National Park, California

SEVERAL HOURS LATER.

Death Valley's infamous heat was, for the moment, cooled by the night sky. A myriad of stars cast a thin light over the valley below. In this immense expanse of land, the Unseen Path's caravan assortment of cars, trucks, RVs, and vans slept peacefully in Mesquite Spring Campground.

The only sign of life was Mitch.

He moved like a shadow, allowing the obscurity of the night to cloak him as he inched to the back of his RV. Every few steps, he'd glance at the other vehicles in the campsite. They stood silent and unlit, the adventurous souls within them ignorant to Mitch's nocturnal activity, which was certainly not a component of the Unseen Path tour he was providing these folks.

Mitch was loaded with gear, giving him a purposeful, if somewhat encumbered, gait. A Bowie knife sat snugly in a sheath on his belt, and a snub-nosed Smith & Wesson weighed heavily in his rear jeans pocket. Draped around his neck were the loops of a pair of large, sturdy sacks—empty, waiting to be filled. Also dangling from a strap on his neck was a camera. It was a simple, everyday model, quite the contrast to Carmen's sophisticated one, an "SLR," he believed it was called. The impending photos would come out clearer and more vibrant with Carmen's device. But this mission was without Carmen's knowledge, so her superior camera and photographic skills were off the table.

Reaching the dirt bike rack on the back of the RV, he stopped and pressed the button on the side of his Timex Ironman. The bold green glow showed 3:07 a.m.

He looked past the bikes to the back side of the vehicle. Just beyond that wall—a few inches of metal and insulation—Carmen was sleeping in their bed.

He paused.

There had been something in her eyes when she'd confronted him at the bikes the previous afternoon. Carmen was on to him. She might not have known precisely what he was up to, but Mitch's wife could spot a deception from miles away, especially from Mitch.

I'll tell her after, Mitch thought.

This brought a quick wave of cheap relief that made him smile.

His fingers felt for the cool metal clasps that secured his dirt bike to the rack. A bead of sweat formed on his brow as he attempted to release the bike without a sound. With each small click and shift of the bike's weight, he expected the RV to rock, to jolt Carmen from her sleep, but finally, the strap was loose. He winced as he lowered the squeaking ramp, and the bike crunched onto the earth.

With one last glance toward the RV, he walked off, pushing the bike beside him.

———

The motor whined across the empty surroundings. A half mile away from Mesquite Spring, when Mitch was as far out of the campground's earshot as he could realistically manage —given the reverberant hollowness of the desert—he'd fired the dirt bike up. But he'd only ridden another half mile up North Highway before he'd had to slow and dip into the wild momentarily, bypassing the orange barrel barricade the NPS had stretched across the road's width.

He'd slowed, but he hadn't come to a stop.

Mitch had never and *would* never let the powers-that-be bring him to a halt.

For the last two miles, he'd rocketed up the shutdown highway with the cool desert nighttime air blasting over his face, through his hair, and the naughtiness of it had been thrilling. He felt almost guilty, knowing he was leaving his intrigue-thirsty tour members behind, clearing a barrier he would not take them past. Later in the day, during the tour, Mitch would take the people as close to the site of the bus tragedy as the law permitted.

But right now, Mitch was going all the way to the crime scene.

On the ill-fated day last week, the Legacy Route bus had been heading for Ubehebe Crater, coming up a few miles short of their destination, not quite making it to their exit— Ubehebe Crater Road—before they were forced off the highway and slaughtered. Naturally, the NPS hadn't told the press exactly where the tragedy had taken place, but if Mitch's estimations were correct, then it—

There.

There it was.

As Mitch rounded a gentle curve and crested a ridge, he saw a crime scene ahead in the moonlit expanse of desert, fluttering police tape draped between orange barrels like those that he'd bypassed at the highway blockade moments earlier.

Mitch figured he should cover the remaining distance on foot, as it was impossible to know who was hidden in the rocky surroundings. He hadn't spotted any suspicious vehicles at the crime scene—no park ranger squad cars or blacked-out SUVs—but the powers-that-be could be anywhere in the desert wild. The Man was elusive, resourceful, and conniving. Mitch never underestimated the Man.

Mitch eased off the throttle, and the bike's knobby tires thumped onto the desert floor. After rolling to a slow, quiet stop, Mitch stowed the bike behind a large stone with a clump of twisted shrubs. He glanced at the crime scene. It was maybe an eighth of a mile away. Easy. Still, he'd have to be careful. If there were powers-that-be in the area, they would be hidden away.

Which meant Mitch would need to be especially stealthy. He would approach from the ridge to the east. This would add time to his hike—taking him several hundred yards in the wrong direction—but the precaution would be more than worth the effort.

His leather boots crunched against the earth, the camera bumping gently against his chest with each stride. A fusion of excitement and trepidation surged through him.

Nearing the crest of a rocky outcrop, Mitch crouched low, using the cover of stones and scrub plants to mask his approach. He looked to the left. The crime scene stretched out before him, and since he'd climbed in elevation, he now had a more bird's-eye view of it.

And it looked like...

Nothing.

No blood. No bodies. No debris.

Just more of the same, more desert.

For all its beauty, Death Valley held secrets, and right now, it seemed, one of those secrets was encircled by flapping crime scene tape.

But it was dark outside. Moonlight only reveals so much. Yes, Mitch would find something once he finished looping the ridge and climbed down to the edge of the tape.

If nothing more, he'd get his photographs.

Planting a knee into the rock, he brought the camera to his face, lined up the crime scene in the viewfinder.

Yes, yes, this bird's-eye view was excellent.

Click.

His mind conjured images of the next Unseen Path newsletter's front page: a large photograph of the Legacy Route bus tragedy crime scene, perhaps with a provocative headline.

He smiled.

Just as he was about to take another shot, a soft noise pricked his ears—a distant rumble, like stones cascading down a slope.

Mitch froze.

Every bit of his old Army training, every bit of his distrustful intuition screamed at him to remain still, to assess the situation.

It could be some sort of desert creature. A coyote. Some kind of bird—a roadrunner or the like.

A loose rock, maybe.

Or was it the powers-that-be?

The Man.

Had Mitch been careless? Had he let his guard down, foolishly disregarding his innate paranoia, forgetting the genuine threat of government forces hidden away in the rocky outcroppings to his left...

...his right...

...his six?

Mitch spun around, putting his hand on his sheathed Bowie knife.

Before he could analyze further, the soft rumble transformed into an unmistakable sound—a mechanical roar that shattered the stillness. Dark figures emerged in the pale moonlight from behind another rocky ridge, moving swiftly. Their silhouettes elongated, ghostly apparitions against the desert floor.

It took Mitch a mere fraction of a second to discern the shapes.

Motorcycles.

Men on motorcycles.

Not dirt bikes like Mitch's—big ol' Harleys.

Mitch did a quick count. Five of them. There were *at least* five of the bastards. Probably more were imminent, not yet seen.

Five government men, closing in rapidly, engines roaring. The bike's movements were coordinated, deliberate, and they were converging on Mitch's position. Retreating on foot wasn't an option—not with them advancing so quickly. His only hope was to make it back to his own bike, a true *dirt* bike, more adept at off-roading than the other men's hogs.

He spun around, searched, and located it: the outcropping where he'd left his bike. It was now a hundred yards away, and one of the other motorcycles lay in the path, rocketing in his direction, a cloud of dust forming behind.

No chance to get there.

Hell with it, then.

There was no better way for Mitch Lockwood to go out than with a literal fight to the death with the powers-that-be.

Mitch pulled the Smith from his back pocket. With his other hand, he yanked the Bowie knife from its sheath. Then he crouched into an aggressive position, swinging his dual weapons in broad arches, prepared to use either.

The roar of the engines grew louder. Deafening. Drowning out the quiet night. Mitch's fight-or-flight instincts kicked into overdrive. Every muscle in his body tautened, ready to spring into action. And just as his finger tensed on the Smith's trigger...

...he saw something.

A several-yard gap in the motorcycles' formation. The Harley he'd spotted a moment earlier had veered to the west, which afforded Mitch a straight path toward his concealed dirt bike.

Without further thought, he bolted.

But the riders were no amateurs. The momentarily disorganized formation regrouped with strategic precision, tightening and closing in. The engines howled.

Mitch's heart thundered in his chest, but his survivor's spirit and his deep-seated training propelled him forward. Ducking into a narrow crevice, he scrambled over boulders, seeking the shadows and using the natural terrain to his advantage.

A quick glance over his shoulder revealed a biker closing in.

Mitch ran harder than he had in years. Decades. Lungs burning, legs pumping.

The outcropping was closer now, and he caught his first glimpse of his dirt bike—a tiny glimmer of chrome. To his left, just as he sprinted even stronger, another Harley appeared, driving him further back.

This Harley was close enough that Mitch finally got a good look at one of the riders.

The man didn't look like a government operative at all.

He looked like a legitimate biker—long salt-and-pepper hair; leather attire; jowly, stubbly face with missing teeth.

Mitch didn't take a moment to process this.

Instead, he jerked to the right, avoiding the bike as it whooshed past him by a yard, a burly hand reaching out to grab him.

Free of the man's reach, Mitch had another clear shot at his bike.

Which was just ahead now.

But then there they were.

The formation swooped in from all angles.

One by one, the motorcycles tightened around him, closing off the path to his bike and any other means of escape.

They slowed but didn't stop.

Engines growling.

Forming a tightening circle.

The scent of gasoline, hot metal, and dust filled the air. Mitch coughed. The headlights blinded him.

He raised his gun.

But just as quickly, he lowered it.

Because there were other guns, all pointed in his direction, all aimed not by suited federal agents but rough-and-tumble bikers. Revolvers. Automatics. A couple of sawed-offs.

Mitch stood still, wheezing, his mind racing. The camera strap weighed heavily around his neck. The riders—some of their faces obscured by helmets and the night, others out on full display—remained on their bikes, engines idling in a low growl.

Mitch dropped his weapons.

The knife, then the gun.

Clank.

Clunk.

And he raised his hands.

CHAPTER THIRTEEN

HOURS LATER.

Mesquite Spring Campground was warming under the first beams of the sun, which announced itself inside the RV as a thin beam that sliced through a tiny gap in the curtains, resting on Carmen Lockwood's face.

She stirred, shifting under the weight of a light blanket...

...lighter, even, than usual.

Her body sensed the absence of warmth next to her. Turning, she found the opposite side of the bed empty.

"Mitch..." she said aloud in a coming-awake tone somewhere between annoyance and burgeoning worry.

Every so often, her husband's penchant for adventure would get the best of him. This wasn't the first morning Carmen had awoken to find the opposite side of her wedding bed abandoned.

She sighed as she brushed tousled black hair from her eyes. For a moment, the quaint surroundings of her bedroom faded, replaced by a vivid memory. Her mother's stern face—blockish, dark-skinned, keen-eyed—materialized in her thoughts.

You do not know what it means to marry such a man, Mamá had warned. *Adventure will not fill your table, niña, nor will it keep you warm at night.*

Carmen put her hand on Mitch's half of the bed, into the time-forged indentation of his two-hundred-twenty-pound frame.

It was cold.

Warm at night, indeed.

Carmen hated it when Mamá's words of yesteryear proved eerily accurate. She recalled the fire in her own rebuttal, the stubbornness of youth, the insatiable pull of passion that had led her to Mitch.

To which Mamá had said, *You'll always be chasing after him.*

Brushing the thoughts away, Carmen slipped from the covers, letting her feet hit the RV's cold vinyl floor. She pulled on her clothing, her mind still lingering on the empty side of the bed. She imagined Mitch, maybe atop some craggy rock, staring out over Death Valley's expanse, caught in the grip of its desolation and beauty, some fool notion in his head, some paranoia sparkling in his eyes.

"He's fine," she muttered to herself.

Yes, her husband was fine because he was in his element—the national park system. She remembered nights under open skies with Mitch, looking up at the stars, finding the constellations, while Mitch would regale her with stories of government conspiracies. Naturally, they'd been dark tales, but something about how he'd told them had made them comfortable and cozy.

He had that effect on people. He had that effect on her.

She wasn't naturally paranoid like him, but she'd bought into his ethos, and now they were two souls on a similar journey, bound by a love for America's open roads and its conspiracies.

Carmen yanked her hiking boot laces tight, then swung

open the RV's door, immediately squinting in the light. The air held a touch of morning chill, a deceptive precursor to the inferno of the upcoming Death Valley day.

Throwing on sunglasses, she looked around the Mesquite Spring Campground. Members of the latest Unseen Path tour —eccentric adventure-seekers with spare cash and spare time —were stirring about the grounds, having left their vehicles as they prepped for the day's journey. Carmen and Mitch were their guides.

And one of those guides was gone.

Taking a deep breath, Carmen tried to suppress the growing unease in her heart. She told herself that today was just another day, and Mitch would return, laughing and chattering about his newest discovery. That disarming smile of his. Gray hair. The belly that Carmen enjoyed both playfully poking and curling up on at night.

The campground was a bustle of early morning activity, the aromas of sunscreen and spray deodorant mingling in the air. Vehicle doors opened and closed, and the collective energy of excitement was unmistakable. After spending an extraordinary amount of money on short notice, these travelers had come from all over to experience the mystery of a story ripped from the headlines—not a typical Unseen Path mystery of time-faded legend, but one that was fresh, immediate, in the news.

Naturally, the anticipation had been substantial.

And, naturally, Mitch had done everything he could to tease that excitement to a fever pitch.

Mitch, who was now missing...

"Morning, Carmen!" a bright-faced woman with a camera slung around her neck said. "Looking forward to today's adventure."

Carmen forced a smile. "Morning, Sandy. It's going to be a great day."

Another voice piped up, a young man with a sunburned nose. Nick.

"Carmen, I hope we can get close enough," Nick said. "Do you know how far back they shut down North Highway?"

"We'll get plenty close, don't worry," Carmen said. "We'll be following the exact route of the Legacy Route bus."

Another older couple approached, their eyes twinkling with joy. But the void left by Mitch's absence lingered.

Trying to keep her voice casual, Carmen scanned the growing crowd surrounding her and said, "Has anyone seen Mitch this morning?"

A few of the members looked around while others shook their heads. One said, "Thought I saw him near the RV last night. Working on something?"

The gears in Carmen's mind shifted. Her thoughts raced back to the evening before. Mitch. Grease stains on his fingers. He'd been tinkering with the dirt bikes.

Her heart pounded harder, the dread undeniable now. Without another word to the group, Carmen sprinted to the back of the RV, praying she was wrong.

But what she saw confirmed her fears.

Only one dirt bike on the two-bike rack.

Mitch had left the camp, gone out into the depths of Death Valley alone, and from the looks of it, he had left in the dark.

"Damn you, Mitch," she whispered.

While Mitch's zest for discovery had always been sheer charisma, it also had its dangerous edges. And now, with a group to manage and a husband unaccounted for, Carmen felt the weight of it all bearing down on her.

Carmen exhaled and headed back around the RV to rejoin the tour group, finding Sandy already approaching, a frown replacing her earlier cheerfulness.

"Is everything okay, Carmen?"

Carmen took a deep breath, aware of all eyes now on her. "There's been a slight change in plans," she began, fighting to keep her voice loud and confident. "Mitch has gone ahead to scout out some special locations for us. He always has his surprises."

She forced a chuckle.

But inside, her mind raced. How long had Mitch been gone? Why had he left without telling her?

And, most importantly, where exactly had he ventured?

She couldn't share the truth with the group, not yet. With Mitch gone, they were depending on her leadership more than ever—they just didn't know it.

Looking away from all the faces, her attention went to the earth. Fresh tire tracks stretched away from the RV. Thin with a knobby pattern. They mocked her.

Waves of resentment surged within Carmen, amplified by the weight of the expectant eyes boring into her from every side.

She heard Mamá.

A man of whims will leave you chasing shadows, mija. One day, you might not catch up.

Those words, once defied with the stubbornness of youth and love, now twisted in Carmen's gut. She'd chosen Mitch and, with him, a life of uncertainty.

But she hadn't signed up for this shit.

...being forced to stand alone, facing a crowd that wanted answers.

The tour group chattered among themselves, their voices a murmur whose energy was gradually shifting to one of unease. The day, which had promised exploration and discovery, had now taken on an uncertain feeling for them.

And, of course, they were already a highly paranoid bunch.

Drawing a deep breath, Carmen made herself face them. She smiled.

"Folks. Folks!"

They stopped chattering. Suspicious eyes turned her way.

"Why don't we all have some cowboy coffee?" She forced the smile wider, more inviting. "It's the perfect way to hit the trails of the American West. How about it?"

CHAPTER FOURTEEN

Pahrump, Nevada

THE BLUE BARREL Lounge opened at 11 a.m.

Silence arrived at 11:03.

As luck would have it, SnakeNeck—the tattooed behemoth who had watched Silence the previous night—was there, too, waiting at the door. And by the man's dark stare, it was apparent SnakeNeck hadn't forgotten about Silence.

The not-quite-afternoon sun blazed over the quiet desert town, casting stretched-out shadows over the cracked pavement of the parking lot. SnakeNeck leaned against the doorframe, his squinted eyes glowering beneath a baseball cap. He wore faded jeans, black motorcycle boots, and a skin-tight black T-shirt.

Clad in his ensemble of gray five-pocket trousers, light-weight Henley, and black chukkas, Silence wasn't much of a contrast, but enough to be apparent. As he approached the entrance, the other man's scowl deepened.

"Saw you across the street last night, creep," SnakeNeck

drawled, puffing out his chest. "You honestly think you're gettin' in here?"

"Yes," Silence said.

SnakeNeck stared, as much in reaction to Silence's response as to his terrible voice.

A moment passed, then, "Last night, the lady told me you were stalking her."

Silence shrugged. Technically, she hadn't been lying.

SnakeNeck scoffed. "Get the hell away from here, bro."

"No."

Another pause.

Then SnakeNeck tensed, ready to lunge.

"Stop!" Silence barked, sending a jolt of pain down his throat.

SnakeNeck indeed stopped, frozen mid-action as his eyes went fractionally wider. Frame tensed. Arms lifted. Fingers splayed wide.

"I don't want..." Silence said and swallowed. "To put you down."

He honestly didn't.

Despite the naturalistic, undeniable tension that there'd been between the two of them since the staring incident last night, Silence knew SnakeNeck's antagonistic attitude came from a false belief that Silence was the mystery woman's overzealous ex-boyfriend or something of the like. The bouncer had an unpleasant air about him, but as far as Silence was concerned, SnakeNeck was nothing more than a man doing both his job and his best to defend a lady.

SnakeNeck scoffed—a hearty, genuine reaction.

"Don't worry," he said. "You won't."

The man's arrested response came into motion again, and he moved forward, bringing a beefy hand barreling toward Silence's throat. Silence dodged, bringing his arm up to deflect the attack, sending SnakeNeck reeling to the side.

With a quick sidestep, Silence was behind him, encircling the other man's neck in a rear naked choke hold. He applied pressure.

Lots of it.

The flesh-colored, non-inked swaths of SnakeNeck's skin flushed red, bulging with veins.

The man groaned.

"A sleeper..." He gasped. "Hold? That's a ... dirty..." Another gasp. "Move."

"Oh, well," Silence said.

More pressure.

And SnakeNeck went limp in his grasp.

Silence bent at the knees, easing the man's girth to the pavement. Slower yet, he transferred SnakeNeck's head to the ground. The bouncer now lay in a surprisingly comfortable-looking position on the sidewalk outside the Blue Barrel's doorway. The angry red color continued to recede from his neck, the coiled rattlesnake glowing back into full prominence.

See? Silence thought as he looked down at the slumbering giant. *I'm not such a dirty fighter, after all. I laid you down like a gentleman.*

Moments earlier, Silence had been rather sanctimonious in his decision not to have an altercation with SnakeNeck, as the bouncer likely deemed him a ne'er-do-well. Still, he couldn't deny that he felt a twinge of silly pride at having won their twelve-hour battle of wills.

He suppressed a grin, stepped over the body, and pushed through the door.

The interior of the Blue Barrel was like a set piece from a bygone era—a drop-tile ceiling hung low over a mishmash of neon beer signs and threadbare bar stools. The smell was a blend of cheap beer, stale smoke, and the faint trace of dead-end pessimism. It was a sprawling place, and there were no customers yet, but Silence could picture it soon filled with the same sort of people he'd seen the night before—a few bikers in leather jackets, a handful of low-lives hunched over their drinks, and several nondescript individuals nursing their midday sorrows with amber liquid.

"Hair of the dog, huh?" a voice said from the back.

It was the bartender behind the counter, the only other person in the place—a short man in a plain white t-shirt, sparse hair swept to one side. He had the weary look of someone who'd seen too many desperate faces reflected in his array of liquor bottles.

"You here last night?" Silence said, leaning into the counter.

The bartender hesitated, narrowing his eyes as they flicked toward Silence's throat. He didn't take long pondering Silence's voice, though. It took a lot to bewilder a guy like this.

After the brief moment passed, the bartender grunted a noncommittal, "Maybe."

Silence responded by pulling the printed photograph from his pocket. He unfolded it, handed it to the man.

"So was she," Silence said.

The bartender took a cursory glance at the photo of the mystery woman and shot Silence a skeptical look.

"So what?"

"You're the bartender..." Silence said and swallowed. "The man with the answers..." Another swallow. "She would talk to you."

Yes, all signs pointed to the mystery woman being a seasoned investigator. As an investigator himself, Silence knew the best place to get answers was the watering hole. It was some sort of ancient impulse, going all the way back to the earliest of days, to the crawl out of the primordial ooze— people liked to talk in the presence of liquids.

Drunken barstool ramblings. Coffee-fueled morning chatter. Water cooler gossip. Mimosas with the girls. Beers with the boys.

As such, bartenders were privy to lots of valuable intel. They were an investigator's dream, some of the best individuals with whom to make inquiries.

"Maybe," the man said again.

"What'd she want?"

Skepticism multiplied in the old salt's eyes, gathering like dark clouds. "Can't remember. Lots of folks come and go."

Silence let a long moment draw out, then he pointed at a tiny black-and-white monitor perched over the line of liquor bottles and said, "Think harder."

The bartender turned around, looked.

On the screen, a high-angle viewpoint looked down upon the Blue Barrel's entrance. There was SnakeNeck—on his back, asleep, chest rising and lowering in a peaceful cadence.

"Shit! What'd you do to Bruce?"

The bartender whipped back to face Silence, his mouth now open. He licked his lips, swallowed, and glanced at the printout on the counter below.

"She was asking 'bout the Lost Jackals, all right?" the man said, his voice almost a whisper. "And some guy named Draper."

Draper? There were a few Drapers in Silence's extensive mental databank, none tied to the Jackals.

"What first name..." he said, swallowed. "Did she give with 'Draper'?"

The bartender shrugged. "Can't remember."

It was an honest response; Silence could read that much in the man's body language.

"All I know is that the guy sitting there," the bartender continued and pointed to one of the empty stools, "told her Draper went to Furnace Creek."

Furnace Creek. Silence knew the name. It was a tiny town in Death Valley, home to the park's headquarters.

"Did she mention..." Silence said and swallowed. "Adrian Hirsch?"

There was no recognition in the bartender's eyes.

"Never heard of him," he said, shaking his head. Again, the man's truthfulness was evident.

"Did she mention..." Silence said and swallowed. "The Boston Legacy Collapse?"

The question perplexed the bartender even more than the last. His brow knitted.

"You mean all those folks who died back in the '80s in Beantown?" He gave Silence a long, appraising look, then shrugged. "No. Why the hell would she ask about that?"

Silence didn't respond.

He gave the bartender a nod of thanks, folded the paper, returned it to his pocket, then pushed off the counter and left, his mind swimming in a pool of fresh intelligence.

The Draper name was an intriguing mystery. Of the handful of scumbag "Drapers" in Silence's mental files, none had ties to the Lost Jackals or even a reason for an affiliation. If the woman's investigation was correct, and the Jackals were the gang responsible for slaughtering the tourists, logic said the Jackals' leadership would be involved.

But Silence and the Watchers knew the gang was headed by a man named Higgins in Bakersfield, California. The other regional chapter was in Vegas, led by a man named Bonilla.

Higgins. Bonilla.

Not Draper.

As Silence stepped outside, the bright afternoon sun was harsh after the dimly lit Blue Barrel Lounge. He threw on his Ray-Bans. There was SnakeNeck—or Bruce, rather—on the pavement just outside the door, still immobile but blinking into consciousness. He squinted up at Silence.

Silence gave him a two-finger wave/salute and walked off.

CHAPTER FIFTEEN

Mojave Desert, California

THE HEAT HIT MITCH FIRST, suffocating him.

He coughed, gagged. Saliva speckled his chin; his lips were coated with it.

He blinked into consciousness.

The world was shadow and light and momentum, spinning around him. Slits of daylight weaved through gaps in the metal interior—the backside of a van. A large one. A panel van. He was lying on the floor.

The light seeping into the van's windowless walls was bold and bright, indicating the sun's position high in the sky.

Which meant...

Hours.

Mitch had been out for hours. Last he remembered, it was pitch-black. Nighttime desert. A star-pricked blanket of sky.

His wrists ached. They were bound. So, too, were his ankles.

Beads of sweat covered his forehead, merging in rivulets

that traced down his temples. Puddles of sweat shimmered on the corrugated floor beneath him. Moisture had gathered around the collar of his T-shirt, too, soaking the fabric until it clung to his skin.

The van lurched forward. Tied up on the floor, every motion sent Mitch sliding, colliding into the unforgiving metal walls. And legs, too. Boots. He kept smashing into *people*.

Mitch gasped as this realization brought a fresh wave of cognizance crashing upon him, snapping him fully alert.

There were other people in the back of the van with him.

Several of them.

He blinked, brought his head off the floor, found men looking down upon him.

Rough-looking types. Two sat on stools; two were on the metal bumps of the van's wheel wells. They watched Mitch's struggles, sliding and flopping with the van's movements. The slight upturn of their lips and the occasional outright chuckle showed their cruel pleasure for his discomfort.

Leather pants. Leather vests. Shiny chrome studs and spikes. Beards. Sunglasses.

Bikers.

Motorcycles...

As more acuity crystalized, Mitch's thoughts returned to his most recent memories. Yes, his side mission to the bus tragedy site on North Highway, the crime-scene-tape-encircled patch of desert glowing under the moonlight.

Figures had closed in around him, appearing out of the rocky wilderness.

Men on motorcycles.

These men.

Mitch had dropped his knife and his Smith on the desert floor. He hadn't been willing to give up without a fight, but not knowing the men's full intentions, he'd thought that lifting his hands in a show of mild submission would lessen the intensity of their attack.

It hadn't.

The men had rushed him, thrown him to the rocky ground. Blood had gushed through Mitch's mouth as his cheek split against his teeth. The metallic, sharp taste mingled with the earth's grit. Someone had twisted his arm behind his back. Pain jolted from his shoulder, and Mitch had thought his rotator cuff had torn. He'd screamed. Something on his face. Cloth. A noxious taste.

And then everything turned to black.

And remained so.

Until Mitch had woken up moments earlier, sliding about the hot metal floor of the van.

Panic flushed over him, prickling his wet skin. Had Mitch become another statistic—one of the mysterious national park disappearances he'd researched and written about so extensively?

He'd dug too deeply. They found him. After all these years, they found him. *God dammit!* All the work he'd done with Unseen Path—it had led him here. Captured. In the back of a van. With four government men looking down on him, laughing as he bashed about the metallic environment.

Heart pounding, he tried to take stock, discerning any identifying traits from his captors. Their rugged exteriors didn't paint them as federal agents, military contractors, or off-the-books black ops guys. They looked like motorcycle gang members, like quintessential Raven's Ride ruffians.

But the powers-that-be were good. They were talented at hiding in plain sight. The idea that they had men who readily passed as outlaw bikers was entirely believable.

The van took a turn, and Mitch went tumbling to the left, bashing into a pair of boots. A round of deep laughs rumbled out of the faux bikers. The back of Mitch's shirt rode up, exposing a patch of skin that scraped against the floor. The burn of it mingled with the heat.

Amidst the chaos of thoughts and pain, Mitch's mind fought for clarity, tried to find a tether in this storm. But answers remained elusive, and the clattering noise jumbled with memories, taking him further back than he'd been a few moments earlier, before the abduction in the desert...

...and back to the previous afternoon.

At the back of the RV. When he'd been preparing the dirt bike. The skeptical look on Carmen's face. She'd known. That intuition of hers.

She'd known.

What are you up to, Mitch? she'd said.

And Mitch had lied.

For over a day, he'd somehow convinced himself that he'd done something nobler.

But he hadn't.

He'd lied to Carmen.

Maintenance, he'd said, indicating the ill-fated dirt bike. *I want us to take some rides after the tour.*

Carmen had been worried, and Mitch had seen it, felt it. But he'd waved it off, pushed her concerns to the back of his mind.

In the stifling heat, with ropes digging into his wrists and ankles, the truth loomed large. He'd lied to Carmen, and he'd disregarded her.

Carmen always warned Mitch that his impulsiveness would catch up to him.

Now, tied up and surrounded by government toughs, she'd been proven correct.

Unable to see the stark desert outside, Mitch could only imagine the heat blurring into a hazy mirage as the van sped on. But within, a cold realization settled over him, overpowering the fever: he might never experience another adventure, never feel the thrill of discovery, never uncover another mystery.

Worst of all, he might never lay eyes on Carmen again.

That thought was a dagger, piercing deeper than any of his physical pain.

Suddenly, something entirely foreign to him overwhelmed everything else: desperation. It was the realization that he, of all people, Mitch Lockwood, founder of Unseen Path, might soon be erased from this world—another statistic, another lost soul, another unsolved mystery of the national parks.

CHAPTER SIXTEEN

Furnace Creek, California

BLOOM WAS BACK in Death Valley.

A few days earlier, her investigation had begun there before she followed leads that took her outside the park's boundaries and out of the state of California, touring her around several small towns and one big Sin City.

Now, she'd returned to the Valley of Death.

Although, if she didn't know better, she might have forgotten she was surrounded by an unending desert landscape.

Because, at that very moment, she was in an oasis.

A literal oasis.

The census-designated spot Furnace Creek—right in the middle of the massive national park, engulfed in desert—was not only home to DVNP's visitor center, museum, and headquarters, but it was also a true natural oasis that had been developed into a manmade marvel, replete with a resort, a golf course, palm groves, gardens, and perfectly manicured streets.

As such, the Furnace Creek Café's interior was not the quintessential California highway all-American greasy spoon. Far from it. Though the place served traditional diner food—burgers, shakes, all-day breakfast—it went about it in a highly polished manner. Everything was new and clean, from the spotless chrome accents to the checkered tablecloths to the nostalgic photos and decorations on the walls.

Bloom was in one of the plush red booths by the windows. She pulled her arms in against a chill. The air-conditioning was cranked. Freezing. This sensation was a bizarre, almost discordant juxtaposition as she looked out the window —past a line of picture-perfect palm trees and a stretch of green grass—to the twisted, brown expanse of one of the most extreme environments on the planet.

The thirty-something waitress approached wearing a smile and a high-end take on a classic diner uniform—a powder-blue, short-sleeved dress with white piping, cinched at the waist by a narrow belt. Her polished name-tag said *AGNES*. Bloom wondered if the dated name was another component of the retro costuming or if the woman really was Agnes. She didn't look like an Agnes.

Agnes reached into one of the capacious pockets of her white apron and took out an order pad and pen.

Bloom gave the surroundings a broad sweep of the eyes and said, "Real nice place you guys got here. You part of the park?"

The other woman shook her head. "Privately owned. We belong to the resort."

While Agnes's order pad remained at chest height, she pointed with her pen through the windows on the other side of the cafe where an elaborate hotel lined with palm trees basked in the blinding sunlight.

"I see," Bloom said. "Did Kaveny buy you guys out, or are you independent?"

Agnes bristled, lifting her chin. "No, ma'am. The Parnes family would never sell out."

Bloom lifted a hand in apology. "Sorry, I ... I'm from out of town. I heard about Kaveny buying up private hotels and resorts in the area, upsetting people, and ... I ... sorry."

Agnes's professional smile returned, and she waved it off, bringing her pen back to her order pad.

"What can I get you, ma'am?"

"Black coffee and a cherry Danish," Bloom said, pointing to the glass display case full of pastries by the cash register. She paused a beat. "And perhaps some information."

Again Agnes stiffened, pen halting as she looked up from her order pad. A flicker of something indefinable crossed over her eyes.

"Information? What, are you a cop?"

"I'm someone ... with a personal interest in what happened here last week."

This seemed to soften Agnes somewhat—tense cheeks slackening, lips parting—as though she assumed Bloom had lost a loved one to the murders.

"Raven's Ride," Bloom continued. "You're surely seeing a lot of bikers come through here lately."

"Of course."

"The Lost Jackals?"

A slight pause. Then Agnes nodded. Something in the eyes again, this time more akin to anxiety.

"Ethan Draper," Bloom said. "How about *that* Jackal? Has he come through lately?"

Another pause from Agnes, longer than before. Her lips parted—

But before the conversation could continue, the jingle of the entrance bell drew Agnes's attention. A family of four in wide-brimmed hats and hiking boots entered.

Offering Bloom a strained smile, Agnes said, "Just a moment, ma'am," and left to accommodate the new arrivals.

Bloom watched. The way Agnes talked to the children with soft-spoken kindness, the way her brow furrowed in concentration as she took down the family's order, said Agnes was a staple at the Furnace Creek Cafe, a part of the restaurant's fabric. If anyone had the information Bloom needed, it was her.

Bloom took the brief interruption to gather her thoughts. Her lead on Draper had been thin but solid enough to pursue. It was all she had, the only tie—abstract as it might be—to the negligence of more than a decade earlier. Whoever he truly was, Draper was the connection between Adrian Hirsch and the negligence in Boston so many years ago.

Negligence...

The theme of Bloom's life.

She thought of Saeed then. What could have happened, the near miss, the disaster averted. Funny how what-might-have-beens can affect a person as much as events that actually occurred.

Agnes returned, the aroma of freshly brewed coffee wafting with her as she placed a mug in front of Bloom, followed by a plate with a perfectly golden-brown cherry Danish.

"Thank you," Bloom said. The two women stared at each other for a moment, the café's bustling noise fading to a distant hum. Then, with a deliberate steadiness, Bloom said the name once more. "Ethan Draper."

She hadn't said it like a question. She just put it out there, waiting for Agnes to take the reins.

Agnes's shoulders dipped before she gave Bloom a nod. "Yeah. Yeah, he was one of the Jackals who came through here."

"Last week?"

Agnes nodded. "We don't ... we don't normally see a lot of biker gangs. I mean, look at this place." She waved a hand at the glistening perfection. "But it's Raven's Ride, you know? They're all over the area. They just finally started leaving for the big finale tonight in Ridgecrest."

"The day of the bus slaughter," Bloom said slowly, steady, keeping her eyes trained on Agnes's. She didn't want to scare the woman off, but she needed a clear understanding. "The Jackals were here, weren't they?"

"I mean, lots of bikers came through that day, and—"

"Including the Jackals?"

Agnes bit her lip. Hesitated again. Frightened. Finally, she nodded.

"You recognized the name Ethan Draper," Bloom said. "So you met him, then?"

"I served them. The Jackals. Four of 'em. This guy, this 'Ethan,' did all the talking. He was dressed just like the others, but he was different, like he was their leader or something. Loud, obnoxious. But also ... kind of ... I don't know, distinct, smarter."

"They say where they were going?"

"No," Agnes said, getting louder, breathless. "And like I said, there were other bikers in that day. Just 'cause they were here, doesn't mean they were the ones who—"

"You're safe," Bloom said.

"But you don't understand these gangs," Agnes said, voice shaking, no longer hiding her fright. "The Jackals especially. They'll—"

"You're safe," Bloom repeated. "No one'll find out you talked to me. I swear it."

Agnes took in an unsteady breath. Nodded weakly. And left.

Retreating into her own thoughts, Bloom leaned back into the cushion—which wheezed and squeaked—and took a bite of the cherry Danish.

It tasted just as perfect as it looked, though she couldn't savor it.

CHAPTER SEVENTEEN

Bakersfield, California

HIRSCH'S POLISHED oxfords crunched through dust and sparse gravel.

The motorcycle junkyard was full of warped metal, scattered parts, and decaying frames. An aroma of rust, oil, and dry California soil permeated the air. Though miles and an ocean away from his German origins, Hirsch sensed an eerie kinship with the junkyard's despair. Certain types of darkness were universal.

This secluded location on the outskirts of Bakersfield belonged to the Lost Jackals, and it had an almost sacred presence—a testament to the Jackals' reverence for their rides, even beyond repair, beyond mechanical death.

It was also the ideal spot for certain types of activities.

As Hirsch delved deeper into the graveyard, with Westlin marching alongside, a voice called out.

"Adrian Hirsch. How's it hangin', bud?"

The American drawl—one that Hirsch immediately

recognized—sliced through the faint hum of distant traffic, dripping with a confidence that bordered on impertinence.

Out of the mechanical tangle stepped Ethan Draper.

This was Hirsch's first time seeing the man since the incident. The dark hair, dark eyes, and slightly olive-toned skin were as he remembered. The height, just below average, was consistent, too, as was the nondescript physique and the nondescript body language.

Yet, something was different.

Maybe Hirsch just hadn't noticed it when they first met: the dead quality of Draper's inky eyes.

On a different face, their oversized appearance would have projected a sense of artlessness. They seemed to absorb every detail, sparkling with a misplaced mark of curiosity. The eyes of a man untethered from the collective.

The air grew thicker, charged with an unspoken animosity as Hirsch's gaze fell directly upon those strange eyes. This wasn't a mere meeting between allies; this was a confrontation. Though they'd spoken briefly the night of the bus attack, Hirsch's sense of betrayal flared further seeing Draper in person for the first time since then—echoes of that deviation from the agreed-upon plan, its nature still elusive.

Draper extended a hand well before he was within reach.

Hirsch waved it off, didn't break stride.

"Let's not waste time," he said, dispelling any pretense of cordiality.

A mocking smile tugged at Draper's lips as he fell into line beside Hirsch and Westlin.

"Fine. Follow me."

A few meters farther into the detritus, Hirsch said, "Tell me what happened."

Draper turned to him. "Huh?"

"It was supposed to be MacLeod and Shapiro."

Draper shrugged. "I told you; it's a long story. You said

you didn't want to waste time. I'll fill you in soon. Don't worry yourself, Adrian. You're in no danger. The Jackals got your back."

Hirsch bristled.

The bastard used his first name again.

And he'd avoided the question once more like he had on the night of the attack.

Westlin, ever watchful, caught Hirsch's eye. A minute nod passed between them—a subtle yet robust language shaped over years of shared dangers.

The trio delved deeper into the catacombs of metal carcasses, Draper leading the way. Every step amplified Hirsch's unease, each crunch of gravel.

He was *following* Ethan Draper. His contact. *Literally* following the slimy piece of shit.

He had to take a breath to calm his nerves.

Finally, they reached it—a solitary, dilapidated shed standing amid the decay. It was a patchwork of rust-covered metal and fading plastic siding that appeared to have been pieced together from salvaged materials. A stubborn structure, one that refused to succumb to time.

"This is it?" Hirsch scoffed.

"It is," Draper said, that enigmatic smile still spanning his face.

Hirsch took a calculated breath. Whether sanctuary or trap, the shed held answers. And he was about to pry them out.

Draper wrenched the creaking door open with a tug, revealing a dim interior lit solely by the sallow glow of sunlight sneaking in through the translucent polycarbonate roofing. Framed by that sickly light were several members of the Lost Jackals. Ominously silent. Beefy, sweaty frames. Faces marked by hard lives. They wore swaths of black leather clothing. Everywhere were the light blue bandanas—

on foreheads, biceps, even knotted around a few burly thighs.

Patches bearing the Lost Jackals' logo were there at every turn of the eyes, too. At the center of the design was a jackal's head, a side profile. Its ears were erect, and its eyes were light blue, the only color in an otherwise monochromatic design. Sharp teeth were slightly bared in a subtle snarl.

Encircling this central image was a chain, symbolizing the unbreakable bond of the gang members. Above the jackal's head, in a bold, gothic font arched *LOST*. Below, *JACKALS* was written in the same style. Both words were linked by the ends of the chain, completing the circle.

Hirsch let his eyes trace over the bikers as he stepped farther into the shed. In the center of the space, bound with coarse rope to a folding chair, was Mitch Lockwood. Caucasian. Out-of-shape. Late forties or so. His spine was straight, arms tugging at the binds that held him to the metal chair, knuckles white with effort. His gut strained his shirt, which was smeared with sweat and dirt. Stubble lined his jowls. Greasy salt-and-pepper hair. Eyes that flickered with apprehensive defiance.

The oppressive quiet inside the shed mingled with the tension that had already flared between Hirsch and Draper. The assembled bikers lining the walls looked like an Americanized, Warholian take on ancient gargoyles, perched and ready for a fight but holding their peace—for now. None of them met Hirsch's gaze or dared to speak; their role was that of an added layer of security and intimidation for the coming confrontation.

The weight of all eyes was upon Hirsch as his gaze turned to the man in the chair, then flicked back to Draper, a silent acknowledgment of the stakes involved. This man, Draper, was why they were here, the reason for this uneasy collaboration.

He brought his attention back to the captive.

"Mitch Lockwood," Hirsch began, letting the name fill the air before it dissolved into the stagnant atmosphere, "my name is Adrian Hirsch. I have some questions that require immediate answers. What were you doing past the NPS highway barricade at three thirty this morning?"

Lockwood's eyes darted from Hirsch to Westlin and back again.

"Freelance journalism," he said in a sarcastic tone, letting everyone know he was aware they understood his true identity and purpose.

"You're a 'journalist,' *ja*?" Hirsch didn't allow Lockwood a moment to answer the rhetorical question. "More like the founder of Unseen Path, a newsletter and tour group that concerns itself with U.S. national park mysteries: deaths, disappearances, and the like."

Westlin shifted past Hirsch's side, moving subtly closer to Lockwood.

Lockwood swallowed.

"What were you doing at the crime scene?" Hirsch said.

Lockwood's eyes scanned the faces again: Hirsch, Westlin, Draper, the bikers. He didn't respond.

"Speak!" Hirsch said.

As if on cue, Westlin moved toward Lockwood again—more quickly and aggressively—stopping inches from the man.

Lockwood leaned back as far as his restraints would allow. His lips opened—quivering, wet. But he still said nothing.

This was a proud man, indeed. But Hirsch couldn't be sure yet if his muteness came from bravery or just the opposite: utter fright.

Hirsch's eyes lingered on Lockwood for a moment longer, contemplating the strange duality of the man tied to the chair. Lockwood's earlier sardonic response veiled more than it revealed. Perhaps this conspiracy-obsessed quasi-journalist really had ascertained the reason for the bus slaughter.

Or...

Maybe he'd deduced something that had eluded even Hirsch's vast and intricate understanding.

Maybe he knew what Ethan Draper was refusing to reveal.

The thought was as compelling as it was unsettling.

Hirsch looked at Draper for a moment.

Those dark eyes.

That smug grin.

No matter what Lockwood knew, it was time for answers.

Hirsch turned to Westlin, said nothing, only gave a subtle nod, the same form of communication he'd offered in the desert last week before commanding Westlin to slaughter MacLeod and Shapiro.

It was all that was needed.

Westlin stepped toward Lockwood, a dark glint flashing across his eyes.

CHAPTER EIGHTEEN

Furnace Creek, California

SILENCE PEERED through the gap between a pair of luxury RVs. He was in the Wrangler, parked in an immaculate blacktop lot across the street from the Furnace Creek Cafe, watching the restaurant from his place of concealment. The mystery woman sat alone at a booth behind one of the front-facing windows.

The town of Furnace Creek was an actual oasis, and its caretakers had taken full advantage. Towering palms rustled in the hot breeze. Lush green lawns. A sprawling resort lay beyond the cafe, and farther back was a golf course. The standard Death Valley desert landscape surrounded it all, encircled by a line of mountains.

Silence's earbuds—whose wires draped down his chest to a 3.5mm jack—transmitted the noises an electronic listening device picked up. The device was about six inches cubed with a miniature parabolic dish, which Silence was pointing toward the cafe. The staticky din in his ears relayed subtle indications of the mystery woman munching on a cherry Danish and sipping her coffee, cutlery and ceramic clanking in the background. Several minutes had passed since the woman asked the waitress her questions. Now, she seemed to be taking a few moments to recharge while she processed the information.

Silence's mind also churned through the mystery woman's interrogation. The way she'd questioned the waitress—there had been a finesse to her questions, a rhythm that spoke of expert training. Earlier in the investigation, this would have been further confirmation to Silence of the Watchers-prompted assumption she was an FBI agent.

After the previous evening's confrontation, though, Silence was no longer operating on that assumption. He knew better now.

His hand went to his left ribcage, and he winced at the slightest pressure from his fingertips. That's where the mystery woman had gotten him, her best shot.

But there'd also been the Krav Maga attack, the Pencak silat palm strike, the Systema maneuvers.

She might be a talented inquisitor, but the mystery woman had an entirely more deadly set of skills, too. Both a bloodhound and an operator.

Silence's gaze shifted to his PenPal notebook, sitting on the center console, its blue-and-gray-striped cover turned back, mechanical pencil laying diagonally across the notes he'd taken, ready for further use should the woman across the street ask the waitress more questions. He picked the notebook up, put the pencil aside, and studied the notes he'd taken a few minutes earlier.

His eyes found a line that had been an after-thought at the time he wrote it, but had somehow been tickling the back of his brain ever since: *Kaveny International Hotels & Resorts.* The mystery woman had asked the waitress about Kaveny's recent controversial purchases of numerous privately owned hotels, motels, and resorts in the American Southwest.

Kaveny had another reason for being in the news lately. Though the woman had not mentioned them, Silence had added two related names to his notes: *Santa Barbara* and *Elysian*. He took the mechanical pencil from the PenPal's spiral binding and added another note: *50th anniversary tonight*.

Tonight...

Santa Barbara...

Could be a coincidence. But Silence wasn't a big believer in coincidences, particularly in his line of work.

I wonder... he thought.

Among the other notes, a name stood out—*Ethan Draper*. The name had teased the periphery of Silence's memory but refused to leap into full focus, so two minutes ago, he'd called a speed-dial number on his phone, reaching out to the network of Watchers Specialists to confirm his suspicions. As always, the call had been routed to a random Specialist, and Silence had made an "information retrieval" request. These things never took long; he would receive a call at any moment.

On cue, his cellular phone chimed. He checked the number on the multiplex and flipped the phone open.

"A-23," he said, using the abbreviated form of his full Watchers numerical title, Asset 23.

"We have your information," the Specialist replied.

It was a different Specialist than the one he'd spoken to minutes earlier. That one had been a middle-aged guy with a low smoker's grumble; this one was a female with a nasally lisp. The network of Watchers Specialists was spread out across the country in a web of interconnected lines of communication.

Specialists were the lifeblood of the Watchers organization. While the higher-ups made the decisions and Asset assassins like Silence worked in the field correcting failures in procedural justice, Specialists provided weaponry, channeled money secretly around the globe, surreptitiously navigated the legal system, and provided all other logistical needs for the Watchers' mission.

Accordingly, they managed the Watchers' copious intel.

"Ethan Draper," the Specialist said. "The name popped up. Your gut feeling was correct, Suppressor."

In addition to the title Asset 23—or A-23—Silence also had the codename Suppressor.

"An 'Ethan Draper' was investigated regarding domestic terrorist events in both North Carolina and Iowa."

The woman cleared her throat, and when she continued, her flat tone of voice said that she was clearly reading information from some sort of computer database.

"Charlotte. Three years ago. Someone sabotaged the construction site of a new mega-mall, leading to significant structural damage and delays in the project. Methods were discreet, involving the slow erosion of key supports over weeks. Cops investigated, consulting with the FBI regarding a possible terrorist connection. One suspect was a twenty-something man named Ethan Draper, but the incident was ultimately chalked up to a contractor error. A costly setback, but no lives were lost.

"Dubuque, Iowa. Last February. Remember that fast-food incident? That ... certain chain of restaurants that had to delay the debut of their latest burger? The company was planning to launch its biggest promotional campaign yet, one that was sure to drive consumption to all-time highs. Just days before the campaign launch, people got sick in Iowa. The meat vendor issued an emergency recall, as you'll ... um, recall, no pun intended, but even though it was ultimately ruled as no foul play, again there was an investigation, and one name that came up was—"

"Ethan Draper," Silence said.

"Right. Another twenty-something-year-old male suspect. The infected food was found at restaurants nationwide, so the feds got involved. FBI. FDA. The fast-food bigwigs were more than willing to comply—public image and all that. One man on their radar, Ethan Draper, seemed to have ties to multiple locations where the food was discovered.

"The feds had a theory that Draper planted the tainted food supplies, hoping for a widespread panic and the suspension of the restaurant chain's upcoming campaign. The resulting scandal would cause a significant drop in sales, thereby sending a powerful message about the fast-food industry's practices. They thought Draper could be a sort of anti-capitalist activist before the trail went cold. Not until your call a few minutes ago had anyone made a tie between the Charlotte incident and the fast food investigation."

Silence had thought the name Ethan Draper sounded familiar, a name that seemed to be connected to disparate events in recent history. Having the notions confirmed stroked his ego slightly but also gave a violent shove to a new set of ideas forming in his mind.

However, this new line of reasoning had a significant obstacle in its path. One piece of information simply didn't make sense...

"The Lost Jackals?" he said.

The Specialist gave a short, exasperated snicker. "Yeah, we can't make heads or tails of that either. We've discovered that there's an Ethan Draper in the Jackals. A low-level guy. No title, no rank. Undoubtedly, this is our man, but we have no other intel on him. We're working on it. We'll keep you posted."

Beep.

The Specialist ended the conversation as abruptly as she started it.

Silence took a moment to marinate in this new intel. Ethan Draper and corporate terror incidents and the Lost Jackals motorcycle gang. All of them connected.

But...

What about the mystery woman across the street, finishing a cherry Danish and sipping her coffee? Her unwarranted FBI searches?

The FBI had investigated both the mall attack in Charlotte and the fast food tampering, so this seemed to play into the Watchers' initial conclusion that the mystery woman was a rogue FBI agent.

But again, Silence's mind flashed on the woman's fighting acumen. The strength. Precision. The telltale signs of elite training.

She was more than a special agent.

She *had* to be.

And then there was Adrian Hirsch, the German criminal, someone with zero reason to be involved in the slaughter of tour bus members in the American desert, a middle-aged lawbreaker elite with a penchant for torture who certainly had no apparent association with a young American man attacking shopping malls and fast-food chains.

Silence's chaotic mind space began to spin. He felt it tumbling. He quickly reached out for his mindfulness techniques, beginning a five-second meditation—

And he stopped.

Because there was yet another maddeningly discordant layer to his investigation. An architectural disaster. Years in the past.

All the way back in the *previous decade*.

Frustrated, Silence mentally cast aside his notion of a five-second meditation. He reached toward the passenger seat and grabbed a manila folder, pulling it open. He shuffled through its contents until he found the section marked "Boston 1983," flipping to the list of names involved in the Boston Legacy Center's creation—city officials, architects, engineers, artists, interior designers, landscapers, and a copious number of investors and donators.

His PenPal was still open on his thigh. He flipped a page there, too, going back to a note he'd made the previous night after cross-referencing a pair of his resources. Another list of names, much shorter. He'd labeled it *BUS SLAUGHTER VICTIMS*. Fifteen people, thirteen of whom he'd crossed off. He had circled the two remaining names—*Scott MacLeod* and *Milton Shapiro*.

He took his attention back to the sheet of paper in the folder. The names at the top of the longer, printed list—five names—were printed in a larger font than the others, denoting their significance. Silence had circled two of the five: *Scott MacLeod* and *Milton Shapiro*.

The Boston Legacy Center Collapse.

An architectural disaster...

Should Draper's plan have succeeded in Charlotte three years earlier, there would have also been an architectural disaster at a North Carolina shopping mall.

A decade had passed between the two events, Boston and Charlotte. The Specialist had said Ethan Draper was a "twenty-something-year-old" suspect at the events in Charlotte and Dubuque, Iowa. At the time of the Boston Legacy Center Canopy Collapse, then, Draper would have been a teenager at best, possibly even a child.

So ... a connection there made no sense.

Silence's exhale turned into a growl.

He considered a five-second meditation again but looked out the windshield instead. Across the street, the mystery woman had finished her Danish. She had her coffee mug to her lips. Her eyes were distant but intensely focused.

Not only was she an elite operator—like Silence—but it had become abundantly clear that she was also a dogged investigator—like Silence. He wondered if this investigation's discordant strains of intel were bothering her as much as they were him.

She took another sip, and Silence observed how her jaw muscles worked as she drank. A strong woman. Large and strong. Those jaw muscles on that sharp angle of her face reminded Silence of someone else.

Someone else with prominent jaw muscles.

The man Silence had seen in Pensacola the night before he left for the Southwest.

The man in the alley behind Black Jack's, a seedy bar known as a hive of illegal gambling.

The man with piercing blue eyes who stared with cold intent in Silence's direction as Silence had sat parked, observing, much like he was now—but in the darkness of a muggy Florida night, not the dry heat of a desert day, in his BMW, not a Wrangler.

All of this pulled his abstract reasoning toward a memory.

It brought him back to his old mentor.

It brought him back to Marvin Tanner.

Two weeks in a row, Silence had followed Tanner to Black Jack's, to that hub of illegal gambling that Silence now understood to be the latest satellite of Labyrinth.

The memory was an unwanted visitor, disrupting Silence's current train of thought. He couldn't get distracted, not with the ridiculous level of confusion already present in his mission.

Yet...

There was his cellular phone, resting on his thigh, right

above the PenPal, where he'd placed it after his phone call with the Specialist.

The phone was a link not just to the web of Watchers Specialists...

...it could connect him to anywhere in the world.

It could take him out of the desert for a moment and back there.

To Pensacola.

His hand went to the phone. He flipped it open, punched in the number. Two rings, and there was an answer.

"Hey there, friend," Elsher said in his slight Scottish accent. "You must have ESP, because I was gonna call you in just a few."

"Update?" Silence said.

"Marvin Tanner's been busy. After watching him go to the ATM yesterday, I did a bit more digging. Seems that wasn't an isolated occurrence. He's been making regular withdrawals there for a couple of weeks."

A pit opened up in Silence's stomach.

"Now, that doesn't prove Tanner's involved in illegal gambling," Elsher said, "but ... it looks pretty damn bad."

Silence exhaled. "It does."

"And I've got an ID on the man you mentioned—the bright blue eyes, big jaw muscles."

Silence sat forward.

"I poked around town today, met a few lovely people." Elsher's rendition of *lovely* oozed with disgusted sarcasm. "The man's name is Liam Rourke. Labyrinth sent him over from New Orleans to start up the new cell."

Labyrinth. The illegal gambling network. They'd infiltrated the city of Pensacola. *Silence's city*. They'd ensnared Silence's former mentor into a life of sin.

Now, the faceless organization had a face, one with deadly blue eyes.

...that flashed at Silence again, out of the haze of memory, from the darkness of the alley...

But the blue eyes had a name now as well.

Liam Rourke.

Silence felt an overwhelming desire to take action, to peel off in the Jeep and drive thirty hours straight back to Pensacola.

And kick some ass.

His fists tightened.

"I'm looking into Rourke," Elsher said. "I'll let you know."

"Thanks."

Beep.

Elsher was gone.

But Silence hardly noticed.

It had been a stupid idea to reach out to Elsher with his mind already spinning from the inharmonious threads of confusion relating to his current mission. Now, his mind was an absolute tempest. He felt himself slipping. He desperately needed to halt the chaos.

He called out to her.

C.C., I need you.

But before his deceased fiancée could reply, another memory assailed him, one more recent than following Tanner from Pensacola Beach to Black Jack's, more recent than the bright blue eyes and bulging jaw muscles in the alley, more recent even than the meeting at the bayside bar with Elsher, laying out the parameters of the surveillance and investigation work that the private detective was to complete while Silence was on the other side of the country.

The memory was Silence, back at his house after meeting Elsher, stripping naked, climbing into the sensory deprivation pod.

Then, a memory within a memory.

As he'd floated, Silence had slipped back in time, back to when he was Jake Rowe.

Jake had been in the man's office. His lieutenant's office. His *mentor's* office.

Marvin Tanner's office.

Jake had told Tanner he had solid evidence that Mr. Martinelli—a respected Pensacola shopkeeper known for his community work—was a crook. Jake had told Tanner that Martinelli was malignant, that there was solid evidence against the man.

And Tanner, with that patient yet damn smug smile, had told Jake that even the most unexpected people can harbor secrets, but those secrets weren't always nefarious.

It had been condescending, maddening.

In a fittingly patronizing tone, Tanner had asked Jake if he was *sure* Martinelli was crooked or if he was letting emotion cloud his judgment.

At that point, the buzzer in the sensory deprivation pod had sounded, tripped by the motion sensor outside Silence's home. It had been Lola and Mrs. Enfield returning, ending the memory but also signifying that Silence could finally get the damn drooler, Baxter, out of his house.

Now, in Death Valley, Silence could do nothing about the situation in Pensacola, nothing for Tanner, nothing to stop Labyrinth.

He needed to focus on his mission.

But as he closed his eyes, he didn't enter a five-second meditation.

Instead, he went back to his interrupted memory of Jake Rowe, back to Tanner's office years earlier, back to the argument about Martinelli.

———

Jake slapped a palm on Tanner's desk. He yelled at the older man, contending that, no, he wasn't letting emotion overrule his logic.

In response to this outburst, Tanner said nothing. But his mustachioed grin grew even smugger.

The irony wasn't lost on Jake. He scowled.

Then he looked away from Tanner and back to the materials, flipping through them with as much anger as zest. He told Tanner there was even more evidence against Martinelli, not simply the insinuations Jake had brought up a few minutes earlier.

He showed Tanner that there were even strong suggestions that Martinelli had ties to organized crime, to Pensacola's Farone crime organization, a history of interactions, verifiable interactions.

After being smugly silent for so long, Tanner finally spoke again. "People and situations aren't always what they seem, Jake."

Jake bristled. The older man's condescension was beginning to eat at him.

And, with Tanner's stalwart quasi-defense of Martinelli, Jake was beginning to feel the first inclinations of distrust.

Paranoia, even.

The Farone crime organization had a firm grip on the Pensacola region, with tentacles reaching the tightest corners and the highest positions of power. It would seem they'd gotten to a good man like Martinelli.

Maybe, even, they'd gotten to a good cop.

Like Tanner.

Jake shuddered as he looked back at Tanner, that seemingly warm smile.

No. No, Jake wouldn't believe it. Not yet. He would give his mentor a chance to prove himself before he thought the worst possible of him.

Jake told Tanner that if the lieutenant knew something that Jake didn't, he'd better tell him now. Right now.

Tanner eased forward, the springs in his old chair squealing as he crossed his arms on his desktop, now much closer to Jake.

"What you don't understand about Martinelli, Jake, is that—"

———

Silence gasped.

Much like the first time he slipped back into the memory of the meeting in Tanner's office—floating naked in his pod in Pensacola—something urgent jolted him back to the present.

But unlike last time, it wasn't the shrill electronic beep of an alarm.

It was movement.

Across the street, the mystery woman finally stood up. She slid a greenback beneath her saucer and headed for the exit.

Silence removed his earbuds, slid the listening device's power switch to *OFF*, and placed the device on the passenger seat. As he watched the mystery woman leave the Furnace Creek Cafe and head for the old Nova, he flipped open his cellular phone and pressed and held the 2 button. Speed dial.

One ring, and a Specialist picked up. By coincidence, it was the same one he'd talked to moments earlier—the female with the nasally voice.

"You again?" she said. It wasn't the standard greeting of simply: *Specialist.*

Nonetheless, Silence proceeded with protocol, issuing the standard Asset introduction. "Suppressor, A-23."

"Confirmed. State your business."

"Information retrieval," Silence said and swallowed. "Another name. Liam Rourke."

For better or worse, Silence couldn't shut down the thoughts of his old mentor's slip into illegal gambling, of the Labyrinth organization infecting his beloved home city of

Pensacola, of the man with the deadly blue eyes and bulging jaw muscles.

Elsher had said he would look into Liam Rourke.

But Silence didn't have the patience to wait for a private detective to dig up information.

To Hell with that.

He had much more powerful resources at his disposal—an intricate network of the most detailed intel in the country.

There was a slight pause from the Specialist.

"I don't see that name in the mission notes," she said. "New lead?"

"You could say that."

Another pause from the Specialist. "Are you up to something, Suppressor?"

Silence's reputation for stepping outside the Watchers' standard protocols was well-known within the organization, including the copious Specialists. He was, after all, the top Asset. One can't hide one's reputation when one is the top dog.

Silence didn't respond.

The Specialist sighed. "We'll look into Liam Rourke for you."

Beep.

She was gone.

Across the street, the Nova turned out of the cafe parking lot onto Highway 190. Silence watched it roll past through the gap between the RVs.

Then, without hesitating this time, he put the stick into first and followed the mystery woman.

As with the situation in Pensacola, it was time to up the ante in Death Valley. With the information he'd gotten from the Specialist regarding Ethan Draper, Silence was ready to contact the muscly, tall, blonde-headed professional once more.

This time, Silence wouldn't be caught off-guard. He was prepared for whatever bullshit she had up her sleeve. Krav Maga or Pencak silat or Systema ... it didn't matter to him now.

Let's get reacquainted, lady.

He took off after the mystery woman.

CHAPTER NINETEEN

Death Valley National Park, California

CARMEN TRUDGED along the periphery of the Mesquite Spring Campground, boots crunching on stone. The canvas backpack tugged on her shoulder. The harbinger of its contents weighed even heavier than the tattered notebooks themselves. For the last two hours, she'd poured through Mitch's materials, trying to find any clue regarding where he might be.

She'd found no clues.

All she could fathom was that Mitch had gone past the NPS/police barricade on North Highway.

At night.

Before anyone would notice.

Before *she* would notice.

As to why he hadn't come home...

Carmen could only assume the worst. But she wouldn't. Not yet.

It was 11:20 a.m. The tour was to have begun twenty minutes earlier. Today's' excursion was to be the highlight of this trip—the point at which the Unseen Path caravan would retrace the path of the ill-fated tour bus, leaving DVNP and coming back, going all the way to the barricade on North Highway.

For the first five minutes past the scheduled tour time, Carmen had hidden in her RV. Knowing she couldn't delay any longer, she'd then stepped outside, assuring the tour members that there was a brief delay, but they would soon hit the road. She'd spent the next ten minutes pacing around the campground, never staying in one place for long, avoiding people's questions of *Where in the world is Mitch?* and *Are there refunds?* as she desperately poured through Mitch's materials that she'd gathered in his ratty old backpack.

Carmen jumped.

Sandy had come out of nowhere, blocking her path. "We've been waiting fifteen minutes, Carmen. This isn't what we paid for!"

Trying to remain composed, Carmen raised her hands, calling for patience as the rest of the tour members came in their direction.

"I understand your concerns," Carmen began, looking over the group. "Mitch... he must have gotten sidetracked with some research, or maybe lost track of time during his morning walk. You know how he gets with his investigations."

But even as she spoke, she recognized the futility of her words. All the people surrounding her were members of Unseen Path. They knew Mitch well. They were accustomed to his idiosyncrasies but weren't about to suffer them.

A rush of anger swept over Carmen as the flustered, sun-tan-lotioned, ball-cap-wearing faces closed around her.

Mitch! she thought.

And yet, beneath that anger, an undercurrent of genuine concern bubbled. Carmen knew the perils of her and her husband's chosen life, the potential dangers lurking in the vast expanses of the national parks. Mitch might be out there being Mitch, sure...

...or something might be terribly wrong.

Mamás voice came to her again.

That Mitch, Mamá had warned, *his spirit is free, too free. You'll always be chasing after him, mi hija. Be prepared for that life.*

Carmen exhaled.

Shut up, Mamá, she thought.

Now wasn't the time for introspection. It was the time for action.

"This is ridiculous!" came a voice, cold and accusatory. "We paid good money for this tour, and you can't even keep to a schedule?"

It was Richard, a long-time follower of the Unseen Path newsletter but a first-time participant in their tours. His eyes were alight with anger.

Carmen, already on edge, felt a rush of fury.

"Mitch and I have been doing this for years," she said, stepping toward Richard. "He's ... he's fine."

All eyes were on Carmen now, and she felt the weight of their collective gaze. Taking a deep breath, she nodded, smiled, and brought her tone back to a friendly level.

"Folks, I'm ... I'm sorry. Today's excursion is going to be delayed."

Groans. Exclamations. People threw their hands into the air.

Gathering herself, Carmen stepped forward, pushing through the group and stomping to her RV. She called out over her shoulder.

"I understand the inconvenience," she added, her voice stronger now. "I know you've all been looking forward to today. I appreciate your understanding during this unexpected situation."

She kept moving, eyes locked on the rack jutting off the rear end of the RV.

At the one empty slot.

And her dirt bike.

She heard footsteps behind her as she reached up and started unstrapping it.

Carmen, what is going on?

What do you mean by "delayed"? How long are we gonna have to wait?

She slid off the last strap and pulled out the ramp. The screech of metal against rusty metal. She took the handlebars, eased the bike down.

Carmen, wait! Tell us what's happening?

Do you have any clue where your husband is?

At this, Carmen whipped around, keeping her hands on the handlebars.

"No, Sandy!" Carmen shouted. "No, I do not!"

She threw her leg over the bike and kicked it started. With a twist of the throttle, she was off.

CHAPTER TWENTY

Bakersfield, California

THE PLACE WAS AN OVERSIZED, overcrowded, overheated tomb.

Or, at least, that's what *they* thought it would be: a tomb. Mitch wouldn't give them the satisfaction. Some folks— survivors, you might call them—had an obnoxious tendency toward persistence. Among Mitch's long list of grating quali- ties, persistent survival was one of them.

The steel shed's stifling atmosphere was both cramped and paralyzing. Burly federal agents lined the walls, standing at a piss-poor rendition of military attention but ready to pounce at any moment. Mitch was bound to a metallic folding chair—arms and legs immobilized—feeling its chill against his skin. Every sound made him bristle, but he refused to show any signs of fear, forcing his heart to slow its pounding.

A faint glimmer of hope poured in from above, a literal glimmer— muted light filtering in from the cracked and discolored plastic roofing. It showed Mitch that this place *wasn't* a tomb. It was only a shed. By association, it showed Mitch that the other men—no matter what institution they belonged to—were flesh and blood, no different from Mitch, just people, nothing more.

The man standing in front of Mitch—the poised and polished fifty-something with designer clothes and perfectly coifed gray hair—had done all the talking and did so in a distinct German accent. He must have been a West German Cold War relic, now lending his covert "interrogation" skills to the Americans.

...Americans, such as the federal agents along the wall, who were using both their burly builds and surprisingly authentic biker attire to pose as outlaw motorcycle gang members.

The air grew thick, laden with unspoken threats, as everyone in the room waited for Mitch's response to the question posed by the man with the accent.

Mitch set his jaw. He'd be damned if he was gonna spill his soul to these government lackeys.

A moment passed, and the man with the accent turned to his associate, the younger man with the leather wristband—which bore elaborately engraved symbols—the only other man in the room not adorned in biker gear. He was a muscle-bound creep with buzz-cut hair and a trim beard, clearly the German accent man's lieutenant, standing just a few feet from the older man.

The man with the accent nodded at the one with the wristband, and the latter stalked toward Mitch. There was no warning, no hesitation, just a flash of movement. The man's fist drove into Mitch's gut.

The impact knocked Mitch's breath out, the edges of his vision blurring into dark smudges. Unbearable pain pulsated from his midsection.

As Wristband retreated, the man with the accent leaned in.

"Let's try again, shall we?" he said.

Mitch clenched his jaw and inhaled, nostrils flaring, using his non-response as defiance. He braced himself for whatever would happen next.

Wristband raised his knee and sent it rocketing into Mitch's ribs. It came like a sledgehammer, and Mitch doubled over in his binds, ropes digging into his wrists, his biceps, mouth straining wide to suck in the air that had been knocked out of him once more.

Sharp twinges of pain crackled through his body. Every breath was like drawing in broken glass. White spots twinkled in his vision, dancing in the encroaching dark periphery, and icy cold flashed over his skin.

His gaze darted about the metal shed. Somewhere—there in the corner! Or over there, beneath the overhang—were hidden cameras peering from its rusty facade. He couldn't see them, but they were there, definitely.

The shadows danced and twisted, and the biker toughs altered before him, morphing into silhouettes of suited men, physiques trimming into athleticism, leather and denim replaced by dark suits.

Secret agents.

Dark emissaries of the institutions Mitch had long feared and written about.

That's what this was, this interrogation, this torture; it was the perverse retribution for Mitch's years of nosing into things these people wanted left alone. The powers-that-be had sent their men in black.

"Unseen Path's time is up, wouldn't you say?"

The words had been uttered in that familiar German accent, but Mitch could no longer discern the distinguished-looking man in the swirling haze.

"Why not make it easier on yourself, Mr. Lockwood?"

Hearing the creep vocalize the name, Unseen Path, Mitch's life's work, the sanctuary for truth-seekers, made Mitch's jaw tighten. His teeth ground together. He said nothing.

The tension shattered as Wristband lunged out of the murk, his knee driving into Mitch's ribs with sickening precision. The room spun, and for a moment, Mitch tasted copper.

His mind unspooled.

The walls of the shed closed in, shadows mutating along menacing silhouettes—suited men, secret agents, bureaucrats —all symbols of the institutions that he knew were out to get people like him. They were proof he was onto something big, something the government wanted to keep hidden.

As Wristband pulled back for another strike, Mitch's eyes slipped out of focus. The shed's walls stretched and wavered, turning into a lush canopy of intertwined branches. He was in a small village at the edge of a vibrant Mexican jungle, the air rich with the scent of earth and vegetation. Carmen was there, years younger, her raven-black hair cascading down her shoulders, her laughter bubbling through the trees.

They'd met there. When Mitch and a pair of buddies had been on weekend leave. On the outskirts of a small Mexican village. Carmen's eyes had locked onto his from across a sunlit courtyard. She was a descendant of routine, born to a tequila distiller and a school teacher, a life bound by the tick-tock of the distillery and the school bell's toll. But there, in the cusp between civilization and nature—languid ceiling fans and belts of laughter and humidity-dampened skin and bottles of beer with slices of lime—she was untamed, just like Mitch.

A jarring impact yanked Mitch back. It was Wristband's boot, crashing into his ribs. The force of the blow left Mitch gasping, but his mind clung to Carmen.

Their first time camping under the stars. They'd been nestled in a forgotten corner of Yellowstone National Park. Carmen had organized everything with meticulous attention to detail, her logistical prowess transforming a mundane camping trip into an unforgettable experience. She'd cooked a feast using a simple camp stove—tacos seasoned just like her mother used to make in their tiny Mexican kitchen. The way she'd looked at him that night ... her eyes luminous in the dim light, an immensity of warmth and understanding.

With a shudder, Mitch was torn away. The man with the German accent leaned close, his voice a venomous whisper.

"Your obstinance is goddamn annoying, Lockwood. It's a luxury you can't afford."

Mitch tightened his jaw, absorbing the weight of each word. He said nothing, and doing so triggered another strike from Wristband, a clenched fist that met the side of Mitch's face with a sickening crunch.

His head snapped sideways. His vision spun.

Carmen was with him then—not in the village, but *there* in the steel shed.

Stay strong, you stubborn fool. Te amo.

Mitch blinked, and for a fleeting moment, he felt her hand over his. Then he felt a curious resolve solidify within him. The room, the agents, and even Wristband and German Accent all faded into shadowy outlines.

If not for himself, if not for Unseen Path, he would survive this for Carmen.

His eyes met those of the German-accented man, and for the first time, Mitch allowed a smile to form on his bruised and bloodied lips.

"Is something amusing, Lockwood?" the man said.

Mitch's smile widened. "You have no idea."

CHAPTER TWENTY-ONE

Furnace Creek, California

BLOOM DIDN'T CARE that the Chevy Nova's upholstery was cracked and faded. Nor did the radio's intermittent buzzing bother her. She didn't even mind the putrid smell of the cigarette burns in the seats. What annoyed her about the few-hundred-dollar last-minute purchase she'd picked up at the start of her self-assigned mission was the absence of air conditioning.

One did not want to face this issue in Death Valley, the hottest place on Earth.

Comparatively speaking, she'd felt cool and comfortable during yesterday's sun-scorched afternoon in Las Vegas despite the temperature being north of one hundred. She'd been sweaty there, but at least she hadn't found herself driving in a seat soppy with her own perspiration.

Now, back at DVNP, she had the Nova's windows rolled down to catch the occasional desert breeze, but it only ushered in more oven-like air. It was a no-win situation.

Distracting herself from the beads dripping down her face

and neck and even her elbow pits, she turned inward to her churning thoughts and dissected the information she'd gleaned from Agnes at the cafe. Bloom now had confirmation that Ethan Draper was in Death Valley with the Lost Jackals contingent on the day of the bus tragedy.

A series of interconnected thoughts darted through her mind, with Draper at the center. The man was a terrorist. Not a suspected terrorist. *A terrorist*. If they'd just *listened* to Bloom years ago, they'd know that!

But she couldn't dwell in the past.

She had a bad habit of that.

Coming back to the present, she thought of what she'd learned from Agnes, the waitress. One piece of the conversation kept replaying, and it wasn't a piece she would have thought her subconscious would find significant.

Kaveny.

Agnes had said the folks in Furnace Creek hadn't been bought out by Kaveny International. Bloom had asked out of curiosity, not the mission, as she'd heard so much gossip, so many angry rants about the Kaveny purchases during her mission.

And for some reason, it forged a link in her mind between two notions that she wouldn't have otherwise connected. She'd found out that tonight, on the coast in Santa Barbara, Kaveny was holding their grand opening celebration of the first in a line of high-end resorts—the Elysian Resort.

"Tonight..." Bloom said to herself. "Santa Barbara ... Adrian Hirsch. Tonight..."

Her words drifted off into her thoughts.

A significant grand opening celebration—replete with dignitaries and celebrities—for a worldwide hospitality conglomerate that happened to be causing great consternation in the region...

...only days after the bus tragedy?

It could be a coincidence. But Bloom didn't believe in coincidences.

I wonder... she thought.

A connection between international criminal Adrian Hirsch and Kaveny International made sense. It fell into a logical pattern, and Bloom liked this because Bloom liked logic. What remained clouded in confusion—completely *illogical*—was the tie between Hirsch and Draper.

Adrian Hirsch was European, sophisticated, well-connected, and as money-hungry and materialistic as they come. It didn't make sense for a man like that to have ties to a man like Ethan Draper.

Unless there was some sort of mutual benefit.

Unless there was some sort of connection Bloom just wasn't seeing.

Her eyes absently drifted to the rearview mirror, and she spotted it again—the gleaming, predatory silhouette of the silver Jeep Wrangler.

Kai.

The mysterious man who'd trailed her the previous day, ultimately ending in their confrontation in the starry desert night outside Pahrump.

When they'd fought, she'd detected a remarkable amount of skill. Kai was a fellow elite. Some sort of agent, maybe black ops.

With his bizarre plastic card, Kai had revealed himself as a member of some enigmatic "organization." But the way he moved, the way he anticipated her actions, it was all eerily reminiscent of her own training.

The dark thought had begun to coil up in the back of her mind: Kai might be one of hers, someone sent to retrieve her, to take her back to the other side of the country for whatever sort of fallout awaited her after her recent course of actions.

When they'd separated, after she'd given Kai the final

strike that sent him reeling, Bloom had felt a moment of triumph. It stayed with her as she scrambled back into the Nova, speeding away, leaving Kai to nurse his wounds. It wasn't until she was a mile down the road that something had dawned on Bloom.

Something about the moments-earlier memory felt off.

She'd replayed it again and again. The strike she'd given Kai, the way he'd doubled over.

It was almost as if...

He'd been feigning.

Pretending.

This had erased her earlier thought that he might be one of her own out to get her, to bring her back, to face the consequences of her dissent.

Since her epiphany, Bloom had wondered if Kai let her go because he'd determined she had nothing he needed, that her rogue behavior was not worth his time.

But now...

There was Kai's silver Wrangler.

Again.

She'd thought she'd caught glimpses of the Jeep throughout the day, but she'd subsequently waved it off as paranoia, knowing there was no way Kai could have tracked her all the way to Furnace Creek.

But there he was.

And this time, he was so close that there was no mistaking—he *wanted* her to know he was back there now.

Bloom's grip on the steering wheel tightened, knuckles going white. As the weight of her revelations bore down on her, she felt the subtle weight of the gun holstered at her side, a silent promise of protection. If Kai was indeed after another confrontation, he was gonna get one.

But it would be on her terms, not his.

Furnace Creek was a tiny place, and the oasis's greenery

quickly gave way to the typical expanse of barren desert. There were still a few side roads and gravel paths this close to the little blip of civilization—dusty alleys and lanes branching off the main highway. Each one was an opportunity.

Years of training and evasive maneuvers played in Bloom's mind, each scenario running its course, assessing its feasibility. She needed the element of surprise, an unexpected move to throw Kai off, even for just a moment.

So, without giving it any more thought, Bloom acted.

With a sudden jerk of the wheel, the Nova broke its straight trajectory, making a sharp turn onto one of the side roads. Dust and stones flew as the tires lost and then regained their grip on the uneven surface. The world outside the windshield became a blur of brown and gold, the horizon tilting as the car threatened to lose balance.

Adrenaline pumped through Bloom's veins, sharpening her focus. For the briefest moment, the roar of the Nova's engine was the only sound in the world, drowning out all thought, all doubt.

But then, as quickly as it began, it ended.

The car steadied itself on the new road, a cloud of dust settling behind it, obscuring the view of the main highway behind.

Bloom took a moment to catch her breath, heart pounding. The weight of her decisions, the cat-and-mouse chase, and the uncertainty of Kai's intentions pressed heavily against her.

So did the gun against her ribs.

CHAPTER TWENTY-TWO

"No, honey, I haven't seen Mitch," Agnes said, her eyes filled with genuine concern.

Agnes was a Furnace Creek Cafe waitress, a fixture in the retro-chic eatery, someone Carmen met two years ago when she and Mitch visited Death Valley on a solo trip unrelated to Unseen Path. Two mornings earlier, the trio had been reunited.

Agnes reached her hand across the counter to touch Carmen's, patting it gently.

"I've not seen him since you two had breakfast the other day," Agnes continued. "I'm real sorry."

Carmen's heart sank.

"Okay, thanks, Agnes."

She turned to leave, but Agnes's hand tightened on hers.

"Wait," Agnes said. "Another woman was just here, asking all sorts of questions. You think that's got something to do with Mitch's disappearance?"

Carmen squared to the counter. "What woman?"

"I think she was some sort of ... investigator. She was blonde, tall, muscular build. She was asking about the bus murders, of course. Seemed to think the Lost Jackals were involved. And some guy named Draper, too."

None of the details Agnes provided made sense to Carmen. She had no clue how they might relate to the murders, even though Unseen Path was in Death Valley for a tour centering on the bus tragedy. Still, she wasn't a believer in coincidences, and it seemed odd that Agnes would get a visitor asking strange questions on the day Mitch disappeared.

They were the very type of questions that Mitch himself would ask...

I wonder... Carmen thought.

"I don't know any woman like that," she said, her voice drifting off as her intuition called to her like it had the previous afternoon and that morning. "But something's not right. Something's going on. Did she give a name?"

Agnes shook her head.

"Did you see what she was driving?"

Agnes nodded. "She got into a rusty old Chevy, and—"

The squeal of tires cut Agnes off, a harsh, jarring sound that drew Carmen's attention to the window. Everyone else in the restaurant turned too, immediate fixation, instant whispers.

Carmen bolted to the window, her eyes wide and searching. Down the street, she saw a car peeling around a corner.

A rusty old Chevy...

Tires smoking. Engine roaring.

A silver Wrangler followed, closing the gap, its movements precise and predatory.

The Chevy vanished from view. A half second later, so did the Wrangler.

A cloud of dust twisted in their wake.

Hushed awe swept over the cafe. More whispers. A few laughs. Some of the patrons ran to the far window, hoping to see more. A few even bolted outside, jingling the bell on the glass door.

A shiver swept over Carmen's flesh. Her intuition again announced itself, this time as a sense of significant and terrifying recognition.

The woman who'd questioned Agnes.

The car chase outside.

All of this had something to do with Mitch.

Carmen could feel it.

Mitch, damn you!

The reckless fool...

Without a second thought, she bolted out of Furnace Creek Cafe.

The heat hit her first, then the sunlight, squinting her eyes for a split second before they adjusted. She pushed through the gawkers.

Her dirt bike was there, waiting.

She sprinted to it, climbed on, and with a surge of adrenaline, she drove her boot down into the kick starter. She twisted the throttle. The wheel spun on the blacktop, shrieked, caught hold, and Carmen rocketed off.

CHAPTER TWENTY-THREE

THE ROCKY HORIZON blurred as the roar of engines filled the vast emptiness of the desert. Silence tightened his grip on the steering wheel, every instinct honed into the chase, zeroing in on the rust-pocked rear end of the vehicle ahead. The Nova had just taken a sudden, screeching turn off Highway 190 onto a side street called Airport Road.

Even in the rush of the pursuit, Silence was struck by the bizarre juxtaposition. To his left, south of the road, was a golf course. To his right: an expanse of empty desert with craggy mountains in the distance.

Furnace Creek had a small airport, Silence knew, and he could see the tower at the end of this straight stretch of appropriately named road. A dead end. Even though the Chevy was gradually pulling away from the slower Wrangler, Silence pondered the futility of the mystery woman's efforts.

A dash to the airport? Did she truly believe she could just hop onto a plane and elude him? If so, she'd surely succumbed to panic. Maybe she wasn't the elite operator Silence had thought she was.

But just as Silence was speculating about these notions,

the Nova suddenly yanked to the right, going off the road and into the flat desert, instantly sending a plume of dust into the air. The car rocked violently, tearing to the side.

And Silence felt a devious grin form on his lips.

He'd really been hoping for an excuse to take the Wrangler off-roading.

Bam!

He left the smooth surface of the road with a jolt. As with the mystery woman's car, the Wrangler also sent up a cloud of dust.

In front of Silence, the Nova swerved hard left, then right. It seemed like an attempt to circle back toward the main highway. But the Wrangler's fat tires made quick work of the terrain, and its suspension soaked up every bump and rock with ease, allowing Silence to cut the woman off at every angle. He kept the gas pedal firmly pressed to the floor and steadily reduced the distance between them.

The Nova clunked and wheezed as it drove farther into the desert, away from Airport Road. Silence frowned, wondering why the hell the woman was taking that old car deeper into the rugged wild with a fully capable off-road machine in full pursuit.

Before he could ponder the notion too deeply, the Nova bucked in front of him. Brake lights glowed red, the one on the passenger side flickering. With a shudder and a growl of the tires, the Nova came to a crunching stop, sending billows of dust into the air.

The door opened.

It was then Silence realized the mystery woman hadn't been trying to escape into the desert; she'd been leading them away from the road, the airport, the golf course, and the resort. She was trying to put distance between them and the town of Furnace Creek, trying to keep civilians out of downrange...

Because she had a gun.

It was a SIG-Sauer P225. Or possibly a P220. Silence couldn't be entirely sure, not with the woman's obscured position crouched behind her open driver-side door, not with the blinding sunlight.

Either way, it was a solid and popular weapon.

Either way, it was a 9mm automatic.

And, either way, it was aimed directly at Silence's windshield.

The instinctual flair of adrenaline brought Silence into a moment of slowed time, a technique C.C. had taught him, a way to make sense of chaotic, split-second bursts of action, stretching them out for analysis and reaction.

In this flash of frozen existence, Silence immediately recognized that he could take cover, draw his Beretta, and win the standoff or gunfight or whatever the situation might turn into. The mystery woman might be well trained and elite, but Silence wagered—*knew*—that he was even better trained and even more elite.

But another piece of mental practice came to his mind during his slowed perception, which he'd learned not just from C.C. but also from his Watchers trainer, Nakiri. They'd both taught him the value of diplomacy at critical moments.

So as Silence brought the Wrangler to a stop, he opened the door, stepped out into the desert heat, and raised his arms into the sky, facing the woman with an expression of blank compliance. He moved toward her, keeping his arms raised.

"What do you want, Kai?" she shouted. "Why the hell are you still following me?"

Silence thought about his reasoning for contacting the woman again: the fact that he'd unearthed details about the connection between Ethan Draper and the Lost Jackals.

But he couldn't get into the details. Not yet. Not with his voice. For now, he just needed the woman to lower her pistol.

"Like my card said..." Silence said and swallowed. "I'm here to help."

"I don't need your help. Stay back! I'll shoot!"

Silence didn't stop moving toward her, still playing his hunch.

"No, you won't," he said, shaking his head. He swallowed. "You're one of..." Another swallow. "The good guys."

"What makes you assume that?"

"Multiple FBI..." He swallowed. "Database searches."

The mystery woman's mouth fell open. Her SIG dipped. For a moment, she stayed in this sort of paralysis as Silence continued to approach. Then, scowling, the woman shoved her weapon back in its holster. She stood up, put her hands on her hips.

"Who are you, Kai? *What* are you? Black ops?"

"Basically."

"Basically? What the hell does that even mean?"

Silence chose to answer her question with a question. "And you?"

The woman hesitated. "I'm CIA."

Now it was Silence's turned to be stunned.

His mind spun in circles, trying to make sense of the fact that the woman he'd been chasing for two days was a CIA operative. She'd been conducting an investigation, but ... the CIA had no law enforcement function. Its mission was related to U.S. policy, not to criminal activity.

Quickly gathering his thoughts, Silence rationalized his approach. Whatever the woman's end goal, she *was* investigating the tour bus tragedy. That much was clear.

"We want the same thing," Silence said, still approaching, still with his hands raised.

He was within yards of the Nova; he could smell its

coolant leak, the sweet scent of antifreeze floating in the hot, dusty air.

"We need to..." he said and swallowed. "Work together."

"You're right, Kai. I'm not gonna shoot you," the woman said, motioning her chin toward her holstered SIG. "But I'll be damned if I'm working with some black ops shadow man. No way in hell. You would have to capture me."

Silence shrugged. "Fair enough."

Silence lunged for her, closing the gap between them in a split second. The woman sidestepped, pivoting sharply and slamming her elbow into the soft tissue below Silence's ribcage.

Fast.

Damn fast.

He grunted, absorbing the blow but keeping his focus. His training with Nakiri taught him to channel pain into action. He pivoted, squared up.

With a sweep of her leg, the woman tried to take him down, but Silence was already in motion, jerking out of the way and countering with a lightning-fast jab. The woman ducked, barely avoiding the blow, and came back up with a vicious uppercut, which Silence dodged in kind.

Tit for tat.

Silence noted the cold, calculated glint in the woman's eyes. This was a person who'd seen some shit, who'd been trained to kill. She spun around, her leg sweeping high. Silence blocked it, wincing as her boot collided with his forearm. Kinetic energy vibrated through his bones.

A battle of attrition, two elite operators trying to find a chink in the other's armor. Silence feinted to the left, then darted right, throwing his hands out, trying to ensnare her. When she proved uncatchable, Silence changed tactics, not dodging her blows but deflecting them, absorbing more of that kinetic energy but also bouncing it right back at the woman.

Return to sender.

The woman was good, very good, but Silence sensed her stamina waning, her movements becoming a fraction of a second slower. Seizing the moment, he went for a grappling maneuver, locking one arm around her waist and the other around her neck, pulling her tightly against him.

The woman countered immediately, smashing the heel of her palm into his jaw. Stars exploded in Silence's vision, but he held on, tightening his grip.

Just when it seemed like he would never subdue her, a noise shot across the desert. Both Silence and the mystery woman looked up. The high-pitched whine was a small vehicle approaching rapidly—a dirt bike.

The operators looked at each other, panting.

And separated.

The dirt bike skidded to a stop, dust swirling in its wake. Out of the settling cloud stepped a Hispanic woman in her late thirties. Her dark brown hair cascaded across her features, and deep concern was evident in her wide eyes. She wore rugged clothing and stood with an air of determination, ready for whatever lay ahead but clearly rattled as all hell.

She called out to the mystery woman. "Are you the woman who was asking questions back at the cafe?"

The mystery woman glanced at Silence, then returned her attention to the newcomer. She nodded.

"Are you ... like, some sort of private investigator?"

The mystery woman hesitated. "Yes."

"Oh, thank God!" the other woman said. "I'm Carmen Lockwood. My husband is missing. Mitch Lockwood. From Unseen Path. You know, the newsletter, the tour group. I ... I need help, and I can't go to the police!"

The mystery woman glanced over at Silence again.

And Silence repeated what he'd said earlier, adding a bit of dire emphasis to his ruined voice.

"We need to..." he said and swallowed. "Work together."

Again, the mystery woman's attention ping-ponged between Carmen Lockwood and Silence, finally locking eyes with Silence.

"Fine."

"Name?" Silence said.

The mystery woman took a half moment to decipher the meaning of Silence's broken English, then exhaled and said, "I'm Bloom. Leah Bloom."

CHAPTER TWENTY-FOUR

Bakersfield, California

THE SHED'S heat was torturous, but for Westlin, it conjured up a vivid memory of another time, another shed of flimsy metal and crooked boards.

He'd been in Mogadishu, Somalia, working for a man named Boulanger—someone not as prominent as Hirsch but nearly as dangerous. The air had been thick with desperation and gunpowder, the room crackling with the charge of recent violence.

Boulanger had given Westlin the green light to extract information from a local rebel leader, a task Westlin had executed with brutal efficiency. Unlike Hirsch, Boulanger had instructed Westlin to cross the final line and snuff out the flame of life that fluttered in the unfortunate captive's eyes.

To finish the man.

The man begged, but he'd still died.

In the here and now, in Bakersfield, California, Westlin looked at Mitch Lockwood's crumpled form, lying unconscious on the metal folding chair.

Unconscious, but not motionless.

Lockwood's chest slowly, almost peacefully, lifted and fell. Westlin had broken the man, just as Hirsch had ordered him to, just as he'd done countless times before.

Yet, there was a line Westlin hadn't crossed—a line that Hirsch had clearly drawn at the very beginning of Westlin's employment. Boulanger had had no such line; the thought wouldn't have occurred to the man. And as much as Westlin told himself that a job was a job, that employment's aim was wealth, not personal satisfaction, the memory of that earlier freedom, that ultimate control over life and death, filled him with something he couldn't dismiss.

But...

He had to stay focused, maintain his objectivity, and keep his emotions in check. He was not his father, a man consumed by the job. Westlin had a purpose and knew why he was doing what he did.

Westlin was a weapon, a precision-crafted tool.

Weapons are emotionless.

Deep breath.

And he was re-centered.

Westlin looked at Lockwood's prostrate body and felt neither pride nor regret, only necessity.

Hirsch was on the other side of the shed, pacing. Every tailored edge of his once-immaculate suit was now disheveled. Westlin felt a momentary jolt of unease. Hirsch had always been a rock—collected, professional, and a source of wisdom. But now, Hirsch's eyes were not the focused blue skies Westlin knew; they were gray and turbulent seas.

For a brief instant, Westlin was reminded of his father.

But he shook off the thought and reasoned with himself. He'd worked for Hirsch for years now and had never seen the man act in such a way. *Everyone has his limits*, Westlin thought to himself. This brought a moment of simultaneous clarity and empathy.

There had been a damn good reason for Hirsch's bizarre trip to the American West. Similarly, there was a good reason for the man's uncharacteristic fraying, something whose roots had dug deep into Hirsch's soul for years—more than a decade—finally bursting forth here in a stuffy shed in a motorcycle junkyard in Bakersfield, California.

Hirsch hadn't spoken for several minutes. Neither had Draper. Neither had the Jackals lined up along the walls. And Lockwood was unconscious.

Hirsch pivoted and addressed Westlin, ending the eerie silence.

"All we got from him," he said, gesturing toward Lockwood's bent frame, "is the name—Carmen. His wife. And he was delirious before we got that out of him."

The weight of disappointment settled between them, floating in the dry heat. Carmen. A name, nothing more, extracted from a man who'd held onto his secrets with a vice-like grip, even as his consciousness slipped away.

Lockwood had been resilient.

Stubborn old shits often were.

Hirsch's voice dropped an octave. "But perhaps this 'Carmen' could be ... useful to us."

The statement echoed in the dank shed, a chill coursing through Westlin's veins.

It was a happy chill.

Because he could feel his mentor's energy radiating, brimming with a swagger that had been degrading for days, finally unraveling during the last half hour in this shed.

Hirsch was suddenly back in top form.

About damn time.

Westlin heard the gentle click of a phone snapping shut and looked across the room. Draper had just concluded a call.

As he approached, he slid the phone into his pocket, his face radiating his eerie yet oddly intriguing presence, those big eyes of his dark as ever but now sparkling with subdued excitement.

"The Jackal scouts did us good, boys. They located Carmen Lockwood," Draper announced as he joined Hirsch and Westlin. "She's in Furnace Creek."

Hirsch shot a quick glance at his watch, its face reflecting the shed's meager light. "The day's Unseen Path tour should have started by now. She'll be wondering where her husband is."

Westlin saw Hirsch's exterior crack again, a fissure in a frozen lake. The man's eyes darkened, his cheeks flushed, and he suddenly lost most of his recaptured poise.

"This is your fault, Draper," Hirsch snarled. "You're the reason we're even concerning ourselves with people like the Lockwoods of Unseen goddamn Path. The targets were MacLeod and Shapiro. *Only*. This operation had boundaries!"

Westlin watched, incredulous, as the always unflappable Hirsch came undone once more, worse than before, worse than ever.

Draper gave Hirsch one of those unsettling expressions of his. He chuckled. "Or maybe if you weren't too chicken-shit to kill people, Adrian, you'd make your life a whole lot easier."

Hirsch stepped into him.

"When all this is over," Hirsch said, "I'll get the truth out of you. I don't care what it takes."

Hirsch hastily composed himself, taking a deep breath and turning away as if trying to put together the pieces of his broken composure.

Westlin looked away from his mentor.

CHAPTER TWENTY-FIVE

Furnace Creek, California

"Thank you, Agnes," Bloom said.

With a slightly confused, slightly alarmed expression, the waitress poured coffee from a pot into a trio of porcelain mugs.

Maybe Agnes realized Bloom was the person who drove the Chevy Nova—the vehicle that had left Furnace Creek Cafe, went peeling off the highway onto a side road that led to the tiny airstrip, then returned a few minutes later.

It would appear she did. Both Agnes's smile and the hand working the coffee pot were shaking.

Bloom was somewhere she never thought she would return: the same booth she'd occupied a half hour earlier when she'd eaten a cherry Danish and downed a cup of coffee. She'd been alone then. Now, she had company. Sitting across from her, squeezed in together on the bright red vinyl seat, were Kai and their new companion, Carmen Lockwood.

A giant man and a small woman.

A person who'd been chasing Bloom for two days and a person who'd just barreled into Bloom's life on a dirt bike.

Surreal...

A rare moment of stupefaction came to Bloom.

To compose herself, she gave a courteous nod to Agnes as the waitress left before taking a sip of coffee; it was just as tasty and fresh as the first cup she had a half hour ago. She then brought her attention to Kai.

The guy was hot.

Dark hair and eyes. Slightly olive complexion. He reminded Bloom a lot of Johnny Depp, the actor from *21 Jump Street*, only much bigger and stronger. Broad shoulders with a powerful build. Well over six feet tall. His clothing gave him an expensive look—a V-neck gray T-shirt, dark denim pants, hiking boots that were surprisingly stylish, and a thin leather bracelet.

Now that Bloom had gotten a good look at him, he didn't look like a CIA agent, as she'd originally thought. She had plenty of experience with CIA members—being one herself —and this guy was different in many ways, not the least of which were his style and predator-like aura, a contrast to the automated aloofness of her male contemporaries.

She was about to say something to him when he spoke first.

"You're CIA," he said and swallowed. "But you ran unsanctioned..." Another swallow. "FBI database searches." Another swallow. "Talk."

She placed her coffee mug before her, giving it an unnecessary straightening.

"I used to be an FBI special agent, but I was recruited into the CIA two years ago." She nudged the mug again. "Now that I'm doing this rogue investigation of mine, I've called in some favors from old friends at the Bureau and used my own ... um, skill set to run a few of the searches myself."

"Hacker," Kai said.

Bloom shrugged. "I dabble."

"Why are you..." Kai said and swallowed. "Doing all of this?"

"It's a ... personal matter. I wouldn't be risking my career and a prison sentence, otherwise. It's just ... Yeah, a personal matter."

She'd blubbered as she said it, staring down at the tabletop. She looked up at Kai, then Carmen, then away from them both to the checkered floor.

"Boston," Kai said with a bit of knowing surety playing through his crackling voice.

Bloom's attention snapped back up to him, mouth agape. "How did you know that?"

Kai just looked back at her for a moment. When he spoke, he didn't answer her question.

"MacLeod and Shapiro. Bus victims." He swallowed. "Boston contractors."

Bloom nodded. "Yes, they ran AeonScape Construction, the primary builders of the Boston Legacy Center canopy. A lot of blame has fallen on them over the years. You'd have thought it would have faded away by now."

She traced her finger along the speckled tabletop, churning her thoughts.

"MacLeod and Shapiro are why Adrian Hirsch came to the States. Some sort of vendetta. Hirsch hired the Lost Jackals—through Ethan Draper—to intercept the tour bus and kill MacLeod and Shapiro. Of course, the Jackals expanded Hirsch's mission and killed *all* the bus tourists."

"Why?"

Bloom shrugged. "Don't know. They were just ... tourists. Rich old folks with no ties to Boston. It doesn't make sense. They—"

"No, why did..." Kai said and swallowed. "Hirsch want MacLeod and Shapiro dead?"

"Haven't figured that part out either. But Hirsch brought his guard dog with him. Luca—"

"Luca Westlin."

Bloom's lips parted. A beat passed, then, "Right."

She was both surprised and not surprised at all. Of course Kai would know about Luca Westlin. Kai and his powerfully omniscient "organization."

His organization...

Maybe this mystery group knew more than the Agency. Maybe they'd deciphered the symbols.

"Westlin's a mystery for us at Langley," Bloom said. "No beginning, no end, just a murky fog of a history. Linked to bloody enforcements in Paris, underground cage fights in Berlin, and roughed-up blackmail victims in Rome. He's rumored to handle all of Hirsch's torture work—mostly beatings. But no killing, of course, given Hirsch's no-kill policy. That's about all we know. But we figure if we can decipher the symbols, then we might unearth his backstory."

"Symbols on..." Kai said and swallowed. "Wristband."

Bloom nodded.

Surveillance images resurfaced in Bloom's mind, photos of the imposing man with the chiseled physique, clad in form-fitting tees, sporting a buzz-cut and a meticulously groomed beard. Bloom had studied the images for so long, straining her eyes to discern the intricate details of the man's signature leather wristband, decorated with elaborate designs woven from brief intersecting lines.

"For a while we thought they might be Ogham inscriptions," she said. "Then Voynich manuscript symbols. But we can't figure them out. You guys?"

"We hit the..." Kai said and swallowed. "Same dead-ends."

He turned away, deep concentration narrowing his brown eyes.

"All right, I told you who I am," Bloom said. "Who are you?"

Kai brought his attention back to her.

"Kai," he said.

Bloom scowled at him before quickly masking it with a diplomatically patient smile.

"I mean, who do you work for?"

"An org—"

"An organization, yes," Bloom said, allowing the scowl to reassert dominance over the smile. "So said your lil plastic card."

Bloom studied Kai with a wary eye. Sure, the guy was dangerous, and he'd seemed suspicious at first, but Bloom's gut told her to trust him. She thought of the tour bus slaughter that had brought them together. Against all odds, here she was, partnered with someone who shared her ambition—doing whatever it took to find out why the murders had happened.

Agnes came back with the food order and placed it on the table: the second cherry Danish of the day for Bloom; a side salad for Carmen Lockwood; and for Kai, a BLT sandwich, chili cheese fries, another side salad, another cherry Danish—Kai had said he'd gotten jealous of the one he'd seen her eating earlier while spying on her, which was creepy—and a chocolate malt shake. When they'd arrived at the cafe as a place to sit, catch their breath, and compare notes, Kai had insisted they eat; he'd said they needed fuel. Both women had said they weren't hungry. Kai had insisted further, imploring prudence and foresight.

Seeing Carmen reluctantly pull her salad closer, Bloom realized she'd forgotten the woman sitting right next to the six-foot-three enigma. The thirty-something Latina's raven-dark tresses framed a heart-shaped face. She wore clothing suitable for the harsh desert landscape—flannel shirt, cargo shorts, boots—well-worn but cared for.

"You know for sure your husband went past the highway barricade to the crime scene?" Bloom said.

"I suppose I'm not certain," Carmen said, "but I found a few notes. And, besides, I still *know*. I know my husband. That's what he would have done."

The innate understanding of one's partner. Bloom couldn't relate. She'd never been married, and her longest relationship was a one-year-three-month disaster. But still, she understood on some level—a kind of inborn femininity, pure humanity.

"Maybe Mitch is still there," Bloom said. "Did you check?"

"*And go past the barricade?* With park police patrolling? I'm one of the founding members of Unseen Path, ma'am. Of course I didn't do that. I'm not as crazy as my husband."

Bloom eyed Carmen, her gaze half-curious, half-skeptical. "Why would Mitch have gone to the crime scene? Is there something he was hoping to find?"

Carmen hesitated momentarily, then reached into her bag and pulled out a weathered notebook. She flipped to a particular page and handed it to Bloom. "See for yourself."

Bloom scanned the scrawled handwriting. It was a list.

photos of crime scene
bloody stones
sagebrush twigs

She looked back up at Carmen. "He was planning to sell these … artifacts and photos on the Unseen Path website?"

"It wouldn't be the first time he's done something like that," Carmen admitted, her eyes avoiding Bloom's. "Mitch has a way of crossing boundaries, both literal and metaphorical."

Bloom closed the notebook and handed it back.

Kai, who'd been silent and motionless for a few moments, turned to Carmen and said, "Why haven't you..." He swallowed. "Gone to NPS or police?"

Carmen looked conflicted. "It's complicated. You need to understand that Mitch had a deep-seated distrust of bureaucratic systems. He was in the Army when he was younger, and some of his experiences ... affected him. Unseen Path—it's on the fringes, you know? We investigate things people don't want to talk about. And sometimes, that means not exactly following the rules."

This seemed to satisfy Kai.

"You two have a reputation..." He swallowed. "Among authority figures."

Carmen sighed and nodded. "Right. Mitch has done this before—disappeared without telling me, only to show up with some new, wild story or artifact. Although this time, something feels different. And yet, if I go to the police, what will I say? That my husband, who already engages in questionable activities, is missing while potentially involved in another questionable activity? I can't risk it."

Bloom looked into Carmen's eyes and saw the tangled web of emotions—love, anxiety, anger. The woman was battling inner fears and intuitions, straddling the line between loyalty to Mitch and the possibility that something terrible had happened to him.

"All right," Bloom said. "Let's see if we can find him without involving the authorities. For now, at least." Then Bloom changed course, trying at consolation. "Maybe Mitch's bike broke down somewhere. Maybe he ... I don't know, got bit by a snake. Maybe—"

"No! I know my husband. He may be a fool, but he's an experienced outdoorsman, and he knows his way around a bike." She paused. "And I can feel it. Something happened."

Kai nodded in agreement.

"And rumors say that..." He swallowed. "Jackal scouts are roaming the park."

This made Carmen gasp.

Bloom shot Kai a look. She'd only known the man face-to-face for less than an hour, and she could already tell he was about as tactful as he was loquacious.

But he was right.

So Bloom nodded.

"Yes, I've heard the same thing," she said quietly.

Carmen's gaze shot back and forth between Bloom and Kai.

"They have him!" she said. "Whoever you two are hunting, they have my Mitch!"

Bloom glanced at Kai.

"Rumor also has it," she said to the big man, "that Ethan Draper left the park, heading for—"

"Bakersfield," Kai said and swallowed. "Jackals HQ."

Bloom's ego whined at her, a little shocked to find that Kai seemed to have the same, if not better, intel than her.

But pride was foolish, especially in her line of work. So she nodded again.

"We go to..." Kai said and swallowed. "Bakersfield after food."

With that, he grabbed his sandwich and took a massive bite. As he chewed, a grin formed.

A grin.

This guy had a face like granite, the sort of visage that wouldn't crack a smile at a Marx Brothers movie. But he was smiling from ear to ear over something as simple as a BLT.

Bloom watched for a moment longer, then took her first nibble of Danish.

And she wondered who the hell she'd just teamed up with.

CHAPTER TWENTY-SIX

Bakersfield, California

HIRSCH WATCHED ETHAN DRAPER.

The worm was at the opposite side of the shed again, cellular phone glued to his ear, taking another call. As he paced the end of the structure—back and forth, over and over—he cut in and out of patches of dust-speckled sunlight. Just looking at the man twisted Hirsch's mouth into a silent snarl of disdain.

Draper.

Of all the rotten alliances Hirsch had formed in his checkered career, this was the one he now regretted the most. A perverse creature, ready to bite when your defenses were down for even a moment. Hirsch remembered the sense of superiority he'd felt when first making a deal with Draper, how he'd thought he could manipulate the situation to his favor. But Draper had proven himself to be as toxic as they come and more innovative than Hirsch had imagined.

Double-crossed.

That notion thrummed in Hirsch's consciousness, an unsettling realization that upended his previously held certainties.

And why? Why had he let his guard down with Draper? Why had he veered off the strict path of calculated moves? *Emotion.* For the first time in his life, Hirsch had allowed emotion to cloud his reasoning, and the realization gnawed at him. All of this—a compromised operation, an unreliable ally, even the very tension in this shed—stemmed from that momentary lapse. This was a stark lesson in why feelings had no place in Hirsch's world.

He couldn't look at Draper any longer. His eyes swept across Mitch Lockwood, slumped unconscious in the metal chair—face battered, body bruised. Collateral damage in a plan that was unraveling.

His eyes continued on, landing on Westlin. At a glance, the man was as impassive as ever, a stone statue, immobile until action was needed. Yet Hirsch could see a flicker of doubt in Westlin's eyes resting where there had been nothing short of reverence.

Across the room, Draper snapped his phone shut with a theatrical flourish and began his approach. Hirsch braced himself, fighting back his revulsion.

"Good news for ya, Adrian," Draper said, a self-satisfied smirk dancing across his lips. "Our scouts in Furnace Creek spotted Carmen Lockwood. She was in the café, talking to a man and a woman. Big, athletic types, apparently. That chick who's been asking all the questions must have called in a partner, and now they've linked up with Lockwood's wife. They left in a silver Jeep Wrangler, taking 190 to Panamint Valley Road to Trona Wildrose."

Hirsch narrowed his eyes. "And you think that gibberish is supposed to mean something to me?"

Draper snorted. "It means they're heading west." He paused with deliberate melodrama. "Toward Bakersfield. Toward the Jackals' turf."

Hirsch glared at him. "Your poor planning has brought us a lot of unwanted attention."

Draper's smirk remained. "Don't worry, Adrian, we—"

"Enough!" Hirsch's voice echoed off the shed's metal walls like the crack of a whip.

The room fell into a thick silence. Even the Jackals lining the perimeter seemed to pull back.

Hirsch sensed Westlin's eyes coming at him from a different angle. His second-in-command had shifted, ever so slightly, as though distancing himself.

Draper opened his mouth, presumably to issue another banality.

But Hirsch cut him off.

His mind was made up. Whatever came next, Hirsch knew one thing for certain: he was still in charge.

"I don't wait for the enemy to come to me!" he shouted in Draper's face.

Draper's smirk evaporated into a look of mild surprise. Hirsch looked beyond him to the Lost Jackals bikers, who stood along the corrugated metal walls.

"Do you hear that?" Hirsch bellowed. "Adrian Hirsch doesn't sit and wait! We'll cut them off."

"But—" Draper began.

"*Shut up!*" Hirsch snapped, barely restraining himself from lunging at the man. "I'm in charge here."

His gaze swung to the Lost Jackals again, making sure each man met his eyes. He swallowed, and in a quieter, deadly tone, he repeated, "I'm in charge here."

Finally, Hirsch looked back at Westlin. Their eyes met. Westlin's face still reflected the confusion, the uncertainty, but Hirsch saw something else: a flicker of the old loyalty, a glimmer of belief.

"Come on," Hirsch said to his lackey.

Without waiting for a response, Hirsch turned on his heel and strode toward the shed's exit.

CHAPTER TWENTY-SEVEN

Mojave Desert, California

FOR THREE HOURS, the Wrangler had been eating up desert roads.

Silence was behind the wheel. To his right, Bloom sat in the passenger seat. Her eyes were concealed behind aviator shades. In back, Carmen Lockwood, also wearing aviators, hers with blue lenses, had one arm stretched out on the rear bench seat.

Heading for Bakersfield, they'd left Furnace Creek north on SR 190. This gradually pulled them west before the highway reached its apex, the point at which the highway has a change of heart, no longer taking passengers in a northward direction, now guiding them southwest. A while later, the Wrangler turned onto Panamint Valley Road, a slightly more rugged affair than 190, going south for another fourteen miles before turning onto Trona Wildrose Road.

They'd been in the wild for some time, but they would soon break through to humanity for a brief while when they crossed through the Searles Valley area—a census-designated spot that included the small and tightly spaced communities of Pioneer Point, Trona, the town of Searles Valley, and Argus.

Had the Wrangler been topless, bathing the travelers in sunlight as arid Death Valley air whooshed through the cab, the scene would have been the epitome of Americana—a lone truck slicing through the desert on an endless highway bearing a trio of passengers, hair flapping in the hot wind, sitting in speechless calm, together but alone in their own thoughts.

Of course, Silence's silver Wrangler bore a hardtop, so he and the women were sealed off from the elements, and the air conditioning was fully cranked. This modern climate control was keeping things as comfortable as possible given the circumstances: a spontaneous road trip to search for someone's missing spouse who had likely been kidnapped and to confront an infamous motorcycle gang, a suspected terrorist, and a notorious international criminal about the slaughter of fifteen souls.

Shouldering that set of circumstances, Silence's contingent needed all the help they could get—not just protection from the heat and wind. They needed to use the relative comfort to both mentally regroup and confabulate, although it had been some time since any of them had spoken.

And it was nearly lulling Silence to sleep.

He blinked hard and purposefully.

The aftereffect of the previous week of poor sleep was coming back to him again—Ohio, Tanner, and that damn drooling Baxter making their presences known once more.

No matter how fragmented and maddeningly disjointed this investigation was, it eventually had to come to an end.

Then Silence could go home. Back to that California-king-size bed of his in Pensacola. And sleep.

And then sleep some more.

The hush was broken as Bloom shifted in her seat, angling

herself toward Silence. "What do you know about Draper?"

Silence flicked his eyes toward her.

"Linked to attacks..." he said and swallowed. "In Charlotte and Iowa."

"That's it?"

Silence nodded.

And he saw a slight smile play on Bloom's lips. Satisfaction. A pride thing. Clearly, she knew more about Draper and was quite tickled with herself at having finally bested the mysterious "Kai."

Or, perhaps, Bloom now felt justification for the risk she'd taken embarking on her mission.

Either way, Silence didn't care. He just wanted the intel she had.

Bloom obliged.

"Draper's not just a thug; he's an idealist. That's why he's dangerous. His family struggled through the early '80s recession. Small business owners. His dad's health fell apart from the stress, and his mom had to be the glue holding everything together. Puts a chip on a guy's shoulder, you know?"

Silence felt a subtle shift. After her moment of pride, Bloom was engaging him now like a full contemporary. It was an unspoken declaration that she viewed him as an equal, a partner in the confusion she'd involved herself in. From a woman living out of a rusty shell of a car, risking her safety and freedom, this was as monumental as any intelligence briefing Silence had been privy to.

"Draper went to college," Bloom continued. "Economics and political science major. But he got disenchanted with the system he was studying, said academia was part of the problem that crushed his family—all talk, but no action; all theory, but zero compassion. He dropped out. That's when he fell in with the Lost Jackals. They gave him a home, a voice, and most importantly, resources."

"Climbed the ranks?" Silence said.

Bloom shook her head. "Barely. Always remained low-tier, a rung or two from the bottom of the ladder. I was confused by this for the longest time until it dawned on me: Draper will never be a *true* biker. Sure, he believes in the Jackals' anti-establishment outlook, their under-the-radar existence, but he has bigger goals. Ideological goals. If he remains a mere lieutenant, that ensures him access to the gang's resources with practical anonymity."

Silence considered this. Bloom was right. Draper would align with his Lost Jackals brethren in broad strokes, but a man like that couldn't care less about trafficking stolen goods or dealing methamphetamines or getting in turf wars with rival gangs.

The man would have *big* goals.

Like any good terrorist.

"So Draper is attacking..." Silence said and swallowed. "Consumerism."

"Right," Bloom said. "Consumerism. Capitalism. Material-ism. Whatever you want to call it. He wants to assault the notion at its root."

Silence let her words sink in. He considered the previous attacks: the mega-mall in Charlotte, the fast food poisoning.

"The Lost Jackals are..." Silence said, swallowed. "Just a home for him."

"Exactly. Another family to belong to, if I may psychoana-lyze for a moment. His ideology married well with the whole outlaw motorcycle club mystique—freedom and nonconfor-mity and all of that. He utilized the Jackals' systems for both Charlotte and Iowa—connections, materials, travel—but it wasn't until the bus attack with Adrian Hirsch that he actu-ally used Jackal men. The attack wasn't authorized by Higgins, the Jackals' leader in Bakersfield; rumor has it Higgins is pissed. I suspect Draper is about to make his exit from the Jackals, leading his battalion while he still can, using them for the remainder of his operation with Hirsch."

Silence considered this. "If Draper is willing..." He swallowed. "To give up being a Jackal—"

Bloom nodded, cutting him off to finish his thought.

"Then he must have something else planned. The bus murders were just the opening salvo. Draper's about to do something huge."

"Which is?"

Bloom exhaled. "I wish I knew."

Silence ran his thumb along the top edge of the steering wheel. Outside, the Wrangler's tires hummed on the fissured two-lane path stretching before him, the epitome of an American desert road—a gnarled but eloquent scar bisecting the untamed wilderness, no beginning, no end.

The tone of the mission was different now. They weren't just battling an adversary but confronting a belief system. Those were the toughest enemies to defeat.

Silence's eyes flicked to the rearview mirror, catching Carmen's reflection. He wondered what she thought of the conversation she'd just heard. It must have played like a movie reel in her mind, a dark narrative in which her husband was a captive character. He saw the strain on her face, the delicate lines of concern.

Yet, he perceived something else—unyielding resolve. Silence sensed that Carmen's resilience wasn't cultivated but innate, a part of her DNA.

C.C. had always said he was good at reading people.

Their eyes met in the mirror. Silence nodded. Carmen nodded back.

His attention returned to the sun-scorched road. The Wrangler rumbled on, each mile eating away at the distance between them and an abyss of uncertainties.

"So ... black ops, huh?" Bloom said, her tone oddly casual

for the weightiness of the subject, almost playful.

Silence looked at her.

"Basically."

"'Basically.' Yeah, that's what you said before." Bloom watched him for a moment. "You know, Kai, a friend of mine in the Bureau—a guy who was a fan of conspiracy theories, mind you—told me there's a covert circle within the U.S. government, a group of self-important do-gooders who correct what they see as errors in procedural justice. He said they have their own assassins, and they send these killers out into the world to right wrongs.

"I didn't think much of what he'd told me—just another wild conspiracy theory. But when I got to Langley ... I found a few clues. I believe the group is real. And I think you're one of them. I think you're one of their assassins."

Silence didn't respond. He kept his gaze on the road, his hands steady on the wheel. In the distance, tiny hints of buildings appeared on the horizon, the first sign of civilization for some time—Pioneer Point.

"I'll take that as a confirmation," Bloom said, an unreadable expression settling over her face.

From behind came a sharp gasp. Silence glanced at the rearview mirror again.

Carmen's eyes were wide, a fraction of vulnerability breaking through the formidable facade. She inched back on the bench seat.

Silence glanced at Bloom.

"You said it's personal," Silence said and swallowed. "Related to Boston."

He was referring to the reasoning behind her self-assigned mission, the notion she'd mentioned in the cafe. His broken English was enough to get his point across: *If I'm going to help you, I need to know the full reason you've involved yourself in this insanity.*

Bloom's gaze drifted away. A moment passed. Finally, her eyes returned to meet Silence's.

"In '83, my father, Clifford Bloom, was a Boston city inspector. Back in the late '70s when the Legacy Center was constructed, he'd raised concerns about the structural integrity of AeonScape's work. No one listened. Then the canopy collapsed. Forty-six people dead. A hundred injured. For five years, my father never gave up. He never *shut* up. But he still felt he could have done more, said more. Absolutely racked with guilt. He … he was that kind of guy. He died five years later. Fifty years old. Heart problems, but I know it was the stress and guilt that took years off his life."

Silence saw her eyes begin to glisten.

"And I guess … I guess I took after him more than a little because, *I've* been racked with guilt too. Since his death. If I'd focused on him instead of my own high school nonsense…"

She trailed off.

"Then there's Elias Saeed," she said, "an informant I was responsible for in the FBI, someone with a tangential tie to a U.S.-embedded terrorist cell. He nearly lost his life—and his family—because of a miscalculation I made. In return for critical intelligence, we promised him, his wife, and his child safety and a fresh start. I underestimated his importance, underestimated how much he meant to the cell. Saeed … and his wife and child barely survived."

She stopped to brush a strand of hair back into a position it hadn't fallen out of.

"I failed my dad. I failed Saeed and his family. So it's no surprise that nobody in the CIA or the FBI would listen when I put the pieces together about the recent bus murders and the links to the Boston event. I decided I had to do something right for once, even if it cost me everything. I bought an old Chevy with cash and took off across the country."

She chuckled wearily at the end of her story, a sound that conveyed her overwhelming fatigue and disappointment.

Silence said nothing. Neither did Carmen.

The Jeep was quiet again.

A loud, peculiar ringtone shattered the stillness, making all three jump. Silence reached under his seat, pulling out a device that looked like it was born from a union between a phone and a small brick—a large rubberized body with an antenna.

His eyes darted to his cellular phone in the center console; its screen displayed *NO SERVICE*. In situations where his regular phone had no signal—such as being in the middle of the Mojave Desert—the Watchers had arranged for incoming calls to be automatically rerouted to another device.

Lifting the chunky contraption, he looked at Bloom, then at Carmen in the mirror, and said, "Satellite phone."

Simultaneously, both women said, "I know."

There had been a matter-of-fact-ness in both of their tones, morphed into a single voice.

Silence grinned.

Of course both of them would know what a sat phone was. Bloom belonged to the Central Intelligence Agency, and Carmen led a conspiracy-obsessed group that trekked deep into the wilderness of the U.S. national parks.

Shaking off his momentary lapse, Silence flipped open the heavy-duty cover. An orange-red multiplex screen displayed a phone number. From the area code/prefix combination, he knew it was the Watchers. He pressed the rubber *ACCEPT* button.

As soon as the voice greeted him, he knew this call was more than routine.

It was extraordinary.

Because he recognized the voice. Nasally. Female. It was the Specialist he'd spoken to earlier.

To speak with the same Specialist three times in a row was a statistical near-impossibility.

She hadn't simply researched the information he'd requested and put it into the system for another Specialist—*any* Specialist—to relay back to him.

No, she'd called him back. Personally. Deliberately.

"Suppressor, I've done some digging," the Specialist began. "Liam Rourke is more dangerous than you thought. He's a known killer, albeit never convicted. Rourke executed a New Orleans councilmember who was getting too close to Labyrinth's operations. It was staged to look like a coke O.D. coupled with autoerotic asphyxiation. Cops suspected foul play, but Labyrinth's web is intricate. All evidence disappeared; so did any trail leading to Rourke." She paused. "That woman didn't accidentally kill herself while she was getting off; Rourke tortured her to death."

"We're certain..." Silence said and swallowed. "Of this?"

"Three hundred percent."

This was the Watchers' theoretical, nominal, and slightly sardonic barometer for their kills. Since their executions were extra-judicial, illegal, and even treasonous, they never killed until they were three hundred percent certain of guilt.

"So that means...?"

The Specialist sighed, a raspy sound buzzing through the sat phone's speaker. "Yes, authorization granted, Suppressor. A kill order."

A storm of emotions whirled within Silence.

He already knew that back in Pensacola, Tanner was dangerously entwined in illegal gambling. But learning that his old mentor was connected to a gangland executioner who tortured and killed a local politician...

That was a whole new level of darkness.

The realization stoked the flames of Silence's already seething anger.

For a moment, he was back there.

Pensacola.

In the darkness at the edge of Black Jack's.

Looking into the alley.

Bright blue eyes in the shadows, staring back in his direction...

"I went out on a limb for you on this," the Specialist said, breaking through Silence's turbulent thoughts.

She had indeed.

The woman—whoever she was, wherever she was, whatever her name was—was breaking protocol, indulging Silence's roguishness. She'd gone above and beyond. *Way* above and beyond.

"Thanks, ma'am," Silence said.

"You bet."

The line went dead, and Silence snapped the sat phone's cover shut. He found both Bloom and Carmen watching him, their expressions a blend of curiosity and concern.

The Wrangler plunged into Pioneer Point, a cluster of low-slung buildings and dusty streets materializing from the shimmering heat mirage. Faded signs. A pair of abandoned gas stations. A few locals moved languidly. Farther down the road, more desert. It would be another mile to the second of Searles Valley's communities: Trona.

But Silence's mind barely registered it.

His thoughts pivoted back to Liam Rourke.

Blue eyes and twitching jaw muscles.

A man who'd executed a local politician.

A man who'd somehow snared Marvin Tanner into his deadly game.

Every fiber of Silence's being screamed at him to yank the steering wheel, to send the Wrangler screeching in the opposite direction, to head back to Pensacola.

The city had been Silence's haven, his home, his place of

solace between murderous missions, and the idea of Liam Rourke's Labyrinth outfit tainting it was too much to bear. The thought of Tanner, who had once taught him so much, now entangled in the corrupt webs of illegal gambling and a man who'd tortured a female to death, wrenched his soul.

The Wrangler rumbled on.

Farther from Pensacola.

Farther.

But Silence couldn't stop the Jeep. There was the mission. The Death Valley job wasn't just another assignment—it was a matter of thwarting a terrorist.

But the notion of abandoning Tanner...

Tanner, damn you!

If the old fool hadn't gotten involved in illegal gambling, none of this would be happening. How had a man like that succumbed to a vice so asinine, so puerile, so pathetic?

They were out of Pioneer Point now. More desert whooshed past.

Farther from Pensacola.

Farther.

A notion flashed through his mind. An admonition that Falcon, Silence's Prefect, his boss, was often forced to repeat.

No involvement in local matters.

Silence sometimes lended his talents to causes outside his Watchers missions. More than once, this had happened in his home city of Pensacola. No matter where it happened, it pissed Falcon off.

Here on the other side of the country, though, getting involved in Pensacola's local matters was impossible, no matter how much Silence wanted to.

An idea came to him, a way to take action against this bifurcated sense of idleness.

With it came another notion, another reason for panic.

...there was another soul he needed to save.

He flipped open the sat phone's cover, stabbed a number into the rubber buttons.

Two rings.

Then a response.

"Hey, what's up?" Elsher's voice crackled through the phone.

"Need you to stop digging..." Silence said and swallowed. "In Pensacola. Rourke is far more..." Another swallow. "Dangerous than we thought."

A pause, then Elsher's voice conveyed more confusion than concern. "Um, you do know *I'm* the private detective, right? I'm looking into this for you, not the other way around. What the hell is going on?"

"It's complicated," Silence said and swallowed. "You must cease." Another swallow. "You'll be well paid."

Elsher offered another pause, this one pregnant with reluctance and curiosity. "Okay. Fine. But you'll want to know what I found out."

Silence took in a breath. "Yes?"

"Turns out Marvin Tanner *isn't* involved in illegal gambling, at least not in the way you thought. He's been trying to get his nephew, Ben, out of a bind. *Ben* is the one who got in deep with Black Jack's and, subsequently, with Rourke and Labyrinth."

Silence couldn't immediately respond.

"Ben? Tanner's sister's kid?"

"That's the one."

Silence remembered Ben. He'd been a toddler. Now, he would be a young man, late teens...

...the perfect age to get sucked into illicit activities.

"Tanner's been trying to free his nephew from Labyrinth," Elsher continued. "He's even attempted to pay off some of Ben's gambling debts. That's why he made so many ATM visits. Tanner's been leveraging his connections, applying just enough pressure on Rourke to make him think twice about keeping Ben around while also trying to pay down the bill and not jeopardize his position with the police department. A delicate balance."

Tanner...

The man Silence had known. The *good* man Silence had known. Jake Rowe's mentor.

He was a good man, after all. All along. Nothing had changed.

Silence felt a mixture of relief and newfound urgency. "Thanks, Elsher."

"So what now?"

"Go back to Mobile. You're not safe," Silence said and swallowed. "Going to pay you..." Another swallow. "Twice what I promised."

Elsher's rise in mood was apparent even through the crackly, multi-state, bounced-across-a-satellite connection.

"Well! Fair enough." A small chuckle. "I'll start packing up. It's been a real pleasure."

"Take care."

Silence ended the call.

The Wrangler rolled into Trona. It was much the same as Pioneer Point with its low-rise buildings, dry earth, and quiet, empty feel—aside from some taller structures on the edge of town. On one side was a busy borax mine full of whirring machines, conveyors, sheds, and silos; on the other side, there was an abandoned borax mine with the same structures, only motionless and in various states of disrepair—rusty, cracked, boarded-up.

As Silence snapped the sat phone's cover closed, he pictured that toddler again. The one in Jake Rowe's memories. He wondered what Ben looked like as a young man.

Rage then.

Protective rage.

And suddenly...

...a wave of relief.

The momentum of the up-and-down mental surge sent him careening upward to something better, to a pleasant thought—the notion that Tanner had been good all along.

Silence had thought there'd been another side to the older man, something to which he'd been ignorant for so many years.

But Tanner had been just as true as Jake Rowe had always thought.

Even in a storm of terrorists, motorcycle gangs, international criminals, and executioners stretched end-to-end across a vast continent, Silence had been afforded a respite.

C.C.'s voice came to him.

That's right, love, she said. *Breathe that in. Good. Yes, breathe it in. Have gratitude, just like I always tell you.*

She paused a beat, allowing him to breathe in his gratitude as commanded.

Then she said, *But don't you lose focus.*

She was right.

Silence snapped back into full cognizance.

The Wrangler's steering wheel in his grasp.

The weight of his Beretta in its shoulder holster resting against his ribs.

Two women in the vehicle he was piloting, both facing missions of critical importance.

Silence honed his senses.

That's when he saw them.

One by one, they began to emerge from the shadowy contours of buildings, creeping into view. Before he knew it, they were converging on the Wrangler from all directions, engines roaring like a pack of wolves closing in for the kill.

Motorcycles.

CHAPTER TWENTY-EIGHT

Trona, California

POSITIONED on the upper tier of what seemed to be some sort of disused tower or silo—part of an abandoned borax mining complex—a shine of equanimity flowed back into Hirsch. Rusty steel beams held up old shelving units. Broken pipes and discarded pieces of machinery littered the floor. Bright light flooded the space through the open window, which was Hirsch's vantage point of the arid speck of civilization below, just past the borders of the abandoned mine complex.

Borax mining was a key industry in these parts. On the other side of town, not a mile away, loomed a facility much like the one in which Hirsch was positioned—except everything was maintained and operational. A handful of men in dark blue coveralls milled the grounds and climbed the metal stairs. Perhaps the company had modernized to a newer facility. Or perhaps the abandoned site and the operational one had been rivals with one clear-cut winner.

Through the lens of his binoculars, Hirsch watched as the

Harley-Davidsons materialized out of Trona. From behind businesses. From foreclosed lots. A few belched to life right below him, rumbling out of the skeletal remnants of the long-forgotten mining facility. Light blue bandanas flashed throughout the tiny, dry town.

Up ahead on the highway, a lone Jeep appeared, cresting the slight rise. Though the bikes had come from different parts of the town, they all angled their trajectories toward this Wrangler.

It was a different attack pattern than they'd used on the Death Valley National Park tour bus the previous week.

But the idea was the same.

Hirsch lowered the binoculars and smiled.

This was order after the chaos of Hirsch's abrupt unraveling back at the shed. Down there in the town, every soldier moved in perfect formation, and Hirsch was their general, reclaiming the command he'd felt slip from his grasp.

Death Valley flashed before him again.

All of those old American tourists. Seniors. White hair and wrinkles. They'd worn windbreakers and khaki pants and khaki shorts and ugly white sneakers and wide-brimmed hats and swathes of white suntan lotion. They'd screamed. They'd been people, and they'd been turned into a mound of bloody flesh.

Hirsch had sworn he would never kill despite being a renowned and feared criminal. And he never had. It had become something distinctive to Hirsch's mystique, his brand. Almost a trademark. Something that made him unique among the criminal elite navigating the underworld of late-to-post-Cold-War Europe.

But somewhere in the background, in the depths, kept way out of view, had been an emotion that could make Hirsch break his defining, distinctive rule. Hirsch couldn't say he'd repressed it all these years; rather, he'd concealed it. He *would* kill for Margot and Jakob.

But he would only kill the ones who needed it—MacLeod and Shapiro.

Hirsch had killed them both.

Indirectly, that is. Ethan Draper had kept his end of the bargain.

But Draper had *distorted* his end of the bargain, too.

Hirsch saw withered hands reaching out, looking into the eyes of rough men with gray beards sporting black leather and oversized sunglasses, some sort of plea, a fruitless attempt at shared humanity.

Gunfire.

They'd all been killed.

Slaughtered.

Hirsch had killed them. Indirectly, Hirsch had killed thirteen people aside from MacLeod and Shapiro.

Hirsch had waited for years, taming the emotion, soothing and manipulating it to the point he had control over it. But, clearly, he hadn't had the control he'd thought. The emotion had led him to a union with someone as twisted as Ethan Draper.

Watching out the window as the bikes rumbled through the town of Trona, Hirsch sighed.

And then he straightened up, pulling his shoulders back.

He was in control again.

He lifted the binoculars back to his face. Though he couldn't tell which bike it was, Hirsch knew that one of the Harleys bore Draper. This sent a surge of satisfaction through Hirsch. For all his bravado, Draper was again a tool in Hirsch's hands. There was a swell of power, a near-intoxicating rush.

He glanced at Westlin standing next to him. The enigmatic man's eyes reflected the respect that Hirsch had cultivated over the years, but still, something was off—a certain spark, an intensity, seemed to have dimmed. It unsettled Hirsch, even as he tried to bask in the glory of his regained control.

He thought of Westlin in the shed earlier, that concealed fire in his eyes as he'd beaten Mitch Lockwood. Over the years, Hirsch had always kept Westlin on a short leash. A man like Westlin had to be restrained from killing. After all, Westlin was his father's son.

He glanced at Westlin now.

Yes, the man was a killer. Like his father. Maybe he'd be better with a lunatic like Ethan Draper.

As his mind flashed to that scene in Death Valley—all those Heckler & Koch MP5A3s spraying bullets, the old people's screams—anger again flashed across Hirsch's consciousness.

Luca Westlin had held one of those MP5s. Hirsch *had* let the man kill.

Tempering the flare-up, Hirsch returned his attention to the view out the window. The Harleys were drawing closer to the Jeep.

He turned to Westlin.

Last week, in Death Valley, he'd given Westlin his commands with subtle nods—one in the truck and one before MacLeod and Shapiro were killed. It was all that was needed. It was all that had ever been needed.

This time, when he gave Westlin a nod, he also spoke.

"Go. Make it brutal."

Without a word, Westlin stepped away, his silhouette blending into the shadows at the back of the room, going for the staircase.

The words replayed through Hirsch's mind: *Make it brutal*.

It might not be killing, but hopefully, it would sate Westlin.

CHAPTER TWENTY-NINE

THE WRANGLER THUMPED over the uneven road, slowing as they entered the town. It had been only a mile since the last Searles Valley spot, Pioneer Point, and now the Jeep's engine grumbled off rows of unassuming structures in a similar location: Trona. Seated on the Wrangler's rear bench seat, Carmen tasted something sweet, almost metallic, in the air. Maybe it was the borax.

But then, she'd heard borax was odorless.

Maybe she wasn't smelling things.

Maybe she was just losing her mind.

Given her recent choices, it would be par for the course.

Carmen exhaled. She leaned her head against the hardtop's window, the glass cold from the air conditioning.

She thought of Unseen Path, the eclectic truth-seekers united by a common goal: unveiling the secrets that governments and corporations hid from the public. Her role was crucial: coordinating operations for her scatter-brained spouse, ensuring Unseen Path's message reached the masses. But in a moment of impulsiveness, she'd abandoned it all, trading her leadership role for the emotional tug of panic, hopping on her dirt bike to find her missing husband.

The two people in the front seats, Kai and Leah Bloom, were enigmas. They were both tall, both muscular, giving them a larger-than-life mystique. Their sharp features were always alert, and their cryptic conversations hinted at a world Carmen had only ever heard of in whispered rumors. She'd heard terms like *CIA, Langley,* and *black ops.* They spoke in codes and exchanged glances that held more meaning than words. They were the embodiment of the shadow government operatives that Mitch had always warned her about, the sort of people she wrote about in the Unseen Path newsletter.

And yet, here she was, in their company, willingly.

Kai had tensed when they'd crossed into Trona a few moments earlier. Ever so slightly. There was something about the set of his jaw, the way his fingers danced lightly on the steering wheel. All Carmen had noticed that could have triggered this change was a pair of motorcycles—one from the east and another in the distance on the far side of town near an abandoned industrial facility—a borax mine, she assumed.

Carmen had dismissed the bikes and Kai's seeming response, thinking any danger was a figment of her frazzled nerves' imagination, but when the female agent, Bloom, had also come alert, Carmen knew something was wrong.

Bloom suddenly leaned forward. Her posture changed, shoulders tightening. Her hand moved toward the small of her back, where Carmen knew she carried a concealed weapon.

"Company," Bloom whispered to Kai.

Carmen's heart raced as more motorbikes materialized from concealed locations around the town. The two she'd noticed before had multiplied, forming a threatening circle of riders moving toward them.

Farther out, faint plumes of dust trailed upwards. Yet

more motorcycles. They speckled the horizon, coming into view one by one, growing as they approached.

Before Carmen could fully process the situation, the desert tranquility was shattered by the sound of gunfire. Bullets peppered the road yards from the Wrangler's tires, sending up dust clouds. Debris clanked off the sheet metal.

Kai, with reflexes Carmen couldn't comprehend, jerked the wheel hard. The world tilted as the Jeep swerved, tires screeching. From the corner of her eye, Carmen spotted the gleaming metal of a tire spike strip lying in wait on the road. They'd missed it by a yard. The Jeep jolted as it went off-road onto a patch of barren earth fronting a crumbling motel-turned-apartment building.

Adrenaline flooded Carmen's system. Her heart raced, palms sweated. She gripped the bench seat tightly. Every bump and jolt of the Wrangler seemed amplified, sending jitters down her spine.

More gunfire outside.

Crack! Crack! Crack!

Kai lived up to the elite operator persona Carmen had built in her mind. The Jeep moved as if an extension of him, taking a sharp turn to the right, narrowly missing a motorcyclist trying to box them in.

Another swerve. Carmen bashed into the opposite side of the hardtop, pain flaring through her left shoulder. The Jeep barely avoided another biker who'd come at them head-on. The engine roared as Kai pulled the Jeep through a veering set of turns, engulfing them in dust.

The passenger-side window buzzed down, and Bloom swiftly retrieved her pistol.

Crack! Crack!

Cover fire.

The roar of motorcycle engines was louder with the window down. One biker was close—*right beside them*—so close that Carmen could see his nicotine-rotted teeth as he sneered at them.

Bloom made quick work of his hubris.

She fired.

The bike's front tire shredded instantly, sending the foul-toothed biker tumbling to the desert floor. A shower of dry earth. The man spun violently, clothing tearing, lost in a haze of dust and gravel.

Carmen's pulse raced. The situation was surreal, like a scene from one of those action movies she and Mitch watched from the safety of their RV. Instinctively, she fumbled in her pocket for her cellular phone. She wasn't a shadow man—or woman—like the other two, but she could do her part. They needed help.

She entered 9-1-1, pressed send, and waited, her gaze glued to the screen. But all she saw was the daunting *NO SERVICE* message.

Panic welled.

They were truly on their own.

She looked back up and through the windshield ahead. Something had happened since she glanced down at her phone. Their assailants were executing a new strategy. Several bikers had sped along, disappearing from view. As the Jeep thundered forward, the reason for their disappearance became terrifyingly clear.

The path led them to the abandoned borax mine Carmen had spotted earlier in the distance. The looming structures of the mine, now in decrepit condition, cast eerie shadows across the earth. Abandoned machinery lay scattered, rusty metal forms gleaming dully in the fading light.

It was the perfect place to get funneled into and pinned down.

A quick glance through the rear window confirmed the

dire situation: the rest of the thugs were closing in, throttles open, a wall of roaring motorcycles.

Kai didn't panic. Instead, he acted. Slamming the brakes, the Jeep's tires dug into the gravelly surface, sending plumes of dust everywhere. For a fleeting moment, the world felt suspended in that dusty cloud. Time slowed as particles danced in the golden light.

Then, with a swift U-turn, the Jeep's nose now pointed back from where they'd come. The bikers behind skidded, trying to halt their momentum or swerve to avoid a head-on collision.

Just like that, the hunter became the hunted.

Kai dropped the stick into second, floored the accelerator, and charged right into the swarm with the Wrangler's engine roaring.

The cacophony of the machines combined into an almost unbearable crescendo. Carmen slapped her hands over her ears. The Jeep barreled over the rough earth as the bikes scattered in front of it, but more bikes weren't far behind.

Carmen, already reeling from the shock, couldn't fathom how they'd escape.

But Kai, it seemed, had a plan.

Of course.

Without a word, he popped open the glove compartment. He retrieved something that made Carmen's eyes go wide—a piece of hardware Carmen hadn't known existed outside of those action films she and Mitch loved.

A grenade.

An honest-to-God grenade.

Its metallic surface gleamed ominously.

Kai quickly handed it to Bloom, his crackling voice urgent but controlled.

"Use it."

With practiced ease, Bloom pulled the pin, took aim, and

then hurled the grenade out the window toward one of the mine's larger, crumbling buildings.

A deafening roar erupted. The air seemed to compress before violently expanding, and a shockwave pulsed against Carmen's body. The sound echoed off the surrounding structures, reverberating through the Jeep's frame and into the seat.

Carmen screamed.

Massive chunks of brick and debris cascaded down, forming a thick barrier between the Jeep and its pursuers. Carmen felt the ground tremble as dust and rocks dropped from the sky.

The once-pursuing bikers were forced to halt, some swerving to avoid being buried under the rubble. One crashed, skidding on the earth, his arm twisting behind his back. The limb yanked in the wrong direction and was nearly torn off.

With the bikers' path blocked, the thunder of their engines waned.

But then a sharp crack resonated above the dying engine roars, distinctly different from the previous chaos—a rifle shot. The rear window of the Jeep exploded inward, showering Carmen with shards of glass. She ducked instinctively, bringing her face to her knees.

She'd caught a glimpse of the sniper just before burying her face; he was hidden in a shattered window of a distant tower.

Kai spun the wheel, and the Wrangler jerked to the side, going down an alley between a pair of two-story brick warehouses. He glanced back at Carmen before swiftly refocusing on the maze-like facility.

Bloom spun in her seat as well.

"Stay down," she hissed at Carmen, eyes scanning the dilapidated structures for further threat.

As they sped along, weaving through the abandoned buildings and rusted machinery, Carmen felt the oppressive atmosphere engulfing them. And then, just when she thought they might be trapped within the sprawling facility, Bloom pointed ahead.

"There!" Bloom yelled.

In the distance, a road stretched out, leading away from the mine. The remnants of a gated barrier stood sentinel at its entrance, the gate itself long since removed or destroyed.

It was an exit—a lifeline.

Kai buried the gas pedal without hesitation, accelerating toward the old barrier.

CHAPTER THIRTY

KNOBBY TIRES KICKED up dust as the Wrangler sped toward the remnants of the barrier. The once-formidable fence gate was now just a twisted pile of rubble that cast long shadows across the ground. Its coils of razor wire swayed in the breeze.

Bloom's senses were in overdrive as her trio roared toward the gate. She felt an extra weight of responsibility.

For Carmen.

Carmen wasn't an operator like Bloom and Kai.

She was just a woman who wanted to find her husband.

They were almost to the mine's threshold, almost out of the trap, but Bloom's muscles stayed tight. Every sound, every movement, every glint of metal in the distance was a potential threat.

The Jeep's engine roared, echoing off the dilapidated structures as they neared the barrier. But then, Bloom noticed a subtle change in Kai's posture. His grip on the steering wheel tightened, and his eyes narrowed, focusing intently on something ahead.

Following his gaze, Bloom's heart sank. Emerging from

behind a massive warehouse was a giant Mack truck, its engine rumbling. It was heading straight for the gate on a perpendicular path to that of the Wrangler, clearly intending to block their escape.

For a split second, Bloom marveled at Kai's perceptiveness. She'd missed the Mack entirely. From Kai's perspective, only a fraction of the truck would have been visible. How the hell had he noticed it before she had?

But the moment of admiration was fleeting, replaced by a surge of adrenaline.

They were running out of time.

...and space.

To Bloom's shock, instead of slowing down, Kai downshifted, pushing the Jeep to its limits, engine screaming. It surged forward.

"What are you doing?" Bloom shouted over the roar.

Kai didn't respond. His focus was laser-sharp, zoned in on the approaching truck and the narrowing gap at the gate.

From the backseat, Carmen's scream pierced the tense atmosphere. "Kai!"

The Mack truck was almost to the gate now, its massive grille gleaming. The gap was closing fast.

Tighter.

Tighter yet.

Too narrow for a Jeep Wrangler.

The world seemed to slow. Bloom heard the pounding of her heart. She saw the determined set of Kai's jaw.

The gap was narrower. The Mack truck closed in rapidly.

Oh shit...

But then, with inches to spare, Kai shifted course fractionally, just a tiny swipe of his wrist on the steering wheel. The Jeep screeched against the truck's grille. A shower of sparks erupted skyward. The impact threatened to topple the

Jeep, sending it reeling to the right and pushing deep into its suspension, but Kai's expert handling kept it upright.

With a scream of tires, the Jeep cleared the barrier. Kai yanked the steering wheel to the side, sending the Wrangler skidding onto a dusty, cracked side road.

The abandoned mine, with its looming structures and the menacing Mack truck, faded into the background.

Bloom sucked in a deep breath. She turned to Kai with a mix of admiration and disbelief.

"That was ... close."

Kai simply nodded, his eyes fixed on the road ahead. "Yes."

Carmen's voice, shaky but determined, called. "Guys? Um ... what's our next move?"

Bloom glanced at Kai, waiting for his response. When none came, she pressed, "Yeah, Kai. What the hell are we going to do next?"

Kai's eyes remained fixed on the road, but Bloom noticed a subtle change in his demeanor.

Shit, not this again.

His grip on the steering wheel tightened, and his posture became more rigid. Following his gaze, Bloom spotted a solitary figure in the distance—a motorcycle.

The Lost Jackals' last hurrah.

Even from a distance, Bloom could tell the man was massive. She saw a thick white beard flowing in the wind. The arms draped over the handlebars looked like they could snap a tree in half.

And, of course, she saw lots of black leather.

The biker was gaining on them, his engine's roar growing louder with each passing second.

Kai's eyes darted to the rearview mirror, then to the rugged expanse ahead. Without warning, he yanked the steering wheel, and the Jeep jolted as it left the road surface and hit the crumbling terrain.

Rocks and gravel pinged off the Jeep's sides. Kai kept the gas pedal floored, pushing the Wrangler away from the road and deeper into the heart of the desert. The landscape stretched out before them, a vast tableau of jagged rocks, scattered boulders, and hardy shrubs with mountains lining the horizon.

Kai executed a series of sharp turns and maneuvers, using the desert's natural dips and fissures to his advantage. Each move was calculated to put more distance between them and their pursuer.

But the biker was relentless, his powerful machine devouring the ground between them. Bloom pivoted in her seat, finding the biker right behind them, light blue bandana whipping in the wind from its position tied around his forearm.

With a sudden burst of speed, Kai downshifted as he straightened the Jeep, flooring the accelerator once more. As they sped forward, he reached to the side, pulling a Beretta 92FS from its shoulder holster. He leaned out of the driver's side window, taking aim.

Bloom watched as he fired a series of shots.

Crack! Crack! Crack!

The bullets thumped into the ground directly in front of the biker's path, ejecting plumes of rock and debris.

The Harley swerved, almost held on, but lost control with the sudden movement and the unstable terrain. It wobbled, fishtailed, screeched, collapsed, and sent the large man tumbling.

Kai yanked on the emergency brake. The Wrangler shuddered. Its tires skidded on the rock floor. Bloom was sent jolting forward. The seatbelt dug into her shoulder, a jolt of fire cutting through her torso. In the back seat, Carmen screamed.

By the time Bloom blinked her eyes back open, Kai was already out of the Jeep, already standing over the fallen biker. With a swift, powerful motion, Kai drove a punch into the man's face.

A sick, wet thud.

The biker's massive frame went limp.

CHAPTER THIRTY-ONE

THE SUN BEAT down on the abandoned motel, casting sharp shadows onto the cracked asphalt parking lot. A few windows were boarded up with plywood, but most were shattered. The paint was faded and peeling. The neon vacancy sign was rusted and lifeless.

It was on the very edge of Trona, so its location, abandoned state, and the horseshoe layout of the buildings provided a decent spot of seclusion. Silence stood at the front of the Wrangler—which was parked to the side of the lot, hood propped open—with the vehicle's battery cradled in his hands.

As he stepped away from the engine bay, the battery's weight solidified the notion that this was now a repurposed tool, a means to an end. Silence knew its potential all too well. Bloom and Carmen waited at the back of the Wrangler, the latter of whose expression was a mix of anticipation and concern.

The biker, the one they'd captured, was seated with his back against the Jeep, his arms and legs bound securely with twine. Silence had wrapped the man's ankles a few minutes earlier while Bloom had handled the wrists. Silence had admired the CIA operative's work, even learned a new technique.

The biker's face was ashen, blending into his graying beard.

Naturally.

People's bodies tend to go haywire when they break a bone.

Silence looked at it—the man's broken right arm. It hung limp at a sharp angle with an unnatural backward orientation between his elbow and shoulder. The fingers of the adjoining hand were splayed spider-like and entirely motionless—a wizard's hand frozen mid-hex. The skin was swollen and discolored, covered in deep purple and blue bruises.

Sweat beaded the man's forehead, glistening on another dark bruise that had formed around his eye. He breathed like he'd run a marathon, sucking each raspy inhale through gritted teeth.

The guy was gonna pass out at any moment.

As Silence approached the man, Carmen's eyes darted to the battery in his hands, widening with fear and confusion.

"Kai ... what are you going to do with that?" she said, her voice barely above a whisper.

Silence didn't respond. Instead, he locked eyes with Bloom, giving her a nod. He'd been in situations like this before, and he wagered Bloom had, too.

He'd never been comfortable with torture, and it was never a choice he made lightly. Fortunately, in many cases, the mere *threat* of pain was enough to get a person talking.

And the battery was one hell of a visual aid.

The biker's labored breathing grew more pronounced as Silence and Bloom closed in on him. His eyes darted between them and the battery, fear undeniable on his blanched, sweaty, bruised, bearded face.

The panic added a layer of complexity for Silence—it hastened the man's impending loss of consciousness. Timing and efficiency would be critical.

Silence squatted in front of the man. Between his splayed knees, he held the battery—one hand on either side—a few inches over the ground. Kept it there for a moment. And released.

Thud.

Car batteries are damn heavy. They make a nice impact noise. This was another powerful boost to Silence's intimidation factor.

The biker looked at the battery.

"Easy way," Silence said and swallowed. He pointed downward. "Or hard way. Your choice." Another swallow. "Talk."

The biker gulped, Adam's apple bobbing.

"I'll talk," he rasped.

Silence felt a wave of relief. He hadn't wanted "the hard way." All along, he'd suspected he wouldn't need it. Loyalty for guys like a Lost Jackal—an outlaw biker—only goes so far.

No honor among thieves.

Nor outlaws.

Bloom stepped closer.

"Why were you trying to kill us?" she shouted.

The man shook his head. "We weren't trying to kill you. We were..." He grimaced suddenly. "We were trying to bring you in."

Silence scowled. "With tire strips?" He swallowed. "And guns?"

The man shrugged. "I didn't plan the operation, dude."

"The bus slaughter," Bloom said. "You sure as hell weren't trying to bring those people in. Who's plan was that?"

"Draper," the man said. "Ethan Draper."

Bloom smirked. "Yeah, but Draper was hired by an outsider, wasn't he? Adrian Hirsch."

The man nodded.

"Why'd Hirsch..." Silence said and swallowed. "Want them dead?"

The biker's eyes darted between Silence and Bloom, weighing his options.

"He didn't," the man finally admitted. "He only wanted *two* people on that bus dead."

Silence looked up from his crouched position, exchanging a glance with Bloom before returning his gaze to the biker.

"MacLeod and Shapiro," Silence said.

The biker shrugged. "If you say so. Draper didn't give us the names."

"The rest?" Silence said and swallowed. "Why were they killed?"

The biker's gaze dropped to the ground, a hint of shame crossing his features.

"That was Draper's doing," he said. "He's got this whole anti-capitalist agenda. Said the snobs on that bus were the very sort of people he despised. Rich, entitled. So he..." The man grimaced, and his body shuddered. Silence noticed he'd gone another shade whiter. "He had us wipe them all out. He ... he gave us a bonus."

Bloom's eyes narrowed. "And what did Draper get in return for killing the two Hirsch wanted dead?"

The biker hesitated for a moment, then let out a ragged sigh.

"Hirsch forged documents for him. Like, some sort of security pass. Something for tonight."

"Tonight?" Bloom said. "What's Draper doing tonight?

"I don't know, lady. It's not a Jackal thing, whatever he's planning. Draper's always got multiple plays running, with or without the Jackals. He said it's his masterpiece—a terrorist attack at the..." He growled as a wave of pain made his body spasm. "At the ..." A weak moan. "At the big event..."

The man fell limp, face dropping to his chest.

Unconscious.

Silence looked up at Bloom again.

"Ridgecrest," Bloom said. "The Raven's Ride finale."

Silence nodded.

He faced the biker and drove a palm strike into the man's bad shoulder.

"Wake up!" Silence barked.

The man screamed as he snapped back to cogent, awful reality.

Silence wasn't going to permit the man his relief. Not yet. There was one more pressing matter at hand.

Very pressing.

"What about Mitch Lockwood?" Silence's voice went lower even than usual, dangerous. He swallowed. "Where is he?"

The biker smirked, and a glint of genuine amusement flashed in his eyes.

"Oh, Lockwood?" he said. "We took real good care of him."

"*What'd you do?*"

The biker leaned back, his head lolling to the side.

"Let's just say he won't be causing any more trouble. Never..." His eyes fluttered. "Ever..." Head drooped. "Ever again."

His face fell.

Unconscious once more.

From behind, Carmen Lockwood let out a bloodcurdling scream.

CHAPTER THIRTY-TWO

BARELY TWO HOURS had passed since Westlin felt a rekindling of faith, a sensation of trust. Yet now, from his vantage point in the crumbling tower, the scene unfolding before him felt like a vicious slap of betrayal.

He was back in his perch above the abandoned borax mine, back to where he and Hirsch had watched the Jackals' motorcycles converge on the Jeep Wrangler, where Hirsch had released him to join the fray with the command of *Make it brutal.*

On the opposite side of the sprawling floor, past fingers of muted light that seeped through gaps in the shattered glass panes, Hirsch and Draper were at it again. Lined along the far wall, like they had been in the shed earlier, was Draper's contingent of Lost Jackals.

Hirsch, who was always the epitome of control, now looked unhinged—cheeks crimson, sweat glistening on his brow. His eyes, usually cold and calculating, burned with fury, locked on Draper.

"You piece of shit." His voice wavered. "How the hell did you and your Jackals let the Jeep slip away?"

As he watched, Westlin felt a cold sensation unfurl within. Each outburst from Hirsch, each crack in the man's once-impenetrable armor, chipped away at the pedestal Westlin had placed him on. It had only been recently, in the orchestrated chaos of Trona, that a fraction of respect had been reborn.

But now Westlin felt that budding respect shrivel and die.

In its attempt to escape the scene in the dusty tower, his mind wandered away to a memory. A different man. Westlin's *real* father. Someone Westlin had spent most of his life despising, questioning, running from.

Yet at that moment, with the echoes of Hirsch's pathetic anger ringing in his ears, Westlin felt a surge of something unexpected: respect.

For his own flesh and blood.

He saw him.

A brief glimpse of a rugged face, worn by time and choices but always carrying an air of quiet strength. Westlin remembered those piercing eyes that seemed to see right through him, always judging Westlin—no, *assessing* him— always calculating, always predicting.

But most prominently, Westlin recalled the gift, the single connection he'd maintained to that rugged face.

Westlin glanced away from the verbal scuffle between Hirsch and Draper, looking down at his arm, finding the wristband. He touched it. The leather was smooth, cool. He traced the etched patterns with his fingertip.

His father's voice in his head.

People get so easily dazzled by the elaborate, Luca. They want to believe in something grand: ideas, symbolism, a more significant meaning to it all. But while they're busy trying to decode the insignificant, they miss the simple, lethal truth right under their noses.

Before Westlin could sink deeper into his past, a brash voice echoed through the room, bringing him back.

"I could use a man like you," Draper said, looking right at Westlin, ignoring Hirsch, eyes confident and smug. He nodded toward the stoic bikers nearby. "My new Jackals unit is missing a key component: an enforcer. Tonight, the world's going to see something they won't forget. And I promise, I'll grant you liberties your current employer seems too scared to allow."

With a mocking smirk, he motioned to the still-fuming Hirsch.

"Liberties such as, ya know," Draper continued, "allowing a killer to kill."

Westlin could see the moment the words hit Hirsch like a physical blow. His eyes widened, and his mouth opened and closed. Nothing came out.

Speechless.

Spineless.

When Hirsch finally found his voice, it was tinged with tremulous disbelief, which he tried in vain to mask.

"You think you can just poach from my ranks?" Hirsch's voice rose to an almost hysterical pitch.

Draper didn't respond. He didn't even look at Hirsch. He just kept staring in Westlin's direction, awaiting a response.

"I'd be honored," Westlin said.

Hirsch whipped around, his face a canvas of shock and mounting anger.

But Westlin wouldn't waver.

By aligning himself with Draper, he wasn't just breaking away from Hirsch's shadow; he was stepping into his own light, forging his own path—a path he realized had been waiting for him all along, as though he'd only now decoded it from the elaborate symbols on his wristband.

The room grew silent, save for the soft whistle of a desert breeze through broken windows. Every gaze was fixed, unblinking. All eyes were on Westlin, waiting for him to falter, to retract his statement.

But he did not.

For a heartbeat, Hirsch just stood there, even more pathetic. Then, with a suddenness that caught everyone off guard, he turned on his heel and stormed across the space, eyeing Westlin as he passed, going to the doorway in the back. He disappeared into the darkness, and for a moment, his footsteps sounded from the stairwell until they faded out of existence like the man himself.

The hush that Hirsch left in his wake was soon filled by Draper's voice.

"Good choice," Draper said.

He crossed the room and stopped beside Westlin.

"My men," Draper said, motioning to the Jackals, "will be at the Raven's Ride finale in Ridgecrest tonight. I'll be elsewhere. They'll need leadership."

Westlin nodded.

"Good. Mitch Lockwood will be with them," Draper said. "As much as I'd like to live up to my promise right away, I can't let you kill Lockwood. His Unseen Path organization has a following. If he goes missing, people will look for him. But ... that tall woman, the one who's been asking all the questions—we know she's working with Carmen Lockwood now. So if she's some sort of cop or detective like we thinks she is, she might come looking for Mitch. If she does..."

He trailed off for Westlin to finish.

"Kill her."

Draper nodded.

And Westlin grinned.

"Tonight, I'm giving the world a message it won't be able to ignore," Draper said. "But there's a hitch."

Westlin raised an eyebrow, intrigued.

"I'm going to wait until I get the man alone," Draper

continued. "In the bathroom, most likely. I have a syringe, already approved for entry into the event given my cover as a diabetic. But if the man has guards, or if I can't get him solo, I'll need something a bit more up-close-and-personal. I don't mind getting my hands dirty."

He smirked wryly.

"I need something I can get past security—metal detectors, pat-downs, the works. I'm guessing a man of your experience might be able to help?"

Westlin glanced at his wristband and back to Draper.

He grinned.

"My father wasn't the world's most elite killer. But he was a master of one technique: the art of concealment." Westlin's fingers danced over the wristband's engravings. "Yeah, I can help you out."

CHAPTER THIRTY-THREE

Mojave Desert, California

SILENCE WAS BACK behind the Wrangler's wheel.

The desert stretched in all directions, presenting a seemingly endless land of jagged rocks and gnarly scrubs. As the late-day sun began its descent, casting long shadows over the terrain, the once clear blue sky transformed, adopting a calmer hue with twilight's approach.

The air was filled with the sound of the engine rumbling and tires humming on asphalt. Every so often, there was an ominous metallic clunk, a reminder of the Wrangler's recent accident with the Mack truck. Ahead, the silhouettes of buildings emerged from the horizon, the first signs of Ridgecrest.

The city's name brought to mind the Raven's Ride Motorcycle Rally. It was the event's last day, and tonight was the grand finale. The city would be alive with energy—the roars of the bikes, the cheers of the crowd. But biker rallies often come with their share of mischief and potential crime. In a smaller city like Ridgecrest, such events could undoubtedly strain the police force's resources and patience to the limit.

A glance in the rearview mirror revealed Carmen, her face pale and her eyes glassed over, lost in her own world. Next to her on the bench seat, Bloom whispered something, her voice too soft for Silence to catch. But the gentle touch of her hand on Carmen's arm spoke volumes. It was a side of the CIA operative that Silence hadn't expected, a tenderness at odds with her tough exterior.

In the back, past the bench seat, hidden from Silence's view, was the tied-up, unconscious biker. Silence was dropping the man off at a hospital.

As Silence drove, a whirlwind of thoughts consumed him. Draper, Hirsch, Mitch—so many unknowns, countless variables. Unpredictability clouded his judgment, throwing his thoughts into turmoil. Every potential decision felt like a reckless toss of the dice. Silence detested uncertainty, and it only intensified the chaos in his mind. Desperate, he reached for one of C.C.'s grounding techniques but was too consumed by turmoil to find his bearings.

He sensed C.C. herself about to make a presence in his mind—to override both his attempts at self-regulation and the mental storm causing the chaos—when suddenly, a commotion from the back jolted him from his thoughts.

The biker, unconscious for the entire journey, was now awake. The man had propped himself up to a seated position. And he was smirking. Bloom was quick to react, her SIG trained on him instantly.

But Carmen's scream cut through everything, raw and pure.

"You killed my husband!" she shrieked, her voice filled with a mix of rage and despair.

The biker's smirk widened, his eyes cold and devoid of emotion.

"Lady," he drawled, "I said we *took care of* your husband." The biker paused then, which seemed almost intentionally poignant once he uttered his next words: "Your husband is still alive."

———

Silence, Bloom, and Carmen were alone in a secluded park in Ridgecrest. To their left, nestled within the greenery, a playground stood silent, void of children's laughter. The swings swayed gently with the breeze, while the deserted slide looked like it had given up hope of obliging its next joyful rider that day. Across a bustling street to their right, the skeletal frame of a hotel tower renovation project—fully stripped of its original facade—rose above them, juxtaposing the park's semi-natural tranquility with a hint of encroaching urban revitalization.

Ten minutes earlier, they'd buzzed through a hospital parking lot, going just beyond the emergency room porte cochère. Silence hadn't even brought the Wrangler to a complete stop, only slowed it enough to give Bloom a chance to shove the biker—who'd been unconscious after passing out once more—out the back. He landed unceremoniously on the pavement and hadn't finished rolling before the Wrangler screeched off.

Now, Silence and Bloom stood several yards away from their companion, respecting Carmen's request for a few moments of seclusion as she tried to process the tumult of her feelings. She paused by a bench, her finger tracing its backrest.

The subtle rise of Carmen's shoulders suggested relief, but recent traumas were clearly lingering. The agony of thinking her husband had perished, only to discover he was alive but still captive, was beyond comprehension to Silence. He admired her strength.

Bloom watched the other woman for a moment before turning to Silence.

"My dad..." She started before quickly trailing off. "He never gave up in Boston. It cost him everything. I thought if I could somehow bring closure to what had happened to MacLeod and Shapiro, there'd be some closure for my father."

Another long pause. She looked at Carmen. When Bloom spoke again, her voice was low.

"I've failed again, Kai. First, I failed my father, then Saeed, and now her." She pointed. "I promised her we'd find Mitch, but here we are, no closer to finding him than when we started."

Silence took in the pain evident in Bloom's eyes. He remembered the fierce determination Bloom had shown when they'd first met—the rogue presumed FBI agent, the woman on a vendetta. Krav Maga. Pencak silat. Systema.

Now, seeing her so defeated, it tugged at something inside him.

His thoughts churned tumultuously once more, and as images of Hirsch, Westlin, and Draper cascaded among a backdrop of slaughtered tourists in the vast expanse of the Death Valley desert, other images overpowered them, somehow fueled by Bloom's notions of her father.

Silence didn't see his own father.

He saw a father figure.

Tanner, going into the seedy dive bar. Black Jack's. It had seemed nefarious.

But it was beneficent.

Just Tanner being Tanner, doing good in the world. Fighting like Hell to save his nephew Ben from a criminal organization.

Labyrinth.

Rourke...

The cold face. Twitching jaw muscles. Blue eyes.

Bright blue eyes staring at Silence from the darkness of the alley.

If only Silence wasn't stuck in the desert on the other side of the country. If only he could get back to Pensacola.

If only—

C.C.'s voice came to him.

Focus, love.

She was right.

And so he focused.

He looked at Bloom. She seemed to be awaiting a response—an expectant, anticipatory look in her eye, something akin to, but quite different from, the softness he'd seen her offer Carmen earlier in the backseat of the Wrangler.

He obliged her with a simple response. "We'll finish this."

He looked to his right, where the hotel project was under construction. The skeletal frame of the building rose high above him. A large sign advertised the artist's vision of what the finished structure would look like—a lavish affair. His eyes were drawn to something at the bottom of this image.

Bloom followed his gaze, her eyes narrowing as she took in the sign. "What is it, Kai?"

Silence didn't respond. Instead, he dashed across the street, dodging traffic, and stopped before the chain-link fence, staring intently at the bottom of the poster beneath the artist's rendering. In bold, stylized graphics was the logo:

Kaveny International Hotels & Resorts

Below that:

Celebrating 50 years!
At the Elysian Resort chain grand opening in Santa Barbara

Bloom, having followed him, came to a stop, breathless.

"What is it?" she repeated.

Silence pointed at the logo and anniversary.

"Kaveny is buying up..." he said and swallowed. "Privately owned hotels in the Southwest."

Bloom nodded. "Yeah, it's causing quite a stir around these parts."

Silence thought for a moment.

"But they also have new chain..." He swallowed. "Of high-end resorts. Grand opening..." Another swallow. "In Santa Barbara tonight."

Bloom's eyes widened in realization. "A *high-end* resort chain. Exactly the sort of thing Draper despises."

Silence nodded.

"His big attack isn't going to be here at the end of Raven's Ride," she said. "It's going to be—"

"On the coast," Silence finished for her.

He looked back at Carmen, still standing by the bench, her face a mask of pain and relief.

"You stay in Ridgecrest," he said and swallowed. "Free her husband from the Jackals. I'm going..." Another swallow. "To Santa Barbara."

CHAPTER THIRTY-FOUR

Airspace over Ventura County, California

ETHAN DRAPER EASED into the plush leather seat.

Disgusting.

The airplane's first-class cabin exuded decadent luxury, a reality far removed from the hustle of everyday life ticking away thousands of feet below. Overhead compartments gently closed, muffling the soft chatter. Dim lights cast a gentle glow on plush seats and sleekly designed spaces. Across the aisle from Draper, men in sharp suits murmured about recent deals while women with tasteful jewelry shared tales of their recent travels and cultural excursions.

As others settled into the comfort, a tension built in Draper's jaw. This space, with its overt amenities, was alien terrain, far from his familiar world, and he despised anyone who seemed to enjoy it.

He was only there because Adrian Hirsch had handled the logistics for Draper's upcoming attack; this had been the German's half of their agreement. Hirsch was accustomed to first-class amenities and had probably not given it a moment's thought weeks ago when he arranged Draper's transportation.

"Beverage, sir?"

Draper's gaze lifted, meeting the eyes of a young flight attendant. Navy blue uniform, crisply ironed. Perfect makeup. Perfect hair. Her smile seemed genuine yet rehearsed, the type belonging to a person who offered refreshments to countless faces, day in and day out. Various miniature alcohol bottles were prominently displayed on her cart.

"Ginger ale," Draper said.

No alcohol. Clarity was paramount now.

The attendant poured the drink with a practiced flare unbefitting the plastic cup she handed him. As she pushed her cart to the next row, he sipped. Perfectly cold. The bubbles did their thing in his throat.

They always had.

Draper had been fond of ginger ale since he was a kid, always getting them at his family store. He pictured himself as a youngster, standing beside his father at the register, handing change back to customers. Draper's dad would come home exhausted after dealing with the difficulties of the outside world but still managed to shelter young Ethan from the most painful realities. The tiny house they returned to was not much, but it was filled with affection and dedication.

But even love had its limits. As large corporations expanded their reach, using ruthless tactics and overwhelming resources, they choked the life out of countless small businesses. The Draper family store was no exception. The recession of the early '80s rolled in, proving the final punch that took the business out.

Draper remembered the hushed conversations between

his parents, the sound of bills being shuffled and recounted, and the slow, painful realization that they might not make it. The sight of his father, once strong and resilient, now beaten down by the relentless march of capitalism, was a wound that never healed.

It was with these memories, these scars, that Draper had entered college—a sanctuary of knowledge and enlightenment.

Or so he thought.

Instead, he found a system designed to perpetuate the same inequities that had torn his family apart. Every lecture on economics, every discussion on political science, peeled back the veneer of the capitalist dream, revealing a rotten core. The gap between the elite and working-class families like his own was not a flaw in the system—*it was the system itself.* The textbooks felt like propaganda, the classroom debates mere distractions.

It was a rigged game, and Draper had wanted out.

So he left, going straight into the waiting arms of the Lost Jackals. These were the free spirits he'd first hoped to find when he'd gone to the ridiculous school. Each of the men bore their own battle scars from the war against consumerism and corporate greed.

With the Jackals, Draper found a semblance of kinship, echoes of the sentiments and simmering anger he fostered. Yet, as much as there was a shared cause, he always felt slightly out of step. The Jackals might've seen potential leadership qualities in him—a blend of scholarly knowledge and gritty experience—but Draper deliberately kept himself away from the limelight, staying lower in the gang's hierarchy.

Now, enveloped by the lavish confines of the airplane's first-class section, he was amidst the very emblems of the world that both he and the Jackals despised. He rotated the plastic cup of ginger ale across his palm.

Those memories of the past—his parents' sacrifices and the Lost Jackals' brotherhood—fueled his determination.

This mission of his was more than an act of defiance.

It was personal.

The Elysian grand opening wasn't merely an event for the elite to flaunt their wealth. It represented something more systemic. It was a loud proclamation of the unending consumption and insatiable greed that Draper loathed.

As the airplane soared above the clouds, he contemplated his mission. His past actions—the shopping mall in Charlotte and the attempt at poisoning the fast-food chain's supply—as dramatic and chaotic as they had been, had merely been a prelude.

The strike at Elysian would be different, massive. Not a mere spark but a volcano erupting.

He pictured the upcoming event—the opulence, the pageantry, the smug faces of those who benefited most from the rigged game. Their laughter, their clinking glasses, the false camaraderie—all a façade hiding the rot beneath, part of the grotesque theatre of capitalism.

In the dimly lit cabin, the soft whispers of businessmen making deals and discussing market trends became distant, a muffled backdrop to Draper's burgeoning resolve.

Soon, at the Elysian grand opening, Draper would wear the mask of someone who belonged, embracing the upper crust's indulgent customs and rhythms—until the clock struck his hour. Then the world would witness his message, a desperate plea for society to snap out of its consumerist daze and see the shackles binding them.

But there was still the journey to Santa Barbara, the first-class flight.

Draper took a deep breath, trying to relax. As much as he detested the opulence surrounding him, he couldn't deny its soothing nature. For now, he would indulge in its comfort.

Even rebels, even terrorists, needed their moments of respite.

The hum of the plane's engines lulled him to sleep.

CHAPTER THIRTY-FIVE

Ridgecrest, California

THE RAUCOUS DIN of the Raven's Ride rally was muffled by distance, but its sound still pulsed through the night air, even this far away. Dusk drew a muted curtain over Ridgecrest, casting long shadows.

Bloom stood on a side street, removed from the frenetic main drag with its revving engines and roaring crowd. Carmen was with her, dark eyes lit with a look of determination. But also contrariness. She wasn't having what Bloom suggested.

"I'm coming with you," Carmen said through her teeth. "He's my husband. I didn't come this far to stay put."

Bloom's eyes never wavered from Carmen's. She recognized and respected the steely glint in Carmen's gaze—it mirrored her own many times over.

But the stakes were too high.

And this woman was a civilian, no matter how many wild adventures she'd been on.

Bloom straightened.

"Carmen, you need to stay here," she said, her voice level but forceful. She pointed to an all-night coffee shop just down the street. "Wait there."

The far-off roars of the motorcycles seemed to echo her plea, growing louder, then fading, as if punctuating her every word. There was the muffled rumble of the crowd.

Carmen, stubborn as ever, looked ready to protest. To argue. Again.

But before she could, Bloom tried something new—an attempt to appeal to the other woman on a personal level.

"Let me help you," Bloom whispered, reaching out and gripping Carmen's shoulder. "I need this. I need ... to help you."

She really *did* need this. She wanted nothing more than to do something right.

Even if it was just this one time.

Carmen bit her lip.

"Fine," she said quietly. "I've seen what you're capable of." She looked away. "Just ... just bring that big idiot back to me in one piece, okay?"

————

At the wild epicenter of the Raven's Ride motorcycle rally's final night, the air was thick with gasoline, the musky aroma of alcohol, and the sense of adrenaline-pumped anticipation. Pure revelry, full of life's most visceral pleasures and distractions—some lighthearted and fun, others falling squarely into the realm of the inappropriate. Or illegal.

Bloom pushed her way through the sweaty crowd lining the main street. Motorcycle engines roared, each vying for dominance in this metallic jungle. The sidewalks teemed with leather-clad figures, their tattoos telling stories of rebellions, regrets, and rites of passage. The reflective gleam of chrome punctuated every turn and reflected the waning sunset glow in a myriad of directions. The main drag of Ridgecrest had transformed into a parade ground solely for the Harley-Davidsons, each set of wheels announced by its rider like a proud warrior showcasing his steed.

But amidst this mayhem, Bloom had a singular focus. She scanned the crowds for the light blue bandanas of the Lost Jackals. She'd been looking for a while.

And she'd yet to spot one.

As the minutes passed, her heart sank lower and lower. A feeling of dread overtook her. But she forced her senses to remain on high alert, picking out snippets of conversation, gauging body language, and always searching for that telltale splash of color.

She'd seen plenty of orange, *Culpepper Kids*; neon green, *Vermin*; and deep magenta, *Los Luchadoras*.

But no Lost Jackals.

Just when despondency threatened to take over, a flutter of light blue caught Bloom's attention at the far end of the street, amidst the crowd. She squinted, hoping she wasn't imagining things. No, there they were—a cluster of light blue bandanas, bobbing just above the sea of heads.

A rush of relief surged through her, and she began making her way toward them, pushing through the crowd. But immediately another sight caught her peripheral vision. Down a less populated side street, she noticed a separate, smaller contingent also wearing the Lost Jackals' signature light blue bandanas. They were hovering near a nondescript warehouse entrance.

A realization struck her. Draper would never put his men in the spotlight, not amidst the main crowd. The main Lost

Jackals contingent in Ridgecrest would naturally congregate on the main drag. But Draper's select crew—which, by this point, was likely a rogue operation—would be tucked away, strategically placed.

Without hesitation, Bloom turned, her pace quickening, the chaos of the motorcycle parade growing dimmer with every step.

As she drew closer, she noticed the unmistakable signs of age on the building. Its facade was a muted palette of decay— bricks eroded by time, graffiti shouting multicolored protests, and metal supports rusted to a deep, cancerous brown. Several windows had succumbed to age and vandalism, the shards scattered haphazardly around its perimeter. The entrance—a large set of double doors—stood ajar, one side torn from its hinges, revealing only darkness within.

The entrance of the decrepit warehouse loomed before Bloom, but her path was quickly obstructed. A few Jackals, their light blue bandanas marking their allegiance, loped forward out of the shadows. Pure swagger and confidence. Mocking sneers. The leader, a large man with a beard that reached his chest, leaned in, smirking

"Lookin' for something, sweetheart?"

"Some*one*," Bloom said. "Mitch Lockwood."

A chorus of laughter erupted from the group. The leader's smirk widened into a full-blown grin.

"And what's a pretty thing like you want with our guest of honor?"

But their amusement was fleeting.

Bloom sprang into action. Her arm lashed out in a blur of motion, delivering an elbow to the ribs of one assailant. He crumpled as another attempted to flank her. She spun on her heel, sending the second man staggering backward with a powerful kick.

As she took down one Jackal after another, more emerged from the shadows—a wave of black leather and light blue bandanas.

Bloom shifted her body weight to the side and narrowly dodged a punch. She brought her leg up, swept the next man off balance, then spun around to deliver a powerful kick that sent the short one in mirrored glasses flying. He hit the ground with a thud.

Bloom's SIG-Sauer remained holstered throughout the tense confrontation, though she was tempted to draw it. But she hadn't wanted to escalate the conflict. Not yet, anyway. And the men had come at her fast.

And then, as quickly as it started, it was over. The once-threatening group of Jackals lay incapacitated around her, their breaths ragged and uneven. The entrance to the warehouse beckoned, its darkness promising answers and, inevitably, more danger.

Bloom took a moment, her chest heaving, adrenaline still coursing through her body, head to toe. Then, finally, she unholstered her gun. It was time to find Mitch Lockwood and end this.

And that was one damn dark doorway in front of her.

She needed firepower.

One step forward, then another wave of Lost Jackals materialized, coming from the pitch-black entrance she was approaching. Unlike their fallen comrades, this group moved with a purpose, an oddly precise synchronization in their steps. Wafting with their approach were the scents of pot and crack and God-knows-what.

They circled her.

Bloom swung the SIG left, right.

The men were unfazed.

Snickering.

These were men unafraid of death on a normal day, but now, at the culmination of this year's Raven's Ride, they were amped out of their minds on an illicit cocktail.

No fear.

They closed in.

CHAPTER THIRTY-SIX

Airspace over Ventura County, California

SILENCE SHIFTED his weight in the plush leather chair of a luxurious private jet.

Nice.

Amidst the pressures of his challenging missions, the Watchers provided Silence with occasional indulgences like this, small respites to ease the tension. And Silence took advantage of every moment.

The setting sun illuminated the cabin with a soft orange light filtering through the windows. At the same time, the quiet hum of the aircraft's engines was barely perceptible. Silence turned his gaze and watched as a blanket of clouds rolled past.

The Watchers had nearly unlimited resources and often sent him literally jet-setting across the nation in private planes like this, but since Silence's work needed to be as low-profile as possible, he did more driving than flying. For now, he would savor the sky.

But only in a detached manner.

Because there was the mission.

On the sleek mahogany table before him was a collection of materials. Some were promotional, others computer-printed, many featuring the logo he recognized from the Ridgecrest hotel construction site: Kaveny International Hotels & Resorts. He reached out, fingers brushing over the glossy brochures, and delved into the intricate web of information about the forthcoming grand opening of the Elysian Resort. The grandeur of the place, as depicted in the pictures, promised an oasis of luxury on par with Silence's current surroundings.

In kind, Silence had prepped for the grand opening by cleaning himself up and changing into a suit. Perry Ellis. Charcoal. Subtle pin-striping. Black shirt. Black tie with offset diagonal stripes.

Silence's brow furrowed as he considered the intel of Ethan Draper's previous terrorist attacks. Both of them had aimed at rattling the cage of consumerism, at jolting the world out of its materialistic stupor. And now, the Elysian opening was the next potential target.

But aside from being a party-crasher, what could Draper possibly want with a yet-to-be-launched resort? There would be no guests to terrorize, no day-to-day operations to disrupt. Silence's eyes darted across the papers, searching for clues, for patterns, something that would hint at Draper's endgame.

Brushing aside the promotional materials, he turned to the printed intel from the Specialists' databases. He dragged a sheet closer, his eyes landing on a neatly typed list: *Elysian Resort Grand Opening - Distinguished Guests*.

Silence's finger traced the names, recognizing many immediately. Some were Hollywood celebrities, their faces often splashed across screens and magazines. Others were tycoons, people who exercised vast influence from behind the doors of their corporate boardrooms. However, what caught Silence's eye next gave him pause. Under the *Politicians* column was a trio of state governors—California, Arizona, and Nevada.

There, at the list's end, was a name that gave Silence a start: Governor Alexander Durand of Nevada.

Rapidly, Silence sifted through the plethora of materials before him, searching for something specific he'd noticed earlier. His fingers found it—a series of news articles and clippings detailing Kaveny International's recent and rather controversial forays. The consortium had been aggressively acquiring regional, privately owned hotels in the Southwest, a move that had not gone down well with the public. The sentiment was clear in the printed words and the photos of protests; many saw it as a hostile takeover, a destruction of local heritage and culture for corporate gain.

Yet, among the sea of dissent was a singular voice of support—Governor Alexander Durand. Where others saw corporate greed, Durand had publicly lauded Kaveny International for their moves, painting a picture of future prosperity and growth for the region, particularly his state, particularly Las Vegas.

Durand had also been on the national news a lot lately for grander, more significant reasons...

Silence's mind raced. Until now, he had been unsure what Draper might have planned for the Elysian grand opening. The only material Silence knew Draper had acquired from Adrian Hirsch—as a payoff for the Boston contractors' murders—was a counterfeited document of some sort. It dawned on Silence that the document must be an entry pass to the resort opening. Draper was aiming to position himself close to the Nevada governor.

Draper's actions were never random; they always bore deeper intent. Each terrorist attack was a calculated move in a broader strategy. With Governor Durand's evident ties to Kaveny International and his anticipated presence at the

Elysian Resort's grand opening, Silence felt he was beginning to see the larger picture.

He gathered the materials, squared them up with a few thumps on the table, then leaned back into his seat just as he felt the plane descend.

———

The jet's engines whirred down to a soft purr as Silence descended the stairs and onto the tarmac. He paused for a moment, the sudden shift in the atmosphere tangible. The coastal air of Santa Barbara was refreshing—a blend of salt and freshness that contrasted sharply with the arid heat of the Mojave Desert he'd been immersed in for two days. He took a deep breath, savoring the shift, the change it brought to his senses.

A gleaming Lexus was parked a few yards away, idling, its polished surface reflecting the waning light. Silence approached and slipped inside.

The cool embrace of the car's air conditioning was immediate, and the plush driver's seat cradled him in luxury, much like the jet's seating just had. There were the smells of leather and brand-new plastic. Every detail in the Lexus, from the gentle hum of its engine to the delicate fragrance that permeated the interior, spoke of opulence—a stark contrast to the rugged interior of the Wrangler Silence had driven through the desert.

For a fleeting moment, the comfort reminded him of his own BMW back in Pensacola. This quickly brought an image to mind.

Tanner.

As if to bring his train of thought to an immediate, authoritative stop, Falcon's words came to him: *No involvement in local matters.*

But it was too late.

Silence felt a deep pang of guilt. So consumed with his present mission, he'd temporarily overlooked the pressing matters in Pensacola. The shadow of Liam Rourke's Labyrinth loomed large, and the thought of Tanner—and Tanner's nephew, Ben—being in potential danger weighed on him. He yearned to be back in Pensacola—*needed* to be there—to protect, to resolve...

...to destroy Liam Rourke.

But urgency of the present tugged at Silence. The mystery of Draper, the unfolding plot at the Elysian Resort, and the new lead about Governor Durand—it was all intertwined in a web that he needed to unravel. He couldn't afford distractions.

There was the mission.

Silence took hold of the steering wheel, the cool leather grounding him. He needed to compartmentalize, to prioritize. Taking a deep breath—from the stomach, a diaphragmatic breath, one of C.C.'s techniques—he pushed the thoughts of Pensacola to the back of his mind. Now was not the time. He put the Lexus into gear and started east for the Elysian Resort.

His focus had to remain unwavering. For now, the mission was all that mattered.

All the same, the gentle motion of the ride, dampened by the Lexus's perfectly tuned suspension, lulled Silence's mind back to Pensacola as he drove.

He needed to finish the memory he'd been working on for days.

———

Tanner eased forward, the springs in his old chair squealing as he crossed his arms on his desktop, now much closer to Jake.

"*What you don't understand about Martinelli, Jake, is that another cop dug deeper into the guy's finances. And you won't believe what he found.*"

Tanner paused, letting the weight of anticipation hang for a moment.

"*Martinelli didn't have a hand in those financial discrepancies,*" *he continued and pointed to the open folder on Jake's lap—all those materials Jake had thought were so conclusive, so damning.* "*Martinelli's name is listed where it should be in those forms. His signature, too. But signatures can be forged. That shit's the handiwork of a bitter ex-employee trying to tarnish Martinelli's reputation.*"

Jake's pulse raced, the walls seeming to close in. All this time, he'd pigeonholed Martinelli into a villain's role. But now, he saw the truth: Martinelli was every bit the man his reputation painted him to be—a businessman who bettered the city with his successes.

A man who, Jake now knew, had been double-crossed by someone he trusted.

Tanner leaned back in his chair, observing Jake's changing expressions. "*People are a mix, Jake. Light and dark. Good and bad. It's not always clear-cut, and sometimes, it's our job to look beyond the surface.*"

Jake opened his mouth...

But for once, he was speechless.

———

The memory slipped away, replaced by the orange-hued sky ahead. Black silhouettes of lofty palm trees swayed along the boulevard. The Lexus hummed beneath Silence while his mind juggled Tanner's advice, the weight of his mission, and the lessons from his past.

The Lexus barreled on toward the Elysian Resort.

CHAPTER THIRTY-SEVEN

Ridgecrest, California

THE METAL FOLDING chair was getting too damn familiar.

Mitch shivered as the cold metal rods continued to press into his clammy skin. Dim light from the fading sunset filtered through a broken, grimy window. The room's rusted steel columns and mounds of aged paper hinted at long neglect. Broken furniture pieces lay scattered. Judging by the remnants, he was in an old office or storage room. Gaps and marks on the far wall showed where a door had been, now just an empty frame. The room's sense of abandonment was unmistakable.

His head throbbed, the memories still disjointed. They'd taken him out of the blistering shed. There had been a blindfold against his eyes. Whispered conversations just beyond his earshot. Then he'd been in a van again. Highway travel. Out of the van. Carried by multiple men up a set of metal stairs. Dropped hard on a concrete floor. And then his blindfold had been removed, and he was in this rotten room.

Since then, he'd heard laughter from outside, rowdy and

unabashed. But among the human cacophony, there was another sound—the unmistakable rumble of motorcycle engines. *Lots of them.*

Naturally, this noise brought a realization: he was at Ridgecrest, somewhere in the vicinity of the Raven's Ride motorcycle rally's final night celebration.

Some of the voices were nearer, more discernible. They were close. In the subdued light, Mitch believed he discerned a metal mezzanine beyond the doorway. Past that structure, a vast, shadowy expanse loomed with metal beams stretching overhead. This supported his theory that the building was some sort of bygone industrial warehouse, and he was in the remains of a second-floor office.

From the nearby laughter, he identified familiar voices— those of the men who had abducted him in Death Valley, dragged him across the desert, beaten him, and then moved him to this place. For a long while, he had believed they were shadow operatives, federal agents pursuing Unseen Path.

But his mistake was now glaringly apparent.

The bikers below, their jovial banter and the undercurrent of threat, had nothing to do with the covert world of the powers-that-be. This wasn't some elaborate ruse, a carefully orchestrated ploy to draw Mitch in. The men were genuine, hardened bikers, and the sinking feeling in his gut told him they were the infamous Lost Jackals. He remembered passing glances at their emblems in various dive bars, the whispered tales of their ruthlessness. But, in his paranoia, he had thought them something else entirely.

And speaking of miscalculations...

Mitch's gaze slid over to the other man in the room. Sitting against the far wall, the dim light cast the figure in a gauzy shadow. But even in the murkiness, one thing stood out distinctly—a leather wristband adorned with ornate engravings. It was the man from the shed. The man who had prof-

fered Mitch's beating at the behest of the man with the
German accent.

That ruthless, cold son of a bitch.

Their eyes met, and a smattering of unsaid words from
the past confrontation lingered in that protracted moment.
But even as the tension brewed, Mitch's thoughts were irre-
sistibly pulled to another face.

A softer one.

Framed by dark locks.

Carmen.

He could almost hear her voice, see the furrowed brows of
her kindhearted consternation, those lovingly anxious eyes.
The thought that she might be out there, worried sick,
possibly in danger herself because of Mitch's impulsiveness,
was devastating. He had promised her, time and again, that
he would be careful.

Yet here he was, captured in a derelict warehouse, at the
mercy of a biker gang and a lunatic who'd already beaten him
within an inch of his life once.

The sheer magnitude of his recklessness came crashing
down on him. The room—with its cracked window and bare
doorframe—felt stifling, the air laden with past mistakes and
regrets. He thought about all the times he'd jumped to
conclusions, acted on instinct rather than reason.

Unseen Path wasn't just about him; it never was. Mitch's
actions had consequences that reached far beyond his own
life, rippling into the lives of those he loved. Carmen, who
had always stood by his side, didn't deserve the fallout of his
recklessness.

A silent promise formed. If Mitch could navigate his way
out of this, things would change. No more hasty decisions
based on irrational fear. No more letting paranoia dictate his
steps.

A sudden surge of noise broke his focus. What had been

laughter from below quickly turned to alarmed shouts. The clangs and scuffles that followed indicated a disturbance. Mitch tensed, his attention now sharply focused on the unseen situation downstairs.

Across the room, the man with the wristband reacted with equal alarm. He sprang to his feet, his earlier calm shattered, and raced to the open doorway. The dim light silhouetted him against the mezzanine. He peered out.

From where he sat, Mitch noticed the man's stance shift. Surprise gave way to comprehension, followed by wariness. As the man's realization became evident, tension filled the room.

The man turned back and faced Mitch so suddenly that it made Mitch jump, the ropes digging into his wrists and ankles.

"You have a visitor, Mr. Lockwood," the man said through a dark grin.

CHAPTER THIRTY-EIGHT

WESTLIN STEPPED through the doorway and took hold of the mezzanine's pockmarked railing. The vast, dilapidated interior of the warehouse stretched out below, barely visible in the shafts of the setting sun streaming through the shattered windows. A stark scene cut through the gloom as his eyes adjusted to the dim light.

Below, Draper's Jackals, the squad of brutes with leather jackets and inked skin, freshly under Westlin's command, had formed a predatory ring. A tall, athletic woman in jeans and a T-shirt stood at its center, like prey encircled by wolves. She was disheveled and soiled from what must have been a hell of a day.

Westlin knew who it must be: the mysterious woman who'd traversed the Raven's Ride area of the Mojave Desert for days, asking questions, prodding the right people and the wrong ones. The person who'd tried to unsettle everything.

And here was Westlin with the authorization to kill...

Oh, how sweet it was.

Taking a deep breath, Westlin bellowed, "Stop!"

The word reverberated, a thunderclap that sliced through

the tense air. The bikers, taken aback, paused in their threatening advance, glancing around as if expecting some unseen force to manifest. But all they found was Westlin's steely gaze pinning them from above.

"Looking for Mitch Lockwood, yes?" Westlin called out to the woman.

Her silhouette straightened, a glint of recognition—or perhaps hope—flashing across her features.

"Yes," came her reply. Her voice was as firm and clear as her response was simple.

Westlin nodded.

"He's up here." In a more commanding tone for the Jackals, he ordered, "Let her pass."

The bikers exchanged fleeting glances. They were surely confused by their newfound lieutenant's forceful authority. But in the face of Westlin's unquestionable dominance, their pride faltered, and they opened a pathway toward the interior.

The woman didn't hesitate, just pushed right past. Her boots crunched on the waste-strewn floor, each step echoing through the cavernous space. After a few paces, she looked up, locking eyes with Westlin across the distance. No fear. No regret.

Westlin's respect for her tenacity grew as she pressed farther into the warehouse. She appeared every bit as resilient as the rumors suggested. And while an impending showdown between them loomed, there was an unspoken appreciation of their respective strengths for now.

From his elevated perch, Westlin's gaze followed the woman's steady progress, her silhouette gradually growing as she approached the stairs. Draper's words echoed in his mind.

The freedom to kill.

It had been years since Westlin had indulged in such brutal spontaneity. Under Hirsch's employ, the missions had been purposefully non-lethal, no matter how depraved the torture. The raw, visceral thrill of the hunt had been subdued, replaced with methodical efficiency.

But Draper...

This wild card offered a return to Westlin's old ways, to the pure adrenaline of life and death played out in real-time. And as he watched the woman's unwavering approach, Westlin realized she might just be the catalyst for that long-suppressed hunger.

The metallic cadence of footsteps on steel drew him back to the present. He watched as the woman climbed the last few steps, her determined gaze never leaving his. She stepped onto the mezzanine, the ambient light casting her features into sharp relief. She stopped a yard from him.

"Where's Lockwood?" she said, her voice steady.

Westlin's lips curled into a sardonic smirk.

"You've found him."

He gestured at the doorway behind them. The woman flicked her eyes in that direction and quickly returned her attention to Westlin.

A moment passed.

Then a storm broke.

Westlin lunged first, his arm slicing through the air, aiming for the woman's throat. But she was fast, ducking and pivoting in one fluid motion, her leg sweeping out to knock him off balance. He sidestepped just in time, the wind generated by her kick brushing past him.

Their bodies became a whirlwind of motion. Each strike was met with a counter, each move anticipated and parried. The woman's elbow arched towards his face, but Westlin caught her by the wrist and twisted sharply.

The woman gasped but maintained her footing, retaliating by driving her knee upwards. Westlin released her, narrowly avoiding the knee. But she was already on him, her fingers aiming for pressure points.

The warehouse echoed with the sounds of their confrontation: the thud of flesh on flesh, the sharp intake of breath, the scuffle of boots on the metal platform. It must have been abundantly clear to the Jackal observers below: these were not mere fighters. They were elite, each honed to perfection by countless hours of training and real-world experience.

At one point, Westlin managed to pin the woman against the rusty steel railing, smashing his forearm against her windpipe. But she wriggled free, using her lower center of gravity to flip him over her shoulder. He rolled and was back on his feet instantly, only to find the woman advancing, her eyes cold, calculating.

Their duel raged. Fists and feints. Grit and determination. Westlin could now confirm that the woman's training was as formidable as the rumors had said. He grunted as her elbow found his ribcage. At this moment, her foot went behind his ankle to bring him down.

Whack!

He was on his back on the platform. The entire mezzanine shook and groaned. Immediately, the woman was atop him, her eyes reflecting triumph as she hooked his jaw beneath the crook of her elbow and clamped down with machine strength.

The edges of Westlin's vision blurred straight away, and his thoughts swerved to his father. To the lessons of patience, of waiting for the right moment. Early lessons. Before Westlin had rejected the man.

The memories came in snippets: the icy glint in his father's eyes, hours in the shop, the awe Westlin had felt at the ingenious ways his father concealed weapons in the most unexpected places.

Wallets.

Canes.

Belts.

Briefcases.

Hats.

...a leather wristband.

The woman's weight shifted, giving Westlin just the fraction of a second he needed. His fingers darted to his wrist, tugging at the black stitching on the edge of his wristband. To an outsider, it might've seemed like a desperate, futile gesture, but as the threads began to unravel, they revealed something far more lethal.

The high-tensile-strength cord—thin yet incredibly strong—came free from the strategically planted grooves between the stitches.

Pop, pop, pop, pop.

For the first time in over two decades, since it was embedded in a leather strap when Westlin was just a child, his garrote was exposed to the outside world.

And with a speed that belied his temporary vulnerability, Westlin whipped it forward, looping the cord around the woman's neck.

CHAPTER THIRTY-NINE

THE WIRE CUT into Bloom's throat. Her breaths became shallow and labored.

As her vision blurred with darkness creeping in, the stark reality of having let down her father and Saeed—and failing to right those wrongs—consumed her. She remembered her father's depressed existence, how she hadn't been able to save him from a premature death. She thought of Saeed, his wife, their toddler. They'd lived. But they could have just as easily died because of Bloom's negligence. Murdered. At the hands of the terrorist cell. The young girl murdered. Throat slashed.

It could have happened.

Could have...

...happened...

While the cold metal of the mezzanine's grated flooring pressed into her back, she felt like she was about to add one more name to the list of people she failed: *Leah Bloom*.

Another letdown.

But just as despair took hold, a flicker of resistance sparked within. Memories of rigorous training flooded back, along with moments of laughter shared with now-absent teammates. She felt a sense of urgency as she recalled the purpose of the mission.

The FBI's mission and that of the CIA.

The mission.

Her mission.

Her self-imposed mission to Death Valley to unravel the truth behind the bus tragedy murders and find a resolution for Boston—the catastrophe that took her father.

Bloom was back.

With one hand clutching at the cord digging into her throat, Bloom's other hand reached back, brushing against Westlin in a desperate attempt to find leverage. Her fingers closed around his belt. Using it, she pulled with unexpected force, thrusting her elbow into the man's torso. The blow elicited a gasp, briefly loosening the garrote's pressure.

Bloom made her move. She spun around, a swiftness in her maneuver that was just enough to catch Westlin off guard. Her leg swept out and hooked itself behind his calf.

But she wasn't done.

Using the momentum, she spun him, wrenching his arm backward in a direction nature never intended. A sickening pop of joints met her ears just before Westlin howled.

The man righted himself, momentarily held his bearings, then stumbled backward. Bloom knew better than to give a man like this even a moment to recover.

She advanced. Her foot shot out, connecting with Westlin's knee, bringing him halfway down onto the metal flooring. She was there as he tried to rise, delivering a right hook that reeled his head back.

She had him now. In one fluid motion, she secured her arm around his neck, getting her leverage and positioning perfect.

And she twisted.

Crack.

Westlin fell limp.

She allowed him to slip through her grasp and gather into an awkward mound on the grating.

Bloom, too, collapsed—onto her ass, wrapping her legs with her arms and letting her head drop to her knees.

As her breathing steadied, her fingers gently touched the inflamed skin of her neck. She winced. An immediate burning sensation pulsed from her fingertips.

With a groan, she used the metal railing to pull herself to her feet. Upright, her gaze settled on Westlin's lifeless form. The garrote, that innocuous-looking string, lay beside him, the weapon's simplicity mocking her. She shook off thoughts of her near demise. There was no time for reflection; she had a mission to complete.

Gathering her resolve, Bloom limped onward, every step echoing in the vast warehouse. She looked over the edge of the mezzanine. The Jackals were gone.

As she rounded the corner, a dimly lit room revealed itself. Within those shadows, she saw him—a figure tied to a metal folding chair, his face obscured, but his posture one of defeat and weariness.

As she neared, the man's features became more apparent. Middle-aged. Paunchy. Graying hair and a three-day beard. The bruised and battered face looking up at her was familiar from photographs she'd seen.

Their eyes met.

She tried to speak. Stopped. Grimaced at the pain—which made her think of Kai—and tried again.

"Mitch Lockwood?" she said.

The man's eyes blinked slowly. The response came out on a tired exhale. "That's me."

Bloom limped closer.

"My name's Leah Bloom," she said. "I'm a friend of your wife's."

Mitch's eyes opened a bit more, the pain and weariness softening. His chapped lips lifted into a smile before parting slightly as if to ask a question. But Bloom cut him off.

"I'll warn you now," Bloom added with a sardonic tilt to her voice. "Carmen's pretty pissed at you."

CHAPTER FORTY

Santa Barbara, California

DRAPER STEPPED out of the black limousine, feeling the cool ocean breeze of Santa Barbara tug at his tailored suit. As the vehicle pulled away, the grand edifice of the Elysian Resort loomed before him—a cathedral to capitalism, each spire crafted in ostentation, each balcony dripping with self-indulgence.

He glanced down at what he cradled in his left hand: an immaculately forged, gilt-edged invitation and a set of credentials detailed to perfection. Adrian Hirsch had truly outdone himself. The glossy photograph, the embossed seal, and the meticulous print suggested Draper was a Portuguese dignitary, a puppet on the world stage of politics and wealth, just like everyone else at the gathering.

Security personnel, bulging in tailored suits that strained to contain the muscles underneath, scrutinized his credentials. Their eyes darted between his face and the forged documents, finally resting on the seal that pronounced him a V.I.P. guest.

The lengths to which Draper had gone to obtain that piece of paper were considerable. He'd organized his band of Lost Jackals, tied up loose ends, and even eliminated two inconvenient individuals who'd crossed Adrian Hirsch's path back in the 1980s—all for the privilege of joining this celebration of greed.

One guard inspected the invitation intently while another motioned for Draper to present the syringe. Draper held it aloft and observed the guard's scrutiny of the clear liquid and the attached label confirming it as insulin. The guard nodded approval, consistent with the story of his cover's diabetic condition.

As this played out, a third guard swept Draper with a metal-detecting wand. When the device beeped over his belt buckle, a smirk tugged at Draper's lips.

"Welcome, *Senhor*," one of the guards said, butchering the pronunciation in his attempt at beef-headed diplomacy as he returned the invitation and waved him past. "Enjoy your evening."

Draper's lips stretched into a smile—artificial but indistinguishable from the real McCoy.

"*Obrigado*," he replied, slipping into the Portuguese persona as easily as he'd slipped into his tailored suit. He crossed the threshold into the grand hall that lay just beyond.

The sacrifices had been worth it, he reminded himself. All the death, all the ethical contortions—they'd led him here to the heart of the monstrosity, the belly of the beast. He was inside, within striking distance of his goal.

The governor of Nevada stood somewhere within these walls, blissfully unaware that he was a guest of honor at his own funeral.

The governor wasn't an official presidential candidate— not yet. But the world had its hunches, and Draper had his intel. Regardless, until he was an official candidate, the man would be without the Secret Service detail that would make an assassination attempt problematic.

Tonight, the man was vulnerable.

And Draper wouldn't waste the opportunity.

As Draper moved deeper into the grand hall, his eyes roved over a landscape of opulence that seemed almost vulgar in its intensity. Gold fixtures gleamed from the walls like the rings on a drug lord's fingers. Decadent chandeliers dangled from the ceilings, each crystal painstakingly chosen to refract light into a kaleidoscope of splendor. Servers glided through the throng, wearing bow ties and cultivated smiles, offering flutes of champagne on silver trays.

While Draper's face remained composed, he inwardly recoiled at the thought of the countless opportunities each dollar represented: meals for starving children, vaccines, educational materials. Instead, those resources were here, poured into this palace of excess.

Just then, the CEO of Kaveny International Hotels & Resorts mounted the stage with a microphone in his manicured hands. Draped in a tux that echoed the price of a year's wage for many, his ample physique and pronounced double chin were unmissable.

"Ladies and Gentlemen," he cooed. "If you would kindly raise your glasses."

As if choreographed, a sea of designer gowns and custom tuxedos turned toward the stage, their hands lifting crystal flutes in a silent toast to their own magnificence.

What a spectacle. A grand facade. These people donned their philanthropy as one would cheap costume jewelry, parading it even as they exploited the world. Hidden beneath opulent attire, they were just predators luxuriating in their golden confines.

Draper scanned the crowd, locking onto his prey—the Nevada governor, Alexander Durand, who stood near the stage in animated conversation with what appeared to be a Silicon Valley tech mogul.

Unprotected. Deliciously vulnerable.

Breaking away from his stationary position, Draper sauntered past a long table filled with an exotic smorgasbord. Sushi flown in from the coastal waters of Japan, black truffles unearthed from the wooded areas of France, caviar that had once called the Caspian Sea home—all of it displayed like artifacts in a museum of excess.

Millions starving, and they feasted like emperors of old. Nero, every one of them, fiddling while the world burns.

He continued past a clutch of A-list actors huddled near an original Warhol painting. Draper drew closer to the governor, now separated from the man only by a tech mogul engaged in a one-on-one with a well-known television anchor.

Draper's fingers subtly brushed the interior pocket of his jacket, reassuring himself that the syringe was still there— filled with a solution that would send the would-be president on a very final journey.

Navigating the crowd, Draper inched ever closer to the governor.

Closer.

A few yards away.

At this proximity, the minute details emerged. The slight creases at the edges of the man's eyes betrayed countless hours in strategy meetings. The hint of gray at his temples suggested his life was one not just of privilege but of pressure. Potent cologne touched Draper's nostrils, a rich blend that hinted at aged cedarwood and subtle spices, both commanding and indulgent.

Less than an arm's length away.

But just as Draper tightened his grip on the syringe concealed in his jacket, a hand wrapped around his shoulder...

..and yanked him sideways.

CHAPTER FORTY-ONE

IN ONE FLUID MOTION, Silence had Draper by the collar, yanking him through the door and into a service hallway. Freshly painted walls. Bright fluorescent lights overhead. Polished concrete floor, gleaming. The sterile ambiance of a new establishment.

Draper was remarkably plain, almost forgettable. Average height and weak build. Dark complexion. Dark hair. However, something in the depths of his unnaturally large eyes seemed to absorb more than they reflected, giving him an unsettling presence.

With a smug grin, Draper reached down to his belt buckle, fingers deftly working to release something.

Whoosh!

Silence jumped back, releasing his grip on Draper, just in time to miss the blade that came within inches of his face.

It was a thin, lethal-looking push knife. The blade glinted menacingly in the bright lighting.

Draper grinned, a wicked sparkle in his eyes.

"My new assistant, Luca Westlin—his father was an artist at concealing blades, bypassing even the tightest security, even metal-detectors. *Especially* metal-detectors. I needed a backup weapon for tonight, and Luca gifted me one of his father's finest works—a shiny ol' belt buckle."

Silence's trained eyes locked onto the blade, recalibrating his approach. This was no longer a straightforward hand-to-hand situation. Push knives were a close-combat weapon with a T-shaped handle, designed to be held securely within a closed fist, nestled between a pair of fingers with the blade protruding outward from the front of the hand.

Holding the knife higher, Draper's eyes burned with malevolence.

"This was supposed to be for Governor Durand," Draper said, "just in case my little syringe trick didn't pan out. But, you know, plans change." His voice lowered, edged with menace. "Now, I think it's got your name on it."

As if acting on some internal countdown, Draper suddenly unleashed a scream—animalistic, raw, full of rage. He lunged, knife leading. The move was wild, uncalculated, driven more by emotion than strategy.

It was also unexpected.

Silence had faced numerous adversaries over the years, but there was something uniquely disconcerting about Draper. Ordinarily, a man of Draper's disposition wouldn't register as a threat to a trained assassin like Silence. But the feral intensity in Draper's eyes, his borderline unhinged rage —it added a variable that Silence hadn't accounted for. Those wild, unpredictable qualities went a long way in evening out the advantage an elite operator held.

It became clear that, in this battle, strategy and skill would be matched against raw, unbridled emotion.

Immediately, Silence tapped into one of C.C.'s techniques. Time slowed. Every sense sharpened. He felt each bead of sweat on his brow. The HVAC's whistle dimmed. Distant sounds hushed. Only the hallway mattered. And the knife-wielding madman closing in.

Silence dodged to the side, but not swiftly enough. The knife sliced cleanly through the sleeve of his suit jacket. Wickedly sharp—unsurprising, given it was the work of a master weaponsmith. In response, Silence aimed a punch at Draper, but the man, driven by his frenzied mindset, danced with a flurry of unpredictable moves.

With another wild swing of Draper's knife, Silence was forced backward, smacking into a metal door behind him. The impact with the door swung it open, and suddenly Silence and Draper were stumbling into an entirely different environment.

The vast expanse of a commercial kitchen.

A cacophony of surprise and alarm erupted as the kitchen staff caught sight of the unexpected intruders. Dressed in impeccable white uniforms, the fabric crisp and unwrinkled, each bore the embroidered logo of the Elysian Resort in ornate gold. Almost as one, they fled, scattering like startled birds at the clear threat of violence in Draper's deranged stance and feral screams.

Silence found his balance, the scrape of his boots echoing briefly. Swiftly scanning the environment, he sought tools or obstacles. He'd been trained to make an ally of his surroundings.

The vast kitchen spread out like a gleaming arena of stainless steel. Massive refrigerators stood sentinel, while overhead, an array of pots and pans hung ready for battle. The gentle hum of ovens; the distant sizzle of a fryer; the bubbling of a rapidly boiling pot. At the heart of the space, a central island was adorned with an array of gleaming utensils.

Feeling the weight of his Beretta against his side in its shoulder holster, every instinct urged Silence to draw the weapon and end the threat. He had the shot. He had the space, all the space in the world.

But the retreating forms of the kitchen staff, innocent bystanders, denied the option. A stray bullet in this environment was too great a risk. Close-quarters combat was the only option.

As if sensing Silence's decision, Draper came charging once more, the knife blade catching the light in spasmodic flashes. More screaming, erratic bursts of it.

Moving swiftly, Silence's hand snapped out to grab the nearest useful object—a steel ladle. It was no knife, but it added both weight and reach to his defense.

Quickly pivoting, Silence used the ladle's bowl to deflect and parry Draper's slashing attacks, while its long handle allowed him to jab and keep Draper at a distance.

Clang! Clang!

Draper lunged, swiped, and slashed with a fury that seemed inexhaustible. But Silence countered, dodged, and retaliated with the honed skills of a man who had faced countless adversaries. The steel ladle clashed against the knife, the sound ringing through the kitchen.

Suddenly, Draper grabbed an improvised weapon, too. A cleaver, dislodged from a nearby counter in the chaos, went airborne. Silence dodged in time, the tool embedding itself with a solid thud into a wooden cutting board.

They continued their frenzied dance, maneuvering through the expansive kitchen. Tables, laden with preparations for the night's event, became temporary barriers. Hanging pots became swinging obstacles, hindering both in their pursuit of dominance.

Close to a tray laden with assorted knives, Silence delivered a forceful kick, unleashing a cascade of steel. The blades clattered, scattering across the floor directly in Draper's path.

Unfazed, Draper, with an agility that belied his rage, leapt atop a counter, momentarily gaining the higher ground. His eyes glinted with mania, the push knife's edge glinting in kind.

Silence's eyes, ever searching, landed on a cast-iron skillet. Grasping it with both hands, he used it as an impromptu club, catching Draper across the jaw with a wet thunk that sent him falling off the counter.

More scanning. To Silence's left, an unnoticed pot of water bubbled feverishly on a range, steam rising steadily.

Draper's next lunge was marked with an overzealous confidence, thinking he had finally gained the upper hand. This was the split second Silence had been waiting for.

With reflexes honed by years in the field, Silence seized the pot by its handle, swinging it wide and dousing Draper with the scalding contents. A mist of steam enveloped them as a shrill scream of pain punctured the atmosphere.

Draper's fingers, now red and blistering, involuntarily released their grip on the push knife, which skittered across the floor and came to rest near the ominous gurgle of a deep fryer.

In a surge of raw determination, Silence lunged forward. A fierce side kick to Draper's gut sent the man sprawling onto a counter, momentarily winded.

Conveniently, the kitchen staff was entirely gone now.

They wouldn't see what was about to happen.

Or hear it.

...or smell it.

Silence advanced, his fingers gripping Draper's hair tightly. With a forceful shove, he pushed Draper's face toward the boiling oil of the deep fryer.

The sudden sizzle was piercing, a gruesome duet of boiling liquid and searing flesh.

The scream was just as sudden, but it didn't last nearly as long. Only a fraction of a second. Draper didn't suffer.

The acrid stench quickly overpowered the once familiar aromas of the kitchen. After what felt like an eternity but was only seconds, Silence let go, taking a step back.

Draper dropped out of the fryer, slapping in a sizzling puddle on the floor.

Silence took a few deep breaths, recoiling at the stench. One last look at the remains of Draper's face, and he left.

CHAPTER FORTY-TWO

Los Angeles, California

AN HOUR LATER.

Hirsch sat in a luxurious leather seat inside the rented yacht, looking through the broad window at a Los Angeles harbor. Surrounding him was the pinnacle of extravagance, the type of opulence that even royalty would envy. He observed the harbor's waters as they captured glints of gold from the distant city lights. Beyond the yacht's polished wooden floors and the sparkle of elegant chandeliers reflected in the glass, L.A. spread out infinitely, pulsating with life.

Conventional wisdom and Ethan Draper had advised that Hirsch remain in the United States a little longer, waiting for the uproar over the bus incident to subside. But Hirsch's patience had worn thin, and he sure as hell wasn't going to take Draper's advice any longer. An awakening sense of purpose had surged within Hirsch after his momentary relapse. He felt like himself again. He felt powerful. And he was ready to go home, back to Germany.

Raising the tumbler of aged scotch, he took a large sip.

The liquid smoldered its way down his throat. It should have brought comfort. Instead, it fueled his impatience.

Hirsch glanced at his Rolex.

Where the hell had Rudy disappeared to? Despite Hirsch having just met and hired the captain earlier that evening, Rudy had struck him as a trustworthy and competent individual. His absence was unsettling.

"Rudy?" he called out toward the wheelhouse.

He waited and cocked his head to listen. Nothing. Just the gentle lapping of water against the yacht and the distant hum of the city.

Then, a faint sound—soft footsteps from behind the wheelhouse wall. Movement on the other side of the glass, a flash of shadow. The door opened.

It wasn't Rudy who stepped out.

Instead, Hirsch was met with a figure who looked like he'd been carved from ice and shadows. Tall—unnervingly so —exuding an aura of cold professionalism. Dark clothing, dark hair, dark eyes. A living void.

Hirsch recognized him—the same man who had been paired with a tall woman, both of whom had been relentless in their investigation of the Death Valley events. The moonlight streaming from behind rendered the man almost spectral, casting a daunting silhouette that loomed larger than life. Even in the soft glow, the man's sharp eyes seemed to pierce through the night.

Hirsch's heartbeat quickened, but despite this internal maelstrom, he schooled his features into an expression of calculated calm.

The tall man's gaze remained unyielding, and without a word, he eased into the plush leather seat opposite Hirsch. They were an arm's length apart now. The yacht's chandelier overhead bathed the man in a pale light, the shadows deepening the lines of his face—all angles and corners.

The two men locked eyes. Seconds past, stretching unendingly thin. The quiet was oppressive, filled only by the distant sound of the harbor and the muffled hum of the city beyond.

Then, breaking the nothingness with a voice so ruinous it made Hirsch jump in his seat, the man said, "Talk."

Hirsch's mouth opened. For a long beat, he did nothing. Then he took a deep breath. The scent of the salty sea air was soothing, at least.

"You're some sort of U.S. governmental agent, *ja?*" he said. "You and the tall woman. Both of you."

Without pausing for confirmation, Hirsch continued.

"I'll admit it. I paid Draper to kill Scott MacLeod and Milton Shapiro. I did."

He leaned forward, locking eyes with the man across from him.

"You've probably heard the whispers about me—the infamous Adrian Hirsch no-kill policy. It's true. A pillar of my operations for decades. Call it a remnant of a Catholic childhood, an irritating bit of conscience. But..." Hirsch sighed. "Less than a week ago, MacLeod and Shapiro became the first and only exceptions."

As if on cue, memories of the Boston Legacy Center tragedy swelled to the forefront of Hirsch's mind.

"November 7, 1983," he murmured. "The Boston Legacy Center was a marvel. A symbol of the city. An architectural triumph."

He took a shaky breath.

"My sister, Margot, she was there. And her son, Jakob, my nephew. They were crushed under that damned canopy. Both of them taken from me in an instant. Until your female associate came along, no one tied me to Boston, because many years prior, Margot had changed their last name, hoping to escape the shadow of..." He paused. "Her criminal brother."

Gathering himself, Hirsch continued.

"MacLeod and Shapiro. They were the ones responsible for the Legacy Center build. It was their company. AeonScape Construction..." He spat out the name with disdain. "Under their supervision, that architectural monstrosity was erected. They cut corners, silenced concerns, all in the name of profit. My sister and nephew paid the price for their greed. So, yes, I wanted them dead. For more than a decade. Every night, Margot and Jakob's faces haunted my dreams. I had to do something, but I had to do it right. So I took my time. Planned it out for years. Waited."

He exhaled.

"And still, after all that time, all that planning, it was an emotional decision, a foolish action. And it's brought a windfall of consequences."

Hirsch looked back at the large man. He'd bared his soul; now it was time to see how the dice would fall.

There was something about this man, an aura of secrets and shadows, which struck a chord in Hirsch's mind, a sort of familiarity, like a link to the criminal underworld.

...the criminal underworld.

He reassessed, adjusting his earlier conclusion.

The man in front of him wasn't a government agent...

"You're one of them, aren't you?" Hirsch whispered.

He leaned in, narrowing his gaze, attempting to read the unreadable.

"A powerful man like me hears rumors. Whispers in the dark corners of the world. Of a group—deep within the bowels of the U.S. government. This organization has a cadre of assassins, but not the usual kind. Righteous murderers, they call you. Individuals who exact vengeance, who balance the scales. Assassins."

He placed his tumbler on the table between them, interlaced his fingers, and leaned even closer.

"Perhaps you're here to kill me because of the bus tragedy. But I think not, because I've also heard your organization is *very* careful with its kills. 'Three hundred percent certainty' is what I hear. And I suspect you also know the truth already—that I hired Draper only to kill MacLeod and Shapiro, that Draper took it on himself to kill the others, part of his vendetta against wealthy people, commercialism, and so forth. You're only here to verify that rumor, to make certain that I *didn't* want all of those elderly people killed."

He waited a long moment, and just when he thought the quiet man wouldn't respond, the man gave a curt nod.

Hirsch smiled.

"Rumor has it the organization's assassins are themselves former murderers, people who killed for just yet illegal reasons," he said, "pulled into this life to atone for their killings, serving some sort of penance."

He paused, letting the words sink in.

For the briefest of moments, Hirsch thought he saw something break in the man's gaze. A chink in the armor. A hint of vulnerability. But just as quickly, it was replaced by that cold, calculating stare of his.

Drawing a deep breath, Hirsch continued, the atmosphere around them growing ever thicker.

"You've killed before, haven't you? Not as an assassin, I mean. Before that. Driven by personal reasons." Another pause. "Much like myself one week ago."

The man remained still, his face a mask of stoicism. But Hirsch thought he detected a brief flash of something—recognition, perhaps, or shared pain—in those sharp eyes.

"You did. I can sense it."

Hirsch allowed himself a moment, casting his gaze to the dark waters outside, illuminated by city lights.

"You know, friend, I think..."

As he turned back around, the words died in his throat

The chair opposite him was empty.

The tall man had vanished.

As if he'd never been there.

CHAPTER FORTY-THREE

Ridgecrest, California

BENEATH THE RED neon letters spelling out *COFFEE*, Bloom walked in the parking lot alongside the Lockwoods. The light from the sign spilled onto the pavement, casting a rosy hue and reflecting softly off the cars parked below. Though the immediate vicinity was quiet, the distant thrum of Raven's Ride filled the night air—the roar of engines, sporadic whoops, and faint strains of music.

Bloom had her cellular phone to her ear, pacing as she spoke.

"I'm glad it's all been squared away, Kai, but after everything I did..." she trailed off. The unsaid thought hung in the air: her apprehension about her position with the CIA.

She reached the end of the sidewalk, pivoted, and glanced at the coffee shop. Inside, customers sipped their drinks and engaged in conversations—the kind of folks who preferred the coffee shop's tranquility over the raucous energy of the motorcycle rally.

"You think you're..." Kai said and swallowed. "Out of a job..." Another swallow. "At Langley after this?"

She sighed. "It's a possibility. No, a *probability*."

Kai grunted, a hint of amusement registering.

"Don't worry about it," he said.

Bloom frowned. "Kai, what did you do?"

There was a pause, just a beat longer than comfortable. "My organization..." Kai said and swallowed. "Has friends everywhere."

Bloom felt her eyebrows raise.

The depth of Kai's connections and the power of his organization became clear to her at that moment. The CIA was not easily overshadowed or influenced.

"Wait, you're telling me you went over the CIA's head?" she said and coughed on her words.

Another borderline laugh of a grunt from Kai. "Something like that."

Bloom let out a small, breathy chuckle. For a moment, exasperation duked it out with relief. She'd quickly grown accustomed to the mystique surrounding Kai and his organization, but it still surprised her occasionally.

"Thank you, Kai," she said, a smile tugging at the corners of her mouth. "For everything. It's been real."

"Sure has."

Beep.

He was gone. And she would never hear from him again. Of this, Bloom was sure. She was accustomed to people like him, situations like this.

After all, she was in the CIA.

She collapsed the phone and turned it over in her hand a few times, letting the conversation's weight settle in. After a moment of this, Bloom pocketed the device and slowly shifted her focus to the two figures illuminated by the coffee shop's ambient light.

Mitch Lockwood was drained, the shadows of recent events still lingering in his eyes. Bruises and cuts and scratches. But despite the ordeal, there was a newfound sense of gratitude in his gaze, directed at his wife, who held him by the arm.

Though she didn't have the same physical wounds as Mitch, Carmen still had visible signs of exhaustion—dark circles under her exhausted eyes, a firm set of her lips, and disheveled hair. The stress both Carmen and Mitch were feeling was evident in her posture; she held him close and yet was strong enough to stand on her own feet. This strength was uniquely hers.

Bloom pointed to the pocket where she'd deposited her cellular phone.

"That was Kai," she said. A half beat. "Everything's going to be okay now."

It was a straightforward statement that carried with it the hope of a better tomorrow, redemption, and a chance to start anew.

Just like something Kai himself would have said.

Carmen shrugged.

"No doubts here," she said, her voice raising playfully. One of her eyebrows arched, that spark of lightheartedness in her eyes making a comeback. It was a signature trait of Carmen's —resilient, humorous, and always spotting the silver lining, even in dire situations.

Bloom smiled. "And what about you two?"

Carmen paused, exchanging a long, contemplative look with Mitch. There was so much unspoken in that glance. Bloom could only imagine.

Turning back to Bloom, Carmen spoke in a tone that was equal parts playful and serious.

"Let's just say there're going to be a few changes at Unseen Path."

CHAPTER FORTY-FOUR

Pensacola, Florida

SILENCE FELT the quiet thrum of the BMW's engine beneath him as he checked his watch in the dim streetlight coming in through his window.

11:27.

Thirty-plus minutes to go.

More than enough for what was about to transpire.

He was parked discreetly a block away from Black Jack's.

There it was, the one-story structure crammed between a closed pawn shop and a line of worn-out apartments. Weathered, windowless gray walls marred by grime and time. That sputtering neon sign, its missing letters amplifying the establishment's grim demeanor.

From the intel Andy Elsher had gathered, Silence knew that Tanner's nephew, Ben, had a midnight rendezvous. While the exact nature of that appointment was unknown, it was never good news to have a scheduled meeting at a place like Black Jack's. And nothing good happens after midnight.

Elsher had relayed that the meeting concerned Ben's debt, a three-strikes-and-you're-out situation.

Ben was on his third strike.

Silence had arrived just in time.

Earlier that evening, before the cross-country flight back to Florida, Adrian Hirsch had divined that Silence had been —in a previous life before becoming a Watchers assassin—a killer, someone who had committed murderous crimes of passion that the Watchers had deemed justifiable.

Hirsch was correct.

Jake Rowe had committed his crimes of passion right there in the same city where Silence currently sat with vehicular air-conditioning blasting over him as he did a final weapons check.

It was time to clean up his home city once more, this time in the aid of Jake's former mentor, Marvin Tanner.

Silence was reaching a helping hand back into the past, doing what the now-extinguished Jake Rowe could not.

The Beretta was out and in Silence's grasp, resting on his thigh with his finger well outside the trigger guard. The gun's weight was familiar and reassuring, but he wouldn't need the weapon for the people inside Black Jack's.

Well, save for one.

Many of the people inside would be patrons, of whom a few might not even know of Black Jack's notorious illegal gambling. Doubtful, but possible.

Those people would not confront Silence.

But others would.

And when they did, Silence would need to be thoroughly non-lethal. Not only could he not discern whether his attackers were run-of-the-mill Black Jack's employees or individuals associated with Labyrinth, but membership in Labyrinth didn't automatically warrant elimination. Besides, even though Assets had considerable latitude in deciding their targets, Silence had just one official kill order for Black Jack's.

The Specialist had gone out of her way for Silence. He owed it to her to keep this thing as clean as possible, especially since he was again bending, twisting, and torturing Falcon's tenant: *No involvement in local matters.*

So, while Silence would bring the Beretta with him, he would only need it briefly. But despite the non-lethal approach for the breaching stage of his assault, he'd still exchanged the Beretta's standard mag for a high-capacity one.

You know, just in case.

Slipping the Beretta into its shoulder holster, Silence climbed out of the BMW into the humid night and made his approach. As he neared the entrance, the music became louder, the laughter more raucous. A few of his long strides brought him to the door.

A man in a leather jacket—not unlike SnakeNeck back in Pahrump, Nevada—held a hand out and said, "Hey, bud. Just a—"

Silence clamped a hand on the man's trapezius, used three fingers to press a pair of pressure points, and clamped. The man collapsed. Silence threw open the door.

The smell was the first thing that hit him—a mix of stale beer, unwashed bodies, and a hint of desperation. A dim haze from a few flickering bulbs combined with a thick fog of cigarette smoke. Faded green gaming tables littered the space. A bar stretched out against one wall, its mismatched barstools hosting an array of patrons, Black Jack's Saturday night crowd, some looking beaten down by life and others, eager risk-takers looking for their next win.

A low murmur of conversations went lower as more people noticed Silence. The clink of glass and the rustle of cards. Rattling dice. An old jukebox playing a garbled blues track.

Toward the back, through an archway, Silence glimpsed a room with people hunched over what appeared to be poker tables. Those were likely the high-stakes games, hidden away from the casual patrons.

The first assailant came at Silence brandishing a pool cue, muscles bulging and veins popping with exertion. He swung, intending to crash it against Silence's skull, but the latter sidestepped effortlessly.

Silence snatched the man's outstretched arm, twisting hard. With a yank, the thug was off balance. He careened into a nearby poker table. Chips flew and cards scattered as the man crashed down.

From his peripheral vision, Silence spotted two more aggressors converging on him. One was bald with a prominent scar marring his forehead; the other had long, unkempt hair and a scruffy beard. They moved with a synchronized intent, but Silence was already two steps ahead.

He sidestepped the bald man with a quick pivot, using his momentum to propel him forward while simultaneously shoving the bearded one. The bald man staggered directly into a dartboard. Darts clattered on the floor a second before the limp man joined them. At the same time, the one with the beard crashed into a nearby barstool.

Before Silence could regroup, a hulking figure loomed in front of him. The man was easily a head taller and twice as broad as the last two. Silence locked eyes with the behemoth.

With a roar, the bruiser lunged, but Silence ducked and, using the man's momentum, landed a devastating punch to the solar plexus. As the man bent over, gasping for air, a swift leg sweep had him crashing to the floor, momentarily incapacitated.

From the corner of his eye, Silence caught movement. The man was a card dealer, as evidenced by the handwritten sticker/name tag with the apropos misspelling *DEELER*. His hand was in his jeans pocket.

Silence lunged, catching the man's wrist, stopping the concealed weapon—a switchblade—just as it came out. With a swift elbow strike, the dealer was out, slumped against the poker table's green baize.

Then, as suddenly as the chaos had begun, it was pierced by a booming voice that carried an aura of authority.

"What the hell is going on out here?"

The fighting, the shouting, the clamor—it all ceased abruptly. All eyes, including Silence's, turned to the source of the interruption.

Next to the archway leading to the high-stakes games, a door that had been closed earlier was now open, revealing a dark office beyond.

In the doorway was Liam Rourke.

There they were, those piercing blue eyes.

The twitching jaw muscles.

That air of tainted professionalism, an entrepreneur who'd lost his way, stumbling right over to the wrong side of the tracks.

"You Rourke?" Silence boomed.

Rourke flinched, the raw texture of Silence's voice catching him off guard. After a moment, he nodded, smirking.

"That's me."

"You kill..." Silence said and swallowed. "The councilwoman?"

Rourke gave him a cockeyed look—confused but intrigued. "Sure did."

Despite having a kill order, Silence had asked his question in order to be one hundred percent certain.

Or, *three* hundred percent, as the Watchers colloquially liked to say.

Either way, it was just a final bit of certainty...

...before Silence un-holstered his Beretta and fired twice.

Crack! Crack!

A double tap. Crimson splashed across Rourke's forehead. Brain matter flew into the dark office behind him.

Rourke collapsed.

Screams. Chaos. Streaking movement from all directions.

Before they could escape, Silence's honed speed and reflexes put him in front of the door, blocking their path. In unison, the people slowed, blinked, and looked at him. The crowd noise hushed.

By now, Silence's gun was already lowered. A trickle of smoke snaked from the barrel, and the pleasant gravel smell of gunpowder filled his nostrils. But though he didn't want to scare these people, he still didn't holster the lowered weapon. Not yet. There was something left to do.

He pointed to Rourke's lifeless body.

"Who here..." Silence said and swallowed. "Belongs to Labyrinth?"

Seconds stretched into eternity as the patrons exchanged fearful glances, trying to gauge whether anyone would dare respond.

Finally, one hand hesitantly rose, then another, and another. The ones Silence had bested earlier—a couple of them still climbing up from the floor—identified themselves.

In total, eight figures admitted their allegiance to Labyrinth.

Silence's eyes narrowed, taking them all in.

"*Get out of my city!*"

He holstered his Beretta.

The eight stumbled in his direction, avoiding his eyes.

Silence held the door open for them on their way out.

———

This is creepy, love, C.C.'s voice said.

I know what I'm doing, Silence replied.

He was parked in the BMW again, this time in the lot outside The Sand Dollar at Pensacola Beach. He rested his head back, exhaling deeply, allowing the weight of the night's events to wash out of him as he stared forward at the restaurant.

The Sand Dollar was open late on Friday and Saturday nights—til 2 a.m. Through the windows, Silence saw Tanner sitting at his same table. This time, though, Tanner wasn't eating shrimp and grits. It wasn't Thursday, after all, so they weren't a dollar off. The cheap bastard. Instead, Tanner was nursing a milkshake.

The other difference to the last time Silence had watched his old mentor through The Sand Dollar's windows was that he had a companion at his table, someone who also had a milkshake in front of him, someone Silence had met before, but only when the individual was a toddler. Now, the young man was right at six feet tall, with clear mocha skin, wild hair, and bright eyes.

Ben.

Both of the Tanner men were all smiles, and those smiles broke into laughter every few moments. The time was 1:04, barely over an hour since Ben's date with terrible destiny had been scheduled at Black Jack's a few miles away.

Silence had a sneaky suspicion he knew why they were so happy so soon after such potential danger.

Arriving at Black Jack's an hour ago, not only would Ben and Marvin Tanner have discovered that Labyrinth had unexpectedly left Pensacola, but also that Ben's gambling debt to the bar had been completely paid off. This would have been utterly confounding, but when they would have asked Black Jack's rough proprietors, they would have been told that an anonymous donor had paid Ben's bill, an "organization" of some sort.

Silence grinned.

He watched his mentor for a moment longer as the man shared more laughs with his nephew, smacking the table in his joy, jostling the milkshake glasses.

Silence had thought Marvin Tanner was involved in illegal gambling, betraying his duties as a police officer.

He had doubted a good man.

But, then, Jake Rowe had doubted Martinelli, another good man, and it had been Tanner who steered him in the right direction.

People are a mix, Jake, Tanner had said. *Light and dark. Good and bad.*

One more look at the Tanners.

All right, C.C., Silence said. *I'll leave.*

He put the BMW into gear and rolled off.

CHAPTER FORTY-FIVE

SILENCE'S EYES FLUTTERED OPEN, the first rays of dawn piercing through a tiny crack in his blackout curtains.

Despite the cool dimness of the room, a golden hue seemed to wrap around him in an embrace. The crisp Pima cotton sheets felt more divine even than usual, more than they had a right to. His face softened into a rare, unguarded smile.

Inhaling deeply, he stretched, releasing weeks of tension. This morning held the promise of a different kind of day. He'd sorted out Labyrinth and Black Jack's the previous evening right after returning from the mission in Death Valley and Santa Barbara. Prior to that mission, he'd had a week of downtime, but he'd spent those days fretting over a supposedly crooked former mentor and an evil tabby cat determined to drool on every inch of his private retreat.

All of that was over now.

Silence had no mission on his docket. Of course, his work usually sprang on him quickly, but Silence suspected he would have at least a few days off. No rush, no impending doom, just the quiet solace of his sanctuary.

He envisioned the next day or two and saw himself perusing the unread books that lined his shelves, catching a movie, or perhaps diving into a series of meditative exercises, allowing his body to move at its natural rhythm while simultaneously expelling more of the built-up stress from the Ohio mission, Tanner's seeming betrayal, the drooling cat, murders, international criminals, multi-state cartels, terrorists, assassination attempts...

...and so forth.

Silence pushed himself up from the bed.

Yes, today was the start of something good. Today was about reclaiming his space, reasserting control. As his feet touched the air-conditioning-chilled hardwood floor, he mentally listed the chores he wanted to tackle. Morning: breakfast and stretching. By midday, he would have gotten a workout in, and possibly a grocery run, if there—

Ring!

It was the shrill tone of the landline. It echoed through the room, jarring him from his thoughts.

He almost never got a call on his landline number.

Only one person called it with regularity...

"Oh no..." he said.

———

An hour later.

Silence stood in the middle of his living room, which once reflected his very essence—clean lines, muted tones, an embodiment of calm and order. Now, it resembled a patchwork quilt of colors and textures, each blanket and faded towel a marker of Mrs. Enfield's literal blind eye thrust upon a carefully crafted world of aesthetic precision.

An orange tabby was cradled in Silence's arms. Large. Warm. The deep rumbling of the cat's purr vibrated against him. Though Silence wasn't looking at Baxter—instead, staring with a sort of stunned paralysis into a spot of nothing on the opposite wall—he knew the drool was already present in his home.

Because he felt it. Dripping on his hand.

Warm.

Disgusting.

The echoes of Mrs. Enfield's voice returned, telling Silence that her house was being sprayed. Pest control. She was blind. She couldn't monitor Baxter's movements, couldn't see where the cat was nosing, couldn't be certain he was staying out of the poison.

It's just for a week, she'd promised.

Another week of drooling...

Finally, Silence could deny reality no longer.

He looked down.

Baxter looked up, met Silence's stare, and cat-smiled.

Silence sighed.

ALSO BY ERIK CARTER

ACKNOWLEDGMENTS

For their involvement with *Muted*, I would like to give a sincere thank you to:

My ARC readers, for providing reviews and catching typos. Thanks!

Made in the USA
Middletown, DE
28 November 2023

43816080R00176